Keep the Change

Nirupama Subramanian was born in Chennai, grew up in Delhi and has worked all over India. She obtained her undergraduate degree from Stella Maris College, Chennai, and her MBA in finance from XLRI, Jamshedpur. Once upon a time, she worked in a bank. Now, she is a freelance corporate trainer and consultant by day and a struggling-to-stay-awake writer by night. Her short stories, travel pieces and articles have appeared in several publications and won awards. She won the Commonwealth Short Story Prize in 2006. She lives in Gurgaon with her husband, daughter and a cupb‍   of books. *Keep the Change* is h‍

Keep the Change

Nirupama Subramanian

HarperCollins *Publishers* India
a joint venture with

New Delhi

First published in India in 2010 by
HarperCollins *Publishers* India
a joint venture with
The India Today Group

Copyright © Nirupama Subramanian 2010

ISBN: 978-81-7223-942-8

2 4 6 8 10 9 7 5 3

Nirupama Subramanian asserts the moral
right to be identified as the author of this work.

This is a work of fiction and all characters and incidents described in
this book are the product of the author's imagination.
Any resemblance to actual persons, living or dead,
is entirely coincidental.

HarperCollins *Publishers*
A-53, Sector 57, Noida 201301, India
77-85 Fulham Palace Road, London W6 8JB, United Kingdom
Hazelton Lanes, 55 Avenue Road, Suite 2900, Toronto, Ontario M5R 3L2
and 1995 Markham Road, Scarborough, Ontario M1B 5M8, Canada
25 Ryde Road, Pymble, Sydney, NSW 2073, Australia
31 View Road, Glenfield, Auckland 10, New Zealand
10 East 53rd Street, New York NY 10022, USA

Typeset in 11.5/15 Adobe Jenson Pro
Mindways Design Pvt. Ltd.

Printed and bound at
Thomson Press (India) Ltd.

To my parents
for always being there and letting go

1

Dear Victoria,

This morning, an elephant fell on my head and I had an attack of extreme short-term memory loss for almost two minutes. I was completely disoriented. I didn't know who I was and where I was. A whole world of possibilities opened up. In those two dizzying minutes, I could have been anybody—a best-selling author who had just won the Booker, a stunning supermodel with a string of diamonds and boyfriends, a famous talk show hostess who turned ordinary people into instant celebrities. Just as those wonderful possibilities were running through my mind, it all came back. I was still at 32 Amman Kovil Street, where I was doomed to spend the rest of my life. I came to my senses and picked up poor old Plato—who seems to have lost an eye and gained a new coating of dirt—and put him back with the rest of the stuffed menagerie on top of the cupboard. That was the most exciting thing that happened the whole week.

Vic, is something wrong with my life? I want to be anyone but me and be anywhere but here. I haven't written to you for a long time now, but there is no one I can really talk to in this moment of existential angst. This is not the life I dreamt of. This is not the life I was meant to be living!

It is my twenty-sixth birthday, and here I am, sitting on our frayed drawing-room sofa at 10 p.m., after another mind-numbing day at work, eating Chocolate Excess by myself and waiting to watch *Sex and the City* on TV. My crossing of the quarter-century mark was not a cause for celebration in our household. It has earned Amma entry into the Community Hall of Shame. To have an aged, unmarried daughter on your hands is cause enough to drown yourself in a vat of idli batter. There have been no gifts, no laughter and cheer, no 'Many Happy Returns of the Day'. Usually, Amma cooks up a storm on my birthday and I gorge my way through a five-course meal and three sweet dishes. Today I ate only two spoons of Amma's reluctant semia payasam in the morning. The Iyer family at SSV & Sons suffers from permanent amnesia when it comes to birthdays and will certainly not be nominated for Employer of the Year. They did not even acknowledge the occasion.

Thanks to Mars taking up permanent residence in my seventh house, I continue to be on the shelf while younger and newer models are snapped up in the marriage mart. Mars in the seventh—or is it seventeenth?—means that there is a dosham, a tragic flaw, in my horoscope. Things do not look good for future in-laws. I believe Rahu has also conspired with Ketu to ensure that chances of progeny are faint. So, either I meet someone who doesn't believe in horoscopes or I have to get a boy whose parents are safely dead and whose horoscope is bursting with the promise of several offspring.

Amma and Appa have done their best. With the tenacity of a pit bull holding on to a hapless ankle, Amma flushes out completely unsuitable boys from the nooks and crannies of the world and throws them in my direction. She and Appa have, so far, gone through fifty-two advertisements in the *Hindu*, exchanged horoscopes with 119 friends and relatives and—short of wandering the streets with a loudspeaker, proclaiming, 'Homely girl from good family, convent educated, 25 years, CA rank-holder seeks well-qualified Iyer boy'—have done just about everything to get me off their hands.

Short serial break. *Sex and the City* has started.

To continue. I can't imagine that Carrie Bradshaw and I live on the same planet. Maybe that's why I watch the show. It has a surreal, as-far-away-from-Amman-Kovil-Street-as-possible feeling about it. I envy the way girls in other parts of the world traipse through life, trying on shoes and men with equal abandon.

I envy you, Vic. I can see you in your short skirt and long boots, on the arm of your latest Hugh Grant lookalike, sashaying into the Ritz Carlton, tossing down a strawberry daiquiri and a snack before heading off to shake your shapely legs at the hottest little club in town. While I was busy trudging through bio textbooks during my adolescence, you were probably conducting real experiments on the subject. I am so far from finding a man that it looks like I am going to be a frustrated spinster for life. Nephews and nieces will talk about the eccentric Damanyanthi Maami who became slightly unhinged after repeated failures in the matrimonial race. Aged female relatives will shake their heads and say, 'Paavam Damayanthi, poor Damayanthi,' and click their tongues and prayer beads sadly.

I have made no progress in my quest independently. At twenty-six, I can count, on the fingers of one hand, the number of times I have had close contact with unrelated males.

1. Pinching the cheeks of Pramod, neighbour's son. Age four years and six months.
2. Shaking hands with Father Macleod, visiting professor from Madras Christian College, after handing over the memento for a guest lecture. Age sixty-five plus.
3. Being pinched on the waist by unknown letch on crowded Ranganathan Street while shopping with Amma. Managed to give a hard push to sweaty back in cheap blue polyester shirt, but could not inflict permanent damage.

I will never find a man. I will never own a pair of Manolo Blahniks either. I will jump into that vat of idli batter along with Amma.

Good night,
Damayanthi.

Dear Vic,

My parents are talking of another boy. How did they dredge out yet another boy for yet another girl-seeing ceremony? In the world of matrimonials, the males are always boys—even if they are a toothless eighty-five with a brood of grandchildren. The women are girls who are very fair and very beautiful and always come from 'high status' families.

In the beginning, I had protested. I hate all this girl-seeing business, I had told them, parading in front of prospective in-laws and husband like a prize buffalo at the village fair. Besides, I did not need to get married. I gave them logical reasons—I have a job, I am economically independent, and marriage is always a losing proposition for a girl. You give up freedom, independence and full control of the remote for a life of subservience under a man who is never worth it and in-laws who never appreciate you.

It probably seems strange to you that while I do want to be in a relationship, I am vehemently opposed to the only possible way of getting into it. The real reason I am against marriage in this way is that, like all girls, I am waiting for the perfect man—who now appears to be a creature as mythical as a flying unicorn. I want to figure out what to do with my life, enjoy myself, explore the world and then fall madly in love.

Elizabeth found her Darcy, Jane Eyre had her own Mr Rochester, even Lata Mehra found herself a suitable boy. Surely there must be some quota of romance for me. All those Georgette Heyers and Mills and Boons can't be absolute fiction. The only problem is that there is no man on the horizon. You, Vic, are at least going through a systematic elimination process in your quest for the perfect man. But unlike you, I can't 'get off my arse and meet some nice guys'. It doesn't work that way in Chennai.

Throughout an uneventful fourteen years at Our Sacred Lady Convent School under the eagle eyes of Mother Superior, surrounded by a bunch of naive girls, followed by another uneventful three years of BCom at St Maria's College under the eagle eyes of another Mother Superior, surrounded by a bunch of frustrated girls, there was little opportunity to meet anyone of the opposite sex. In my class at college, only the Anglo-Indian girls, Candice Stone and Cordelia D'Souza, openly had boyfriends. We watched enviously as they jumped onto their boyfriends' motorbikes and whizzed off on dates. They even went for dances and giggled the next day about Andrew and Albert. There were some anomalies, of course, like P. Lourdes Grace Mary who, despite wearing garish polyester half-saris to college and looking as attractive as a piece of chewed-up bubblegum, managed to elope with a boy from

Pachaiyapaa College. But most of us were dutiful girls who chugged home on the Ladies' Special bus.

There have been occasional glances and polite conversation with a couple of boys during the intercollegiate culturals where we were chaperoned by a teacher who kept a strict eye on us. There was a cute guy whose name I could not find out and who boldly complimented me after I won the debate competition. And the unknown man on the motorbike who whizzed down Amman Kovil Street every evening to some secret rendezvous and once almost knocked me down. And soda butti Srinath from 47 Amman Kovil Street who cast surreptitious glances at my window while passing by. None of my friends had elder brothers. The boys are locked away in boys' colleges and the girls are sequestered in theirs, and the parents ensure that the twain never meet. In other cities and other countries young persons are losing their virginity as quickly as possible, but here in Chennai you must at least preserve the notion of being pure and untouched till you reach the marital bed. The whole system, with its Ladies' Special buses and Ladies' queues, is designed to keep you away from the opposite sex. It's like taking a child to a candy shop, but saying she can't touch anything and the only candy she can have is the one Mom selects. The poor kid stands there drooling and dreaming. No wonder we have so many perverts on the roads.

It is not as though I am desperate to have a sexual encounter. My imagination, which is usually vivid and conjures up minute details, blurs when it comes to the actual sexual act. This is probably one of those cases where the build-up to the event is more exciting than the act itself which, I suspect, is a bit of an anticlimax. The few local movies I happened to watch in my teenage years have probably done as much to put me off such encounters as Amma's heavily veiled warnings. In all the movies, raging hormones are vigorously condemned by raging parents. The unmarried girl who abandons herself to carnal desires always ends up abandoned by the family and society. The scarlet letter on her heaving remorseful bosom is invariably a huge 'P' for pregnant. She either ends up paying the price for mortal sin by selfless acts of social service or redeems herself by walking in front of a moving medium of transport. These graphic depictions have probably done more to ensure abstinence and lower the birth rate than all the family planning campaigns put out by the government.

I know this is all changing now, even in India. I saw a Hindi film recently where the heroine has a premarital affair and a live-in relationship with no pangs of guilt or remorse. Not only does she get pregnant, but she also cheerfully looks forward to delivering the baby with her partner. Maybe *I* am the anachronism in this modern world where everybody is having free sex and is in on a conspiracy to keep me bored, single and miserable.

Good night,
D.

❀

Dear Vic,

Today, when the marriage topic came up, I decided to put my foot down firmly. This meant that it was also time for another performance of *The Great Amman Kovil Melodrama*.

> Cast of characters:
> Amma, as distraught, dutiful, long-suffering mother, playing the lead.
> Appa, as distraught, dutiful, long-suffering father, playing a supporting role.
> Damayanthi, as wicked, heartless, rebellious daughter, playing the vamp.

'Daamu, what do you have against marriage anyway? We will never force you into doing anything you don't want. But everybody gets married, you know'. Long-suffering look from Appa.

'It is not marriage, Appa, it's the process. It is so degrading, all this seeing business. It's like being displayed in a shop. It hurts my self-esteem. How can I make up my mind after one meeting anyway?'

'I said yes to marrying your father after seeing the photo only, and that was also only a formality. I *trusted* my parents to make the right decision for me. Everybody gets married like this only.' Amma, with an anguished expression.

'That was thirty years ago. I want to wait a little longer.'

'How much longer? Till you become an old woman and your teeth fall out and hair turns white?'

Gnashing of teeth and frustrated sigh from wicked daughter.

'It is sooo difficult to get a qualified boy for someone of your age. And what with Rahu being in the seventh house. This one is so good,' Amma wails on.

'So why don't you marry him?' says wicked daughter, with a nasty laugh.

'Hmph! I should never have let you do all that studying or a get job. What is the use of all those big-big qualifications? I did not get the chance to study like you. I was in first year of college when the marriage proposal came. Did I protest? Did I argue with my parents? No, I listened and got married according to my parents' wishes. And did the sky come falling down? No. Did the earth split open under my feet? No. I thought, let my daughter study. She will become something in life. And what, what do I get for all the trouble? A daughter who does not listen to her parents. If only I had gotten you married off to that nice boy, Hema's nephew, after you finished BCom, we would have happily been playing with our first grandchild by now. But…'

'Amma, enough. Don't start. These days, marriage is not everything.'

'Marriage is the main thing for a woman. You have become spoilt from all those English books you have read and the silly English movies you see where all the women wear short-short clothes and have many boyfriends, but never get married.'

'You have degenerated because of those horrendous Tamil soaps you keep watching where the only ambition women have is to spawn male children and make perfect idlis.'

'Hmph! Look at Shanta, and your friends Lata and Sharmila. All have had such good marriages and all were arranged like this.'

'Sharmila got divorced last year! And I am sure Shanta is being treated for depression.'

'That's enough, Damayanthi. Aiyo! When will this girl come to her senses?' The anguished cry of Amma stops further dialogue. Temporary reprieve until the next performance.

Bye,
D.

My dear Victoria,

This evening, Amma dragged me to the wedding of Sow Bhairavi with Chi Ramanan at A.V.M. Kalyana Mandapam. I had no idea who these souls were. Amma claimed that she wanted to meet some distant aunts of mine who were supposed to be there. I had no interest in meeting any of our relatives and even less in attending a wedding which would be a grim reminder of my own unmarried status. But in the end, I was cajoled and threatened into attending the auspicious occasion wearing a dark green, red-bordered Kanchivaram sari. Large gold earrings hung from my ears and a glittering necklace edged with small gold coins lay around my neck, indicating to prospective matchmakers that I had a good stock of family jewels. All I needed was a small star on my head and I could have passed for a Christmas tree.

'Now smile properly, don't laugh loudly and don't give any silly answers,' Amma admonished me as we entered the wedding hall. 'I am going to meet Gomati Maami whose sister-in-law's uncle's cousin has a son who is working for a big company in Coimbatore. He is coming to Chennai soon, and if Gomati says everything is okay, we can meet next week itself. I want her to see you at your best. We will never get another chance like this.'

I tried to protest, but was yanked into the hall and thrust under the spotlight of one hundred pairs of flashing diamond earrings. 'See,' hissed Amma, 'how they are all looking at me! You don't know how it is. There is that Akhila whose daughter got married last month—she was not at all a pretty girl, dark with big teeth like a horse. How she got that Bhuvana married to an NRI boy I will never know. She is looking at me so pityingly.'

I must be crazy to be a part of this, I thought. I should have known that my devious mother had some such plans. Gomati Maami appeared on the horizon. She gave me a quick, appraising look from under her bifocals, storing away information to be circulated to her sister-in-law.

Sometimes there is a little voice in my head that says what I really want to say. The sentence starts off in my head, but stops before it escapes my mouth, and is replaced by a politically correct, socially acceptable phrase. Usually, there are two conversations that happen simultaneously, my world voice and my little voice. This is how the conversation went.

Gomati Maami (GM): 'So, this is your daughter.'

Little Voice (LV): 'No, I'm actually her son. I love cross-dressing for special occasions like this.'

Me: Polite smile.

Amma: 'Yes, this is Damayanthi, my only daughter.' Eager smile.

GM: 'So what do you do?'

Amma: 'She has completed her chartered accountancy exams with all-India rank. Now she is working with the firm of S.S. Vishwanatha Iyer, very old, famous accounting company in Chennai.'

LV: 'I actually scour all the pornography sites on the internet and fantasize about making love to tall, handsome men in public places.'

Me: Polite smile.

GM: 'That's very good. How is the job?'

LV: 'It ranks right next to clipping my toenails on Saturday nights and watching farmers talk about the right composition of manure on *Vayalum Vallvum* on TV.'

Me: 'It is okay.'

Amma: 'In her free time, Damayanthi helps me with the cooking. She makes very good onion sambhar and potato.'

LV: 'Don't believe her. I once burnt water and still don't know how to make filter coffee.'

Me: Polite smile.

GM: 'That's very good. What are your other interests?'

LV: 'I like to go bar-hopping with my friends. We drink toddy in the illegal arrack huts on Mahabalipuram Road and dance naked on the beach on full-moon nights.'

Me: 'I read.'

Amma: 'She has learnt Bharatnatyam for five years and has given an Arangetram also, under the famous Kalavati Ramachandran.'

LV: 'I'm actually an exotic dancer and do some amazing mudras with a greased pole.'

Amma: 'So, Shyamala was telling me about your sister-in-law's uncle… a son of marriageable age…'

GM: 'Yes, Komala's maternal uncle's cousin's boy is in Coimbatore and they are looking out for him.'

This is when I am supposed to fade shyly away into the background and feign deep interest in the wedding party. Unfortunately, there are never any good-looking men at these weddings. I think the guys smartly avoid the ordeal and leave the initial screening to their mothers. The most interesting male I saw was about seven years old and seemed determined to yank off the long braid of a small girl who screamed shrilly: 'Amma, Amma, tell im to thop ith.' He seemed to be having a good time.

I noticed two old ladies in nine-yard saris eyeing me speculatively. I hoped there weren't any more matchmakers lurking nearby. These Great Indian Weddings are really scouting expeditions for prospective brides and grooms. Today, Amma was on the prowl and I was on display.

Vision of myself with a large sticker on my forehead saying 'Bride Available', and a cardboard sheet listing my golden virtues around my neck like those people you see proclaiming The End of the World or urging us to Save the Yellow-backed Indian Ocean Shark. I am standing in a corner and assorted Maamis with oily sons are jostling each other to get a good look. Amma is handing out tokens saying, 'One by one please. No Pushing.'

Amma emerged triumphant from the conversation. 'She has asked for your photo and she will give it to Komala to pass it on. She will send me the boy's horoscope by post. He is twenty-nine and does not smoke or drink.' She was satisfied with her day's work.

'Amma, he could be a bald, overweight midget with chronic constipation.'

'He is not. Besides, you are no beauty queen yourself. He is very nice and eligible in every way.'

LV: 'For you, any Tam Brahm who is unmarried and employed is eligible.'

Me: Deep sigh.

'If he is here next week for a family function with his parents, we can arrange a meeting.'

Amma was already hearing the nadaswarams play at the wedding and seeing me in a nine-yard sari with a heavy gold chain hanging around my neck like a noose. There was no way I was getting married to this guy and living in Coimbatore. It would be like moving from one Amman Kovil Street to the next.

'If they are okay, we can set a date next month itself,' she went on as we waded through a banana leaf dinner, oblivious to the fact that I was trying to keep the rasam from dripping onto my sari.

'Amma, please stop it. I am not meeting anyone and certainly not getting married.'

'Now, Damayanthi,' she said, as though I am four years old. 'We have been through this before many, many times. You are twenty-six years old, not a young girl any more. Look at your cousin Shanta. So happy she is, already mother of a beautiful boy, and her in-laws are so fond of her.'

This is probably the fortieth time I have heard about Shanta. Shanta is my mother's cousin's daughter who lives in the US now. The epitome of all virtues who delighted her mother and saddened mine by dutifully marrying the first man her parents chose. She promptly produced a son within a year. She is only twenty-four now, which makes it worse.

'I don't want to be like Shanta. Do you know she has to do all the housework? Washing the dishes, doing the laundry. Her husband insists on eating fresh rasam and sambhar every day. I don't know how she manages with a kid as well.' I actually felt a little sorry for Shanta. When we last met about two years ago, she had just managed to figure out how the dishwasher works and was learning to drive so that she could go to the Indian store, ten miles away, to get fresh coriander. The highlight of her life was getting the latest Tamil movie on DVD and discussing it with her mother on the Sunday evening calls to Tirunelveli. I am *sure* she is being treated for depression.

'And why did you have to lie about my cooking? You know I don't enter the kitchen if I can help it,' I continued accusingly.

'You can tell a thousand lies to fix one marriage,' Amma quoted for the thousandth time.

I can argue endlessly with Amma with the same result—which is no result. I swore not to attend a wedding again in the near future, not even mine.

Bye,
Damayanthi.

꧁

Hey Vic,

This Sunday, I had wonderful plans to laze around and read the latest Jhumpa Lahiri. But Amma and Appa seemed to have different plans for me. As I came down from my little room on the roof, I was presented with my favourite breakfast of rava idli and coconut chutney. 'Well, we hardly see you at home,' said Amma sweetly. 'You are not eating well these days.' She spooned some kesari as well onto my plate. Sweets in the morning! I should have been suspicious, but instead helped myself to another scoop.

'So how is work?' asked Appa. 'I see you are coming home very late these days.'

'Audit,' I mumbled. 'How's yours?'

'Going on,' he said.

Appa is now senior general manager (Finance) at Tamil Nadu Pumps and Pipes, a stolid old public sector company that makes iron pipes. He also knows Sankaran Sir, brother of Iyer Sir, because SSV does some accounting work for TPPL. That helped to get me the job at SSV. The salary is not much, but perks are great for the parents. The Iyer family keeps a paternal eye on me and will report any strange behaviour immediately. Appa has three more years to go before retirement and is keen to marry me off by then. Then he can spend his retirement in peace, reading four newspapers daily and embarking on his hobby of translating Tamil literature into English.

'Finish your food,' said Amma. 'It's getting cold. I am bringing coffee for you.'

Amma had been on one of her cleaning binges. She does not trust Muniamma, whose cleanliness standards are far below my mother's fastidious norms. Muniamma constantly complains about Amma's Obsessive Compulsive Cleaning Disorder, but after twelve years, they have settled down into a squabbling yet congenial coexistence. There are days when Amma herself gets down on her knees and scrubs the corners of our rooms with a mixture of Sabena powder and vinegar, her antidote for grime and grease. Sometimes I find her diminutive frame perched on a ladder, wiping the ceiling fans and tube lights. Unfortunately, Appa and I do not possess her cleanliness streak and are oblivious to stray cobwebs, coffee rings on the table and the perils of wearing footwear in the house. Today, the home looked as though it had come out of a washing machine. The worn-out mosaic flooring sparkled, the few specks of dust that dared to linger had been chased out of the rooms and the air was filled with the fragrance of the jasmine agarbattis that Amma likes to light in our pujai room.

We sipped our coffee in the veranda, a happy Kodak moment. Little did I know that they were lulling me into a false sense of security.

'Oh,' said Amma suddenly. 'It is almost ten o'clock. They will be here soon.'

'Who is coming?' I asked casually. I should have guessed, of course, that cleaning binges preceded visitors.

'You remember we met Gomati Maami at the wedding,' Amma said. 'She liked you, said you seemed like a nice, quiet girl, not like those silly modern types. Good thing I told you to wear that green sari that day and put flowers in your hair. Anyway, she showed your photo to the boy's parents and…'

'No!' I shouted. 'You tricked me. I am not going to meet any boy. No! No! NO!'

'They really liked your photo and…'

'You sent them a photo! Without asking me! Which one?' I hoped it wasn't that hideous one I was forced to take three years ago at Rani Studio which made me look like a junior artist in a B-grade Tamil movie. My polite smile had weakened into a coy simper as I posed before a bright poster of a shiny red rose sliding up to a shiny pink rose in a virulent green garden.

'We sent them the picture we took on Deepavali. They wanted a natural picture. It is a nice, casual photo, not like the touched-up studio photographs that Akhila got made for Bhuvana. All that make-up and eye shadow, chee! That girl looked like Silk Smita.'

'Amma, you are really devious.' She made Machiavelli look like Little Bo Peep.

'If we asked you, I knew you'd say no. Please, please, Daamu, please. Why do you make it so difficult for us? Why are we doing this? Only so that you can be happy and have a good life.'

Act Two of *The Great Amman Kovil Melodrama*. Amma was in her best pleading mode now—she could give any Tamil movie mother in a white sari and glycerine tears a run for her money.

'Please, Damayanthi,' Appa said. ' I request you to consider this just once.' When he spoke like that in English, as though he was addressing a petition to the chief minister to solve the water problem on Amman Kovil Street, I knew I was in trouble.

Suddenly, I felt sorry for my parents. They looked so old and hopeful and miserable all at once that I felt like a wicked wretch. Maybe it would be fun. I had seen it in a movie once, when a girl who already had a lover was being paraded before a prospective boy. She pretended to be mad and said outrageous things to scare him away.

Vision of myself with a mad gleam in my eyes, a la Norman Bates in the last scene of Psycho, demonic laugh behind wild Medusa hair. I gaze at the boy, my eyes turn a glittering red and two fangs emerge from my mouth. Boy and parents scoot away, terrified...

'Hurry up,' said Amma. 'I have taken out a nice sari. The maroon colour will look very good with your complexion. Tie your hair back in a tight plait, it is always falling all over your face.'

'Why don't I wreathe it in jasmine and wear a nose-ring as well?'

'Please, Daamu, hurry up.' Pressure tactics.

'Why can't he see me in my old nightie with my hair hanging all over my face? That is the real me.'

'Aiyo, hurry, hurry! They could be here any minute.'

So, after her token rebellion is squashed, Damayanthi gets ready and wears the nice maroon sari and meets boy.

The boy was a specimen who deserved to spend the rest of his life in a jar of formaldehyde on a laboratory shelf. They were really scraping the bottom of the barrel since this one was only a lowly finance manager at a Coimbatore company called Gajalakshmi Spinning Mills.

He looked like a fat beetle, ogling my chest from under thick, black glasses. He quickly shifted his eyes when I stared back at him. He was almost two inches shorter than me and had slicked down his hair with perfumed coconut oil. Yuck! He had a little pink plastic comb in the back pocket of his blue polyester trousers. Double yuck! In this unfair world, a boy looking like a constipated blob of ectoplasm can aspire to get a fair, beautiful, well-educated girl who can do the Bharatnatyam while singing Meera bhajans and make ten kinds of rasam, but if a girl, however accomplished or intelligent, has even a tinge of brown in her complexion or slightly crooked teeth, she is immediately rejected. I hated the way he appraised me quickly while pretending to stare at the calendar on the wall behind me.

'I want my wife to be adjusting well with my parents,' the boy declared when we were sent to a corner 'to get to know each other'. He had this irritating habit of popping out his tongue and licking his lips after every sentence.

LV: 'Adjust? Like I adjust my sari pleats with three sharp safety pins?'

'Oh!' I said, a sort of questioning, sarcastic 'oh' which he seemed to take as assent to his statement.

'I hope you are not planning to be employed after marriage?' he continued.

LV: 'If I do give up give up my dead-end, boring job, it is not going to be for another dead-end, boring job as your chief housekeeper.'

I said, 'Yes. I am.'

'Then how will you manage the children?'

LV: 'Duh!'

'What children?' I asked. Was I going to become stepmother to his illegitimate brats?

'Oh, we must have one child within a year of marriage.' His tongue flickered out for a second like that of a lecherous toad about to gobble up a fly.

'At least, two totally. My amma says we should not be putting off for too long. Amma says that she would like one boy and one girl. We must start trying right away, no planning. She is really waiting for grandchildren.'

LV: 'And you are really waiting for unlimited free sex.'

Me: 'Ah-ha?'

'So I think, with two children, my parents and the house to look after, you will be quite busy at home itself,' he continued, blithely ignoring my disgusted expression.

LV: 'I would rather be kissed by a Dementor than come within a mile of your body!'

'My horoscope is not very positive about children, so I don't think there is any use even trying,' I said to him, feigning an air of deep despondence.

Boy returns to bosom of his dear amma. Girl sulks in corner.

Good night,
D.

2

My dear Victoria,

Age has withered my intellect and custom has stultified my senses. I have become an ossified fossil, sitting in Amman Kovil Street and entertaining grotesque boys. I have to get out of here and do something with my life. So I turned to great literature for inspiration—I espied a *Cosmopolitan* at the Murugan Lending Library, which promised '10 Ways to Fix Your Life'.

I brought it in sandwiched between *Kumudam* for Amma and *India Today* for Appa. It was smuggled in because the last time Amma saw it, she said, 'Aiyo, what is all this nonsense you are reading with pictures of indecent women and why must you know "Handy Ways to Hook a Man"? You are not a shameless girl who has to chase boys. Appa and I are looking for a nice man for you. Be patient. God will take care of it.' She probably thought that her good Damayanthi was morphing into a desperate man hunter. I maybe twenty-six, but I still feel like a schoolboy sneaking a peek at *Playboy*. This is how I used to smuggle in those Mills and Boons borrowed from friends in college—sandwiched between the pages of *Basic Accounting*.

On perusing this piece of contemporary literature, I am depressed to see that women across the world are obsessed with their looks—losing them—and men—finding them. Even if you have a successful career, you are a social failure if you are single and unable to mingle. If you have a boring job, average looks and are manless, it is time for a complete overhaul.

I completed a self-awareness checklist designed to discover the inner woman in you. I answered, as truthfully as I could, a list of twenty-four questions ranging from 'I Make a List of Things to Do in the Morning'—choosing from options such as 'always', 'seldom', 'often' and 'never'—to 'I Read Useful Books to Improve Myself'. My score of seven meant—'Take Control of Your Life. Choose Your Destiny. Stop Whining and Start Mining the Gold in You.'

Okay, Vic, I think this is the clarion call, the writing on the wall, time to stand tall or lose it all.

I am not a woman who runs with the wolves. I have been more of the girl who ambles home behind the cows of Amaan Kovil Street. But things are going to change now. I will put in my resignation. I will walk into SSV & Sons and say, 'Enough of boring bank reconciliation statements, enough of preparing tedious trial balances and making sense of ridiculous ratios.' My days in accounting are numbered. I am destined for greater things, for bigger stuff. I cannot imagine doing any more time in this decrepit office with its mouldy registers, stained walls, scratchy steel chairs, drinking any more of the sweet, sweet kaapi that Muthu serves us in cheap eversilver tumblers.

I will start up a hi-tech start-up, doing something universally beneficial, which will be sold for millions of dollars after two years of record profits. Then I will help underprivileged children, travel the world and write a bestseller, which will be made into a movie after several rounds of ferocious bidding from leading production houses across the globe. After rejecting several heroine aspirants, the world-famous director will turn to me and say, 'Damayanthi, I think it has to be you.' Thus my Hollywood career will commence.

Vision of myself in huge sunglasses, climbing down from helicopter, doling out food to small, starving children in Kalahandi, while photographers madly click away and hordes of fans rush to get my autograph. Nobel Peace

Prize winner who looks like Daniel Craig helps me out of the helicopter. I laugh, hair flicked carelessly back from the breeze stirred by propeller blades and raise a hand, blow a kiss…

I WILL NOT PROCRASTINATE. I WILL RESIGN.

Tomorrow.

Yours determinedly,
Damayanthi.

※

Dearest Victoria,

I imagine you have been busy at fundraising events like the Gala Concert to raise money for the Red Nose Day. I on the other hand have begun the journey to freedom, romance and independence. Well, I have made a biodata. I have just about written my name on it, but it is a start.

'Biodata of B. Damayanthi.'

Augh! Whenever I see or hear my name, I still have to suppress a shudder. Why did my parents choose to name me after an *Amar Chitra Katha* heroine who was beset with misfortune to the point of actually loaning her only sari to cover her impoverished, naked husband? Amma claims that she was reading the story of Nala-Damayanthi while she was pregnant and was inspired to name me after the dutiful, righteous heroine, despite opposition from my paternal grandmother, who claimed that Damayanthi was not a nice name for a typical Brahmin girl. Apparently, my grandmother felt that I should have been named Gajalakshmi after her. I can't figure out which is worse.

What is really terrible is the 'B'. B. Damayanthi sounds like a curse, as though a wicked witch had come to my naming ceremony and said, 'Be Damayanthi, be a pudgy, pug-nosed child who won't even be chosen for the part of the ugly step-sister in the school play. Be Damayanthi, dutiful, dull daughter; dreary drudge, doomed to spend her days in the dungeons of debit and credit.'

Why can't I have a nice, new-age name? Like Ria or Dia, or even a Kaavya or Tanya? You are lucky, Vic. Victoria sounds regal and posh at the same time! I am stuck with a ghastly name, gloomy marriage prospects and a godawful, boring job.

I have resigned myself to resigning tomorrow. I WILL do it this time.

Bye,
D.

Hi Vic,

I could not resign since we are closed for Pongal holidays. In the clear light of day, I realize that apart from my job, I don't have anything else to do. All those years of school and college gave me a sense of purpose—study hard, come first in class, move on to the next class. Now my days are just passing by. I feel like a piece of driftwood, floating aimlessly on the river of life. SSV is such a typical, stodgy old family firm that you can't build a career there. But resigning does not seem like a sensible thing to do either if you have no clue about what you are going to do after that. I wish I had some grand passion in life, some splendid dream for which I could chuck everything. I guess even you are passionate about Save the Newts in Worcestershire and Hookers for Horses (how many prostitutes have you rehabilitated by employing them as stable hands?) charities and have devoted your life to unusual but worthy causes. But me—I've got nothing.

Many people seem to know what they want to do with their lives from a very young age. I read an interview with a beauty pageant winner sometime back and she just knew from the day she could hold a lipstick that she had to be Miss India some day. Others were playing chess before they could spell it. A child tinkering with the family television clearly indicated that the family harboured a great scientist… I was never good at sport or anything remotely athletic. Though my parents hoped that classical dance and music classes would trigger off some dormant artistic tendency, nothing of the sort happened. The only thing that interested me was books. I read voraciously, almost every book I could lay my hands on. During one of my summer holidays, I finished off two dozen P.G. Wodehouses from our library in thirty days. Unfortunately, you cannot make a career out of speed-reading fiction. Which is why I took shelter in the groves of Academia. I was good at studies—very good in maths—and managed to come first almost every year in school and got a top 20 rank in CA. I can't believe that I am now vegetating at SSV & Sons.

Vision of myself flinging my resignation letter at Iyer Sir and saying, 'National Geographic is sending me on an assignment to fulfil my lifelong ambition of studying the mating patterns of the Galapagos tortoise.' Or, 'This job means nothing to me. I am going to be assisting Mani Ratnam Sir in his next film. Shooting starts tomorrow.' Iyer Sir falls at my feet. 'Damayanthi, don't go. SSV will collapse without you.' I walk out. Muthu, the office boy, runs after me crying, 'Akka,

don't forget me. Please give me a small role in the film.
Please, akka…'

I wish.

Bye,
D.

⚜

Dear Vic,

Today I did something sensible. I called Sumitra long distance. I thought she would have some options. Have I told you about Sumitra? Sumitra and I were together at college and she is about the closest friend I have today. While I was studying for my CA, Sumitra managed to get through MBA exams and flew the Chennai coop to Kolkata. After an eventful two years, during which she acquired a management degree and a Bengali boyfriend, she got a job at Stanton & Hobbes, one of the large, international consultancy firms. She lives in Delhi now, in some posh service apartment, and keeps travelling around. Stanton has offices across the world and Sumitra recently went to Paris for a conference. I like Sumitra, truly, but I have been jealous. Jealous that while she has been globe-trotting,

I have been doing boring work at SSV, biding time at home, waiting to get married.

All that is going to change now. I decided to call Sumitra on her mobile number. Everybody and their milkman have a mobile phone these days. It's time I acquired one, but I know that the only calls I will get will be from Amma—'Damayanthi, when are you coming home? The sambhar is getting cold.'

I called Sumitra late at night, after the parents had retired to the bedroom.

'Hi, Sumi, it's Damayanthi. How are you?'

'Hey, hey, hey how are you doing, D? I am really pissed off. That asshole boss of mine has dumped a shitty assignment on me and I am sitting on my fat ass at this godforsaken place called Gomia in Laalooland, watching two pallis screw each other on the walls.'

That's how Sumitra talks these days. She has morphed from a paavam Tam Brahm girl to foul-mouthed brassy babe in the last two years. She has cut her hair really short, pierced an extra hole in each of her ears and wears a small Om tattoo on her back. The last time she was in Chennai for holidays, she shocked me and everyone around by loudly saying, 'Fuck you, bastard!' to a letch who was ogling her ample boobs. But she is still a five-feet-one, sixty-five-kilo bundle of bubbling energy and good humour.

'Sumi, I am sick of this job. I am sick of this place. I need to get out soon.'

'About time, D. You are really wasting your life there. Before you know it, you will have married one paavam boy and then you will become proud mother of Ambi and Ambujam.'

'Aiyo! Never! So, Sumi, what do I do? Can I get a job somewhere else?'

'Duh. First, prepare a resume. You've got a good rank in CA, so you could try banks or finance jobs in companies, or even some consultancies. Stanton is not hiring now. I'll send you some names and emails of some placement consultants. Send them your resume. I'm sure they'll come up with something. You can also post your resume on some of those job sites. This isn't a bad time to be job hunting. Something will work out.'

'Thanks a lot, Sumi. So how is Deb?' Deb is the boyfriend—Debapriya Bandopadhyay. I can't imagine Sumitra one day becoming Mrs Bandopadhyay. I wonder if they have done IT, but I can't bring myself to ask her.

'Oh fine. The lucky bugger is off to Bangkok next week for some sales conference. I've told him he'd better not go to those massage parlours and better lay off those hookers. Lay OFF, I said, not lay, just in case…'

'Wow! Bangkok.' The whole world is travelling and having adventures. It is just not fair.

'How about you, D, met anybody yet?'

'Naah! No one remotely interesting. Where are all the TDH ones?'

Sumi and I used to laugh about the tall, dark, handsome heroes of romance novels. The only criterion our local heroes met was the dark one—a rather rich shade of charcoal.

'Look, I'm getting a call from Deb. Have to rush. I'll email you the consultants' names as soon as I get out of this shithole. Couple of days, okay? Bye. Take care, D.'

This is a beginning.

Love,
D.

✿

Hey Vic,

I did it.

I took the first step. I made a biodata. A short history of nearly everything of importance in my life, and I could barely manage a paragraph out of it. I mentioned my ranks, but I wonder if that sounds too boastful.

I wrote it out and went to Balaji Cyber Café—earlier known as Balaji Tiffin Palace—to type it on the computer. As usual, there was no one interesting there. An old man was scanning a matrimonial site, some teenagers were looking at websites of colleges in the US and a middle-aged woman was laboriously typing out an email to someone. 'Please do your pujai every day...' Probably writing to an errant son abroad who is busy looking for girlfriends.

I reread my biodata and found it too short. I read it again and found it too boring. I needed some professional help. After scanning all those helpful websites, I have sent the biodata to www.resumerepair. com, along with draft of Rs 250. The experts at resumerepair have assured me that once they are through with it, my resume will scream HIRE ME to prospective employers.

Vision of Damayanthi in a black trouser suit, hair in chic chignon, swinging a laptop, swishing into a boardroom. I point to a presentation on the screen behind me and say, 'Gentlemen, as you can see, my financial strategy has resulted in savings of $3 million for the company, and we expect to close this year with an EBIT of $5.6 million, 175% above last year.' Claps and cheers all round. Dynamic CEO who looks like Tom Cruise squeezes my hand, looks meaningfully into my eyes and says, 'Excellent work. We'll discuss it further over dinner.'

Please see original biodata of B. Damayanthi. Is it:

a. Boring
b. Boastful
c. Brief
d. All of the above

Yours expectantly,
Damayanthi.

BIODATA

Name: B. Damayanthi
Age: 26 years
Address: 32 Amman Kovil Street, Adayar,
            Chennai

I am currently working in the accounting firm of SSV & Sons as a junior clerk. I passed my CA exams with distinction. I was among the top 20 rank-holders in India.

I completed my BCom from St Maria's College, Chennai, where I got the second rank in the university. I did my schooling from Our Sacred Lady Convent in Chennai, where I got the first rank in school in the Plus Two exams. I also got the Best Conduct Award and the Maths Prize in school.

I like reading. I have also participated and won a few debate, quiz competitions and essay writing competitions in school and college.

❦

Hi Vic,

I have just received my resume back from www.resumerepair.com. They had asked me for some more information that I had emailed across—what came back was completely unbelievable. The folks there must be writing fantasy novels in their spare time. I have been carried away by the new persona they have created for me. I wasn't aware that I had so many skills and such a consistent track record of academic excellence. If I thought my earlier biodata was boastful, this one has trumpets blowing all over! I hope those fellows at www.resumerepair.com know what they are doing.

This is the new improved Damayanthi Balachandran, Manager-in-Waiting, who is about to embark on a glorious corporate career. I have emailed my resume to all the placement consultants and am waiting for the calls to pour in.

Please see new resume of Damayanthi B. Does it scream:

> a.   HIRE ME!
> b.   LIAR ME!

Love,
D.

RESUME

Name: Damayanthi Balachandran
Age: 26 years
Address: 32 Amman Kovil Street, Adayar, Chennai 400091
Email: bdamayanthi@webmail.com
Phone: 044-24304778

Career Objective: I wish to develop myself as a world-class finance professional and make a positive contribution to the organization I work for.

Work Experience: September 2003–present, SSV & Sons, Chennai

I am part of a team of senior accountants responsible for key customer deliverables. I undertake financial analysis, preparation and reconciliation of critical accounts and work on challenging projects relating to direct and indirect taxation. I come forward to take up a leadership role and motivate my team members to succeed in achieving organizational objectives. I constantly strive to improve my own performance and aim for excellence in all my activities.

Academic Achievements: I have a consistent track record of achieving academic excellence.

School: Our Sacred Lady Convent, Chennai

- First rank in school in 12th standard board exams
- Seventh rank in state in 12th standard board exams
- Best Conduct Award
- First prize in maths
- First rank in school in 10th standard board exams

College: St Maria's College, Chennai

- First rank in college in BCom final exams
- Fourth rank in Chennai University
- First prize in Intercollege Quiz Competition
- Second Prize in Intercollege Debate Competition

Hobbies: Avid reader and poet, keen badminton player, music buff

Vic, I had no idea that I came forward to take a leadership role, except when it came to leaving office. Even then, Iyer Saar usually beat me to it most of the time. I didn't even know that I had motivated my team, except to encourage Natarajan, one of the other accountants, to quit the job and become a full-time mridangam player. However, he continues to toil away in Pudukottai and Tiruchirapalli, auditing the accounts of medium-sized firms and dreaming about his dream career. I had mentioned that I knew how to get a shuttle over the net and had written a few poems in my youth. These had morphed me into a poet and a keen badminton player.

Amma says, 'You can tell a thousand lies to get a daughter married.' The same seems to hold for getting a job as well.

Now, I just have to wait for the desperate calls of prospective employers.

Awaiting a positive response from them, I beg to remain,

Yours truly,
Damayanthi.

Dear Vic,

It's been a week and there has been no news from any consultant. Three of them acknowledged my email. Standard replies—'Thank you for sending us your resume. We will get back to you in case of any suitable vacancies.' Most did not reply. I rush to Balaji Cyber Café every evening before I return home in the hope that there will be some news, but am confronted only with junk in my mailbox. I trawl the messages from Dan, promising me a great deal on Mortgages, and Veronique, exhorting me to increase the size of my organ. Today, there was an interesting one from Mabel, which said, 'Meet the right man, right here', along with a free registration offer to an online dating portal. I am almost tempted to start an online dalliance with a mysterious male.

Vision of myself exchanging witty emails with a man who knows exactly what to say. We tease, flirt, discuss, debate, and then we want to meet. I'm sitting in a restaurant with a red rose peering from the pages of The Rubaiyat of Omar Khayyam *and there is an interesting shadow at the door, a shadow that also has a red rose crushed between the pages of the* Rubaiyat. *The shadow approaches me and says—*

'You will take laang? Yit is my time now.'

And I am back at Balaji Cyber Café, with the old man who wants to scan the matrimonial websites urging me to vacate my seat.

Such is my life. I trudged back home, feeling even more dejected than usual. I can't bear to see the Iyer gang every day and go through the stupid ledgers of TVM Pistons. I don't care if the sales manager has spent Rs 22,000 on entertainment expenses. I don't care if the accountant has been embezzling funds, I don't care if Mr T.V. Murugappan is going bankrupt. I feel like throwing the ledgers on the wall and shredding the expense vouchers to confetti and showering them on Sankaran Sir's head.

I am going to finish the Mars Bar I bought on the way back and watch *Lara Croft: Tomb Raider* for the second time on Star Movies. Pray for me, Vic.

Damayanthi.

Dearest Vic,

Thank you, Vic. Maybe you made a wish at the wishing well in the picturesque village of Pokeahole-on-Sea instead of an old-fashioned prayer.

Your wish must have come true, because I got a call! A woman from Perfect Placements called up and told me about a job opening in a bank—First Global. I was so desperate that I said, 'Yes, yes, yes,' without knowing anything about the job. First Global is one of those hotshot foreign banks which have set up shop in India. Apparently, they pay very well and send you on training programmes to places like Macao! So said Prema of Perfect Placements.

Vic, I have an interview next week since a vice president who is interviewing people is in Chennai only on next Friday. So I have to prepare for the first interview of my working life. Meeting Iyer Sir cannot be called an interview. All he said after studying my mark sheets for a long time was, 'So, Balu said you need to do your articleship. Can you start next week?' All I said was, 'Yes, I can.'

Now this is going to be a real interview. I will be up against those MBA types who have learnt to bluff their way through campus placements. This means taking up long-time occupancy at Balaji Cyber Café and picking up interview tips.

I was quite excited and could hardly concentrate at work today. The musty, dusty offices of SSV & Sons, with piles of ledgers and paper everywhere, seemed even shabbier than usual. Iyer Sir pointed out a couple of mistakes I made with some calculations. 'It is Rs 2,922 and 74 paise, not 76 paise,' he said. 'Even two paise makes a difference, maa.' I usually do those calculations in my head really quickly, but today I didn't care. I retreated to my desk and pretended to make some notes on the pale green notepad which said, 'Lashmi Nilayam Hot eels,' courtesy a client in the hospitality sector who had generously offloaded all the misprinted pads onto us.

What emerged was this:

> *There was an accountant named Iyer*
> *Who was a great believer in prayer*
> *He took the Lord's name*
> *And prayed for a dame*
> *Who could quench his burning desiyer*

Then I felt really bad—guilty, scum of the earth—for making fun of my boss in this vulgar manner. So I tore up the paper into tiny pieces and threw it in the dustbin. Looking at Iyer Sir—bachelor at forty-five, short, bald, wearing thick black glasses with vibhuti smeared across his forehead, in those ridiculous, baggy brown trousers—I felt a strong surge of pity. His life revolved around the Amman Temple and this little office where he was still ordered around by his elder brother and father. I tried hard

to finish tallying the ledgers and focus on my work.
I will be a good girl and not think cruel things about
this nice, kind man.

Good night,
Damayanthi.

3

~

Vic,

I messed up. The first and perhaps the only chance to change my life, and I messed up. Maybe it was because the interview was during Rahu kaalam,the most inauspicious time of the day. That is like letting a black cat cross the street in front of me and ducking under a ladder with thirteen rungs at the same time. Maybe if I had told Amma she would have got me to change the time. Actually, I cannot blame anyone but me. If only I could do a rewind.

I walked into the new glass building, First Global's Chennai office, looking outwardly elegant in a black-and-white printed silk sari while a thousand butterflies did somersaults in my stomach. I was met by 'Nagi' Nagarajan, the south regional head, and

Ashok Bhasin, the distinguished VP from Mumbai, suited and booted with a red silk tie. It seemed to go pretty well in the beginning. I had researched their website, read up all the assorted bits of information brought up by Google and prepared my standard answers. Thanks to my thorough, detailed preparation and in-depth analysis of what to say at an interview, almost all the questions went off well. Sample this.

'So what are your key strengths and weaknesses?' Question from Mr Bhasin.

'I have strong analytical skills, combined with the ability to communicate effectively across a diverse audience. I strive hard to achieve my goals along with my team, using my leadership skills to steer my team-mates towards team objectives. My main weakness is that I tend to be a perfectionist, never settling for second best. I get impatient when things don't happen on time and tend to stretch beyond my capability.'

'Why do you want to join First Global?'

'I want to be part of a leading international bank that is known for its innovative customer-friendly solutions. The First Global values of integrity, excellence and customer orientation reflect my own personal values. I believe that I will be able to make a positive contribution to First Global and can look forward to a rewarding, long-term career with the bank.'

All ten 'Key Words to Interview Success' incorporated in ten minutes, with bonus points for using the word team three times. There was no way they were not going to roll out the red carpet for me. I could see Nagi beaming benevolently and that Mr Bhasin was about say, 'When can you join?' I felt like the way Lara Croft did when she finally saw the Holy Grail.

'Who is your role model?'

'Lara Croft, Tomb Raider!'

There were a few seconds of surprised silence. I couldn't believe I had said that.

'Do you mean the heroine in that Angelina Jolie film?' asked Nagi.

I looked blankly at him. My mind had stopped functioning for a few seconds.

'Why is she your role model?' Amused look from Mr Bhasin.

Desperate attempt to recover by Damayanthi— 'Because she is very sure of what she wants, is determined to achieve her goals, faces challenges courageously and is in control of her life.' She is exactly the opposite of Ms Damayanthi Balachandran, who realized too late that she should have said Kiran Bedi or Kiran Mazumdar, instead of blurting out inappropriate, non-corporate answer.

Amused look lingers on faces of interviewers.

This is the last question before Damayanthi is dismissed.

I walked out of the office feeling despondent. I didn't want to go back home or to SSV, so I went to Landmark and moped around while browsing through the bookshelves.

I am too scared to call Perfect Placements and ask them what happened. It is better to delay bad news as much as possible. I knew that I should have gone to the temple. After all, what is the point of living on Amman Kovil Street if I don't seek the blessings of our resident deity? The goddess is angry with me and has ordered Saraswati not to sit on my tongue.

What am I thinking? I am beginning to sound like Amma.

Pray for me, Vic.

Damayanthi.

&

Dear Victoria,

May I introduce you to Ms Damayanthi Balachandran, Assistant Manager, First Global Bank, who is about to embark on a glorious corporate career? Yes, Vic, miracles do happen. Prema called me this morning and told me that I had been selected.

'Nagi told me that at first they were not really impressed with you. You said the same things that everybody else did, but Ashok Bhasin really liked that Lara Croft answer, and of course your academic record is very good. By the way, who is Lara Croft? That American politician?' Prema needs to watch more TV.

LV: 'No, dear Prema. Lara Croft is my heroine, my role model, Saviour of the Depressed, Guiding Light of the Good-hearted.'

'She is a popular character in the contemporary entertainment industry.'

'Oh? So, you are ready to move to Mumbai?' Prema went on.

'What? I thought that this job was in Chennai?'

'But Damayanthi, I told you that you have to be flexible about locations. You filled that in their form also. I told them that it is not a constraint. Don't worry, they will pay airfare and give you accommodation.'

Worried? I was not worried. I was delirious with joy!

Vision of myself in Sin City, wearing backless black silk dress, drinking Bloody Mary at hip club, with gorgeous models and actors lusting after me in the background. I

*laugh, hair flicked back carelessly, and croon, 'Daaarling!'
Gorgeous, obscenely rich tycoon who looks like a young
Harrison Ford gazes devotedly at me and says...*

'Can you join by 10 March?' Prema was
enquiring.

That gives me only fifteen days to wind up my life
at SSV and Amman Kovil Street, but I am ready.

Love,
Banker-in-Waiting.

꘎

Hey Vic

I know you have been telling me to 'get a life' for
some time now. I hope I will get the life I have always
dreamt of.

As expected, the parents were not happy with the
news of the new job. They were more unhappy with
the news of the impending move from Chennai.

'A bank?' Appa pondered aloud. 'Daamu, if you
had wanted to work in a bank, you could have taken
the bank exams and become an officer in SBI. What
is this First Global?'

'One of the leading international banks, known
for their cutting-edge technology and innovative

customer-friendly solutions, First Global is a truly global bank present in twenty-five countries across four continents,' I reeled off from their website.

Amma was first annoyed that I had not informed her earlier about my intentions to change jobs. When she calmed down, she had more mundane worries. 'Where will you live? What will you do for food?'

'The bank will give me a place to stay,' I said.

'Will you stay alone?'

'No, Amma. Usually, it's two boys and a girl to a flat for security reasons. And because of cost-cutting measures, we have to share everything, including beds.'

'What, what?' she spluttered like mustard seeds in hot oil.

It's fun to tease her sometimes.

'Sorry. Just joking, Amma. I will stay alone or with another girl.'

'Hmph! What will you do for food? You don't even know how to cook rice! It is my fault. I have pampered you too much. You were always sitting with your nose in a book. Whenever I called you for cooking, you ran away to the library. Aiyo, what is the use of all that reading if you don't even know how to make coffee? I thought I will give you cooking lessons once your marriage gets fixed. What to do now?'

'I will manage,' I tried to reassure her.

'Shall I give you some eversilver vessels and some pulikachhal mix? It will last you for many months and you can make tamarind rice with it. Maybe you can buy a grinder so that you can at least make the batter for idli and dosai. I will give you a big bottle of avakkai pickle. And I will buy Meenakshi Ammal's *Cook and See* book so that you will know what to make.'

'Amma, relax. I am not going on an expedition to the North Pole. I will fix up a cook or eat curd rice and Maggi. Food is not a problem!'

Appa looked anxious and said, 'You have to be careful. Always lock the house and your bedroom. Don't come back alone late at night and don't talk to strangers.'

'Amma, Appa, I am going to Mumbai, not Bosnia! So many girls go abroad alone these days. Why are you making such a big fuss?'

'If you were married, I would have said, "Go anywhere," and given you my blessings,' Amma sniffed. 'Now you have to be even more careful. So far, we carefully safeguarded your reputation, brought you up with good traditional values.'

'Now my value will fall in the marriage market. Everyone will say, "That Damayanthi, she lives alone in Mumbai! Sinful, wicked woman!" I will *never* get married.'

'This is all a joke to you. Just wait till you have a daughter!' Amma sounded exasperated, but I knew she was genuinely concerned about my well-being. After all, I was going to leave home for the first time in my life.

Anyway, it is about time. They have resigned themselves to the fact that I am going away. I have dissuaded Amma from taking the Dadar Express and coming to Mumbai to settle me down. She was quite disappointed about that. I have to keep reminding her that I am twenty-six years old, fully capable of boarding a flight and arriving in a strange city all by myself. I am sure I am.

Amma is going to make all my favourite dishes this whole week. I will miss her.

Love,
D.

Vic,

Only seven days more. I have resigned from SSV. They were more laconic about my move, as though it was something they expected to happen anyway. Iyer Sir said, 'I thought you will get married soon and go to America. All the smart young boys are there these days.' Instead, I might just turn out to be forty-five and unmarried like him! SSV Sir gave me his blessings and Sankaran Sir said, 'First Global Bank! They have not been in India for very long, have they?' Ten years seems like a long time to me, but compared to the old, respected firm of SSV, which has been around for forty years, it is a fly-by-night operator.

'How much are they paying you?'

I told him.

I was getting a fraction of that at SSV. He tried not to look impressed and said, 'You should see how much you are getting as cash in hand. If you are not living at home, you will have more expenses, and cost of living in Mumbai is very high. So practically no savings. Still, it is not a bad option till you get married.'

I packed up the things from my desk, collected my last pay cheque and took the auto for the last time from SSV to 32 Amman Kovil Street. I already have no memories of the years I spent there. I am surprised I lasted so long.

I have decided to spend my last two months' salary in two days. I need to pick up some decent clothes to prepare myself for Mumbai. I will head to Fabindia and get some of those modern kurtis.

Vision of me walking into First Global's plush offices, radiant in a yellow kurta, hair billowing behind me like in a shampoo advert, new handbag swinging by my side. People turn to stare, faint strains of 'Who's that girl?' in the background. I stride onwards, leaving behind a scent of expensive perfume and dumbstruck bankers clutching their ties…

It could happen.

Damayanthi.

Dear Vic,

I am off tomorrow. Packed, ready and waiting. I have spent Rs 950 on a black handbag. You are probably buying a dashing Jane Birkin bag that costs about the same as what I might make in ten years doing bonded labour at SSV & Sons and I guess you will get bored of it within a week. My most extravagant single purchase to date was the cheapest in the shop. I saw a nicer one for Rs 1,050, but a thousand bucks for a bag seemed a bit too much even when I was on a reckless binge. I also bought some nice Charlie sprays for less than Rs 1,000—Amma would freak if she knew that the Nina Ricci perfume that Kavita Chitti got three years ago from Singapore is almost over.

I could get used to the pleasures of material acquisition.

We dropped in on the grandparents yesterday. They had been eagerly looking forward to a wedding—instead they had to bid goodbye. They acted as though I was really crossing the seven seas and venturing into alien territory. Poor things, they are getting old. Paatti has arthritis and Thatha has some cataract problem. Their health issues overwhelm them. It's really scary to think of growing old. Every time I see them, it reminds me of my own mortality! One day I too will be sans teeth, sans hair, sans libido, etc. Might as well have fun now, before it's too late.

'Odamba nalla patthuko,' said Paatti. 'Look after yourself. Eat regular meals, don't do all this dieting or whatever.' She dropped in a proverb about how you can paint a picture only if a wall is strong. 'Be careful with all those Punjabis. They will cheat you and then accuse you of robbing them!' was her final piece of advice. I tried to tell her that Mumbai is in Maharashtra, the cosmopolitan, commercial capital of India, but she firmly believes that any place where Malayalam and Tamil are not spoken is inhabited by Punjabis. She and Amma are so alike.

Today, Amma took me aside for some last-minute woman-to-woman advice. Which meant she would talk and I would nod.

'It is not that I don't trust you, Daamu,' she began. Warning signal. Beep-beep-beep. Heavy dose of advice is about to be unleashed.

Amma: 'A girl must always be careful. There will be many temptations.'

LV: 'I wish.'

Me: 'Uh-uh.'

Amma: 'You should not do anything silly before marriage.'

LV: 'You mean—Do not sleep around. Preserve your virginity like a precious gem to be gifted to your lawfully wedded husband on your wedding night.'

Me: 'Uh-uh.'

Amma: 'I hope you will not take any... drinks.' Hushed whisper.

LV: 'But I plan to get piss drunk every night and embark on a career as a professional bar-hopper.'

Me: 'Only water, Amma. And buttermilk.'

Amma: 'Daamu, if you do meet some boy, please tell us first.'

LV: 'With my luck, the chances are the same as a polar bear finding a mate in the Thar desert.'

Me: 'Uh-uh.'

Amma: 'We don't mind you finding your husband by yourself. We are not that orthodox that we will insist on an arranged marriage. But of course he must be a Hindu.'

LV: 'Wow, that is very generous of you. That also means you really have given up on finding a boy for me!'

Me: 'Uh-uh.'

Amma: 'And of course he should be a Brahmin. I cannot imagine you cooking non-vegetarian food.'

LV: 'Yes, I will ask all men their food habits before proposing to them. In fact, why don't you prepare a questionnaire for me?'

Me: 'Uh-uh.'

Amma: 'And if he is a Tamilian, it will be so much better for us and for you to adjust with the family.'

LV: 'Great! Now that really increases my sample size.'

Me: 'Uh-uh.'

Amma: 'Daamu, do you understand?'

Me: Shake head all over the place. Meaning, 'Yes I do, but no I won't.'

Vic, I'm ready to take off. I'm looking forward to flying.

Wish me luck.

Damayanthi.

4

⤳

Dear Vic,

I am here at last. It's been just one day and I am still in culture shock. I think India is the only country in the world where you can get culture shock after travelling 100 km from wherever you are. I haven't been to Mumbai before, so it's like discovering a new continent. There is something in the air here—a buzz, an energy, a crackle of things about to happen. You have never been to Mumbai, but I am sure you will like it.

I landed at the Chhatrapati Shivaji Airport at Santa Cruz and took a taxi to a place called Khar. Amma was insistent that I take a flight that landed during the day so that wicked taxi drivers would not hoodwink me, take me to a lonely, unknown destination and execute dishonourable designs on my honour. I had to agree with her. I was a little apprehensive at first about landing in a new city. Appa claimed to have a distant third cousin who lived in a place called Dombivili, but I assured them that I would not need the services of any well-meaning uncle. I passed tall buildings that jostled for space behind shanties that bordered the roads. The traffic chugged along at a smooth pace, stolid red buses bearing the legend BEST whizzed past a stream of cars. We passed a flyover that overlooked a large expanse of water. I could even see small boats bobbing in the sea in the distance.

The taxi driver put on the radio and we listened to a Bollywood number in the car.

'In the Mumbai, all over India

We are the bhaaais, we are the bhaaais…'

I am in the Mumbai and I am glad to be here. We managed to locate my flat in a quiet street in Khar. I am sure I will get hopelessly lost here. I can't figure out where 15th road went. It does not seem to be between 14th and 16th roads. The taxi driver actually gave me back Rs 11 as change, which was a refreshing change from the protracted negotiations with the auto drivers in Chennai.

My new home is 124 Pine Crest, which is a dodgy old building on a bed of snot-coloured concrete. There are trees lining the little street and a small all-purpose Patel General Stores at the corner. There is no sign of any pine or crest anywhere in the neighbourhood. But the name makes me feel like I'm at some mountain resort.

The watchman at the gate handed me the key to the apartment and started telling me the history of the place. I am glad I watched all those Bollywood movies on TV. I could at least understand the gist of what he said in his Mumbaiya Hindi. Then he asked me a strange question.

'Aapko baay chahiye?' Do you need a boy?

A boy?

I froze in shock. I couldn't believe what I had just heard. I had thought that such services were offered only to bachelors living alone. I couldn't believe that the watchman had mentioned it so blatantly even before I had moved in. Maybe news of my unmarried status had already reached the city and eligible bachelors had employed the watchman of Pine Crest as a marriage broker.

'I can send one soon. Very reliable,' he continued.

Vision of a hunky boy ringing my doorbell. 'I am very reliable,' he murmurs meaningfully, showing off six-pack abs under a tight black shirt.

'Madam, Gangabai was doing for the other two also who were here before.'

The gigolo was called Gangabai! Was it a eunuch? And what was it doing for the other two?

'Kya?' I muttered doubtfully.

'Everything, Madam. Gangabai will do all cleaning, vessels and washing clothes also. You can leave the key with her and she will finish everything.'

That was a relief. I have now learnt that the maids here are called bais, not to be confused with the gangster-type bhais, not to be confused with boys whom I will never find even in this city. I told the watchman to send Gangabai to clean as soon as she came and hauled my two suitcases into the creaking lift.

My flat is lovely. Vic, it is fully furnished. The drawing room has warm brown sofas with silky cushions, soft beige curtains and a smooth black Flat TV. There is a Persian rug on the floor and crystal glasses in the sideboard. My bedroom has clean sheets, a lamp at the desk and a spacious cupboard. I am alone now, but someone might be moving into the other room soon. I have grabbed the bigger bedroom with a view of many buildings. The other window opens onto a wall and a pipe. I unpacked and put my few belongings away. I hadn't brought too many clothes. Most of my outfits seemed unfit for the corporate life. I will sinfully spend my first salary on material acquisitions. I wish I could have you here, Vic, as wardrobe consultant. No one—not even I—cared how I looked when I worked at SSV, but here I am already feeling a little inadequate.

Gangabai turned up in the evening. She is a small woman who wears a crisp cotton sari and has an air of brisk efficiency about her. She seemed at home in my new home. She quoted her terms in a no-nonsense manner. Apparently, the two gentlemen who were living here earlier had paid her Rs 900 for her services. She would come in for two hours, from 10 p.m. to noon, during the day and finish everything. If I wanted to cook, she would even chop vegetables and keep them for an extra Rs 50. If I didn't, she would arrange for a dabba from her cousin Jamunabai, who would send it over every evening at Rs 30 a dabba with one dal, one sabzi, three rotis and rice.

She spoke a Marathi-Hindi combination which took a while to decipher, and at the end of her monologue, all I could do was nod in a servile way. I did not fare too well in my first negotiations with my first domestic help. If Amma heard that I was paying Rs 900 to a cleaning lady, she would insist on my doing the jhadoo-poncha as well. That is my new word for the day. Jhadoo-poncha

Tomorrow will be in my first day in office. After some enquiries, I have figured out how to get there by train from Bandra station, which is the closest from here. I have to set out on my adventure at 8:00 a.m. sharp, so as to not miss the 8:32 Churchgate Fast.

I believe it actually arrives at 8.32 and leaves the station at 8.37, but I want to take no chances.

Good night,
D.

✽

Hey Vic,

I have had an eventful day and have returned home a true Bombayvala—or should I say Mumbaikar?

I hailed an auto from here and reached the station in one piece. The station was a chaotic whirl. I am surprised that people function in this messy, crowded, smelly, anarchical place. I bought a ticket and found the platform and awaited the Churchgate Fast. There were all sorts of people on the platform. There were some corporate types in dark blue trousers and white shirts, the tips of their ties peeping from their pockets as they fiddled with their mobile phones. I saw a gaggle of giggly college girls wearing jeans or capris with tight T-shirts and oversized bags. Sari-clad women with black rexin handbags mingled with ladies wearing knee-length skirts and flowery tops who chatted in English. Most people knew each other and new arrivals were greeted with warmth and enquiries about the weekend.

The mood seemed to change when the train pulled in. The stragglers moved in and the ladies arranged themselves in a formation reminiscent of warriors at the battlefield. I was caught up in the middle and quickly propelled into the ladies' compartment. I found a pole and clung to it for dear life, inhaling all kinds of odours and conversations that swirled around me. I knew that mine was the last stop and finally I got a place to sit. The train popped me out after about forty minutes. I stumbled out of Churchgate station and stood in a queue for taxis. I finally hopped into one and declared that I needed to get to Shivaji Towers near Fort. All this strenuous activity will soon leave me too tired to work.

Just as I was leaning back in a relieved manner and regaining my breath in the taxi, I realized that the driver was saying that he couldn't find the office. Great! My first day at work and I was lost. The address clearly said Shivaji Towers. I figured it was a new building since no one had heard of it. All the other buildings seemed at least a hundred years old and vaguely colonial. After wandering mindlessly for a few minutes—the taxi driver was surprisingly patient—I gave up and called the HR lady from the driver's mobile phone. After I communicated the directions she had given me, the driver said, 'Oh, you mean Williamson Chambers,' in a couldn't-you-have-said-that-before voice. Shivaji Towers turned out to be an innocuous brown building we had already crossed three times. There was no signage to indicate that it was called Shivaji Towers. A small First Global sign was there in the lobby. I said a little prayer as I entered the portals of my new employer.

My first day at First Global was quite unexciting. Though I had washed my hair and worn my new yellow kurta, no one gave me a second glance. I walked to the reception with my appointment letter. The lady there took a long time to locate the right person. The HR lady I called was not picking up her phone any longer. I had to amuse myself by reading the newspaper and eavesdropping on the conversations the other visitors were having on their cell phones. Most people were claimed within ten minutes, but I warmed the First Global sofa like left-behind luggage for an hour.

Finally, someone called Madhurima from HR met me and made me fill up a lot forms. I have been allocated an employee code and an email address. You may now address all correspondence to d.balachandran@firstglobal.com.

Madhurima was astounded to know that I did not possess a mobile phone and made arrangements to procure one for me immediately. I don't have a desk to myself as yet, so I've been told to use the workstation of a junior officer who is on maternity leave. After I poured out my morning commuting woes to Madhurima, she advised me to buy a first-class pass and take the 8.42 Churchgate local. Hopefully it will be a better experience.

I spent most of the day gazing at the computer screen and reading the FG intranet. Most of the interesting websites are banned in office, thus forcing employees to concentrate on work instead of surfing job and social networking sites. Then I had to repeat my journey in the evening in reverse. I crawled into 124 Pine Crest at 8.30 p.m.

I hadn't arranged for the dabba yet. I ate two pieces of bread and a cup of chocolate ice cream and zoned out watching TV. I will buy some rice so that I can at least have curd rice for dinner. Amma forced me to carry two huge bottles of lime and mango pickle, so I can look forward to at least three hundred and sixty-five curd rice and pickle dinners in the near future.

Love,
D.

Dear Vic,

No, the Mumbai trains cannot be compared to the London Metro. I don't suppose I will ever travel by the London Metro, but I can imagine how it must be. Just take the number of people who travel by it daily, multiply that by two hundred and fifty-five, add some grime, dust, dirt, heat, peanut shells, candy wrappers, vegetable peelings, throw in some vendors of safety pins, sticker bindis, clips, pens and Gujarati snacks, stir them all together into a giant broth smelling of sweat and yesterday's dinner—and you might just be able to replicate the Mumbai local.

I have spent most of the last two days going around the office and getting to know people. This place is like a mini-India, with a complete set of characters from across the country. I bumped into Balki, an aged gent who floats around in the clearing department. Apparently, he has been there for years, sorting cheques and flinging them into boxes. I was surprised that he hadn't turned senile yet!

'Are you from Chennai?' Balki asked when we met. He seemed delighted to know that I was a Tamilian and launched into a complicated narrative of his history at First Global. 'I will tell you everything about the bank,' he said. 'I have been in banking for thirty-two years and in First Global ever since they started in India. Right from the time of Gowtham Bhargava—now he is heading the bank in South America. Gowtham and I joined the bank together. We used to have lunch together every day...' Yada yada yada.

I have to ensure that I don't bump into him ever again.

I met Jimmy Daruwalla, a new hire like me. Jimmy has been hired from a business school in Australia and is also waiting for his assignment. We will both hopefully get confirmed within six months and embark on a rewarding career with First Global. Jimmy looks like he is still in class ten, complete with Cerelac baby cheeks and dimples. His hair is a frizzy mop of brownish curls and his front teeth stick out a little, making him look like a cheerful Bugs Bunny. He is also two inches shorter than me. He seemed to snigger when he was introduced to me.

'What is so funny?' I asked him later.

'What do people usually call you?' he asked with a serious face.

'Damayanthi,' I replied with an equally serious face.

He grinned. 'Not Dummy?'

'No.'

'Or even better—Dumb Balls. That is a nice name for you.'

LV: 'And I can think of a lot of names for you. None of them are nice.'

Me: 'And I can think of a lot of names for you. None of them are nice.'

Yes, I actually did say that. And instead of thinking that I was rude and mean, he just said, 'Peace,' and made a V with his fingers.

Jimmy has been here for two weeks and already seems to know a lot about the bank. He drew an organization chart for me to know the people around and added a personal tit-bit for each of them. Though this is his first job, he seems far wiser about the corporate world than me.

'Viren Bhatia is the head of retail sales. He's sleeping around with Veronica. Throws wild parties. Last year, a trainee gate-crashed his party and got to smoke some pot! Jagdish Ahuja is head of corporate sales. He's got the hots for Veronica and is waiting for his turn once Viren dumps her. Vikas Bhalla is western region retail head. He and Amrita from treasury are supposed to be having a hot affair. Amrita is married to Amar Achrekar, who is the product head for Corporate Bank. He and Veronica used to sleep together last year. Hates Viren because she dumped him for Viren.'

This is a hotbed of hot beds! I couldn't believe all this was real. Jimmy must have an imagination wilder than J.K. Rowling's. How does he know all this? This must be what they call office gossip. There was nothing remotely close to this at SSV. I tried hard to be blasé and cool about all this, but I'm sure I looked shocked. I could feel my ears turning hot and red. They always do that when I get embarrassed. And Jimmy seems to like shocking me. I guess he thinks I am a prudish, old-fashioned southern maiden. I guess I might be one.

There are not too many women at First Global. The only woman senior vice president is a formidable lady called Renu Kamath who heads the credit function. Everyone is in awe of her. I am more curious about seeing this Veronica and her long line of paramours.

Love,
D.

❀

Dear Vic,

I saw Veronica today. She passed us in the cafeteria, where Jimmy and I were going through our regulation thali. She is the confidential secretary to the Big B. Once you are at First Global, Big B can only mean Ajit

Bhandari, our CEO and big chief in the subcontinent. Veronica looks like a pampered poodle on a bad fur day. She was wearing a tight little black skirt that ended well above her knees and a low-cut, semi-transparent blouse in a shade of lilac. I could almost see her lungs through it. She also wore matching plastic lilac earrings—aiyo! I could see all the males come to life like a bunch of dogs in heat.

'What do they see in her?' I asked Jimmy.

'Don't judge a book by its cover,' he answered. 'Peel off the cover first.' He was leering at Veronica's lungs, but not in a crude, lecherous way.

'Why do you guys always notice a woman's er… er… body first?' I asked. Somehow I couldn't bring myself to say breasts. Boobs sounds so crude. Chest sounds flat.

'Because it's more visible than her brains! And women want us to notice their one big asset.'

'That's not true,' I retorted.

'Ask Pamela Anderson.'

'That's not a benchmark.'

'What do women notice when they look at a man?' Jimmy asked. 'The bulge in his...'

'Pocket where he keeps his wallet!' I finished. My ears were turning hot and red again.

'Seriously, tell me?' he continued.

'I think different women look at different things. Shoes, clothes, eyes...' I remember we used to discuss these things in college. In fact, at St Maria's, you usually had to be content with just discussing these things.

'What about you?' he asked. 'What's your fetish?'

You know, Vic, if anyone had told me two months ago that I would be talking about my fetishes to a strange boy I had known only for a few days, I would have written it off as another misplaced astrological prediction. I had never even thought about specifically what I wanted in a man in terms of looks. What was not nice was a plastic comb in the back pocket (yuck!), cheap, fake branded shoes, shiny, checked polyester shirts and oily hair with specks of dandruff (double yuck!).

'Hair, I think. I like nice, dark hair—the kind that's crisp, not oily and slack. Thick, maybe curly, makes you want to run your hands through it.'

'Like mine.' He extended his head downwards. 'It's crispy, oil-free and delicately flavoured with a fragrant, pine-scented shampoo.'

'Sounds yummy, but I am already through with lunch.' I giggled.

'This is dessert, babe!' He twisted his mouth into a mock salacious grin. It looked like Master Raju trying to imitate Rajnikanth—it was so funny that I almost spluttered out the water I was drinking.

What would Amma say if she heard me talking like this?

It doesn't seem like I've known Jimmy for only four days. We laugh and joke like old friends. Did I imagine that conversation or was that B. Damayanthi exchanging swift, brilliant repartee with a man? Can this be called flirting? I don't ever recollect flirting before. Was it Milan Kundera who said, 'Flirting is the promise of sexual intimacy without its guarantee'? I must remember to use it in one of my witty conversations.

The best part is that I feel so comfortable with Jimmy. This does not sound complimentary to him, but he could have been any of my girl friends. It's like talking to Sumitra. Maybe I can have a wonderful platonic relationship with him. Maybe he is gay. That would make him the first homosexual I have ever known. Here I am, fraternizing with a probable gay friend. Vic, you probably have dozens of them, but for me it is a new experience.

Vision of Damayanthi and Jimmy sharing an apartment like they do in Will and Grace. *Jimmy walks in with probable boyfriend who looks like Leornado di Caprio. Oh god! We are both in love with him. Which will triumph—love or friendship? Leo whispers to me…*

❦

Dear Vic,

Sorry, I fell asleep during my fantasy and will now never know what Leo whispered to me.

Yaaaaaawn. That was my fifteenth yawn. My daily train commute is taking its toll on my health. The journey does have its high points. I amuse myself during those forty minutes by listening to the conversations of my fellow passengers, watching some of them even chop vegetables on the train. It's quite amazing, the lives people lead.

This evening, I performed an act of social service and gave my seat to a pregnant woman. The compartment was quite crowded. The poor woman looked as though she had swallowed a couple of basketballs and was about to regurgitate them any minute. Soon a conversation started about pregnancy and childbirth, to which I could contribute nothing. All the other women were mothers. I think motherhood gives you admission into some secret society with a cryptic language of its own.

'How many months?' asked Woman 1.

'Almost eight,' said the basketball woman.

'First one?' asked Woman 2.

Basketball Woman nodded.

'It will be a boy,' added another one. 'I can tell by the way you are sitting.'

'Have you found out?' questioned another lady.

'No,' she replied. 'We don't want to know.'

'My mother-in-law made me find out for the second one,' added Woman 1. 'The first was a girl.' She spoke in Hindi. I can understand the language very well, having scored top marks in Hindi as second language, but my conversational skills are rusty. I have to start watching more Bollywood movies now that I am close to the Hindi heartland.

Some women nodded sympathetically.

'They don't tell you in many hospitals now,' said Woman 2.

'My mother-in-law found some clinic where they do it. When she knew it was also going to be a girl, she wanted me to have an abortion,' continued Woman 1.

'What to do,' sighed Woman 3. 'It's so difficult these days, everything is so expensive.'

'To aapne kya kiya?' someone asked Woman 1. This was like a soap opera, I thought. One reads about these things, but I had never imagined that such things actually happened to people I might meet.

'What to do?' sighed Woman 1. 'Mita diya. Got rid of it. Good thing next one was a boy.'

'You killed it because it was a girl?' I was shocked and spoke out loud. This was an educated, working woman in a big city. There was a tense silence in the carriage.

'Do you have any children?' asked Basketball Woman, breaking the silence. The other women stared at me. I had no telltale signs of marriage—no mangalsutra, no red kumkumam, no ring.

'I'm not married,' I replied.

Just you wait, Woman 1 seemed to say with a knowing smirk. They lost interest in me after that.

'Mine was a Caesarian,' said Woman 4 suddenly. 'Twins. Both boys.'

'Doctors these days do an operation so quickly,' responded Woman 3.

'Both mine were normal,' said Woman 3. 'But I still had a small operation—the opening was too small. Haaye, it was so painful after that. The stitches were not healing properly also. Bathroom jaate time, oof...'

'I know,' added Woman 4. 'My cousin had continuous bleeding for six months. She had problems for one year after the child was born.'

'I had to have a piles operation after delivery,' contributed someone. Each one had a bizarre tale to tell and they told it with all its gory details. The pregnant woman lay back on the seat and closed her eyes. She looked tired and resigned to her fate.

Vic, I am not going to have kids. I will adopt a little girl—maybe two or three of them—and raise them to be independent, free spirits.

Vision of myself surrounded by my rainbow-children family. Husband who looks vaguely like Brad Pitt holds a little black child in his arms while two blond children run around in the grass with a majestic country mansion in the background. I cuddle a South Asian baby wearing designer rompers and laugh, hair gently stirred by the spring breeze…

Good night,
D.

Hi Vic,

Nice to know that you approve of my rainbow-children family. I didn't know that these days you can get a variety of cross-cultural sperm at Spinoza's Sperm Bank. Is that something you might be thinking of? I somehow still want to wait for a partner—a live, dedicated sperm donor, if you know what I mean.

Meanwhile, life goes on at FG. A funny thing happened to me at lunchtime. Not hilarious funny—

more strange funny. Jimmy and I were halfway through our dal roti when Balki passed by. He was carrying a small steel three-tiered tiffin carrier and was looking hesitantly about. He spotted me and advanced to our table with a smile.

'Don't mind, I am joining you,' he said and sat down. We smiled politely. Then he started off in rapid Tamil, 'Would you like some sambhar rice and poriyal? You must be missing home food.'

I declined his offer politely. I had a vague suspicion that he had a son stashed away somewhere and was eyeing me as a potential daughter-in-law.

He volleyed some typical matchmaker probes at me. 'Where are you from originally? Where are your parents? Are you an Iyer? Damayanthi is not a typical Brahmin name?'

I answered him for some time, toggling between English and Tamil. We discovered a possible common distant relative. He was disappointed to discover that my knowledge of my family tree stopped with my first cousins.

'So you are not married, are you?' Balki asked.

'No,' I said. I was right. I had no intention of letting myself be roped into another girl-seeing ceremony. 'Excuse us, we have to leave now.' I started to get up before he could bring up the topic of his son.

'Neither am I,' he replied in English. 'Confirmed bachelor. Those are my initials also—CB, for C. Balakrishnan.'

Both Little Voice and I were struck dumb.

Jimmy was almost hysterical. I hoped he wasn't going to concoct some story around this incident.

'So Damayanthi has found an admirer,' he laughed later. 'CB and DB—you'll make a nice couple.'

'Shut up.' I was trying hard not to laugh. Now I really have to avoid Balki. He is not eligible even by Amma's standards.

'You Madrasis really ought to stick together,' Jimmy went on with a thick accent. 'Stick closely to him and you can change your initials also.'

Actually, I have found that Tamilians are the ones who usually don't stick together. While Bengalis and Malayalis burst into their mother tongue at the slightest opportunity, we will converse in English even if we meet in an Artic igloo.

I was discussing this with Jimmy later in the day. Apparently, little communal cliques exist even in a professional, multinational organization like ours.

'The Punjus dominate sales and most front-end functions,' he explained. 'All aggressive, go-getting types. Lots of Tams in audit and financial control—number-crunching, brainy kind of jobs. Treasury has a bunch of Gujjus and Maarus—those guys seem to be natural hands at trading.'

'It seems like a local core competency theory.'

'There are some others floating around like me—some assorted Bongs and Bawas, but they don't have a vote.'

This was like politics. 'And so the caste system lives on in this strange way,' I wondered aloud.

'Oh, it's very subtle,' said Jimmy. 'I've heard that our HR head, Jagtiani, has a soft spot for Sindhis, so it's easier to get hired in clerical jobs if you are remotely related to one.'

'I still find it difficult to believe. Is it only here in First Global?'

'Nah, I'm sure it's kind of there in all organizations,' answered Jimmy. 'I heard we cracked a huge syndication deal with one of the large Marwari companies because one of the relationship managers is from the same town in Rajasthan as the VP (Finance). Everyone jokes about it, at least.'

Welcome to the Real World!

'This is so weird,' I said.

'You won't have any problems, anyway,' he went on.

'Why?'

'Women have a major advantage in Big B's regime. I believe there is a little room on the fifth floor.'

'What room?' I asked.

'The casting cubicle.' Jimmy wiggled his brows suggestively.

I was shocked. I couldn't believe such a thing existed. I had read about the casting couch in the movie industry, but here, at First Global—a professional, multinational organization—it was not possible!

Then I saw that the idiot Jimmy was grinning like a clown and I got annoyed that I appeared so naive.

'That is so typical of men,' I retorted. 'You guys think that we just have to open up a button or drop the sari pallu to get ahead. Actually, because of all your stupid notions, we end up slogging twice as hard and getting half the credit.'

'Hey, relax!' Jimmy looked surprised at my tirade. 'I was just joking. Don't do the militant feminist thing on me.'

'But—'

'Unless you want to take off your bra and burn it.' He chuckled. I just can't be serious with him.

This is so much fun!

Damayanthi.

5

Dear Vic,

First Global finally figured out what to do with Jimmy and me. We were getting tired of reading product manuals and pretending to scour the intranet. Apparently, there has been some restructuring of some functions and the jobs we were initially supposed to do don't exist any longer. Luckily, instead of firing us, they have put us on a task force on the special projects team. It sounds very important. I guess they can best use my skills there. We also found out that we have a boss. After floating like jetsam for two weeks, we were both relieved and disappointed that we were going to start work. Our boss is Harish Chopra, an assistant vice president. He is a short, fair, wispy sort of a guy, with thin hair and a droopy, thin moustache.

He always wears an anxious look, as though a bomb is about to go off somewhere near him. He seems surgically attached to his mobile phone and is either talking into it or waiting to talk into it.

Harish told us that we are part of a re-engineering task force that is looking at the bank's entire operations. We will be working with a team of external consultants to streamline processes and discover synergies between the retail and institutional parts of the banks. Harish said that it was a challenging assignment that would give us great visibility, which would be good for our career. I didn't have a clue what he was saying, but it sounded exciting. He seems like a sincere, well-meaning person. Jimmy was on leave today—he has a viral infection—so I need to brief him tomorrow.

My workstation has been reclaimed by the officer who has returned from maternity leave. This woman, Jyotsna, looked really irritated that I had been occupying her place. Instead of being a contented new mother, she seems to be suffering from withdrawal symptoms from being away from her precious workstation for so long.

Jimmy and I are now nomads. We are being temporarily stationed inside a small meeting room called Yen. These little meeting and conference rooms are named after different currencies, probably by some bright spark who thought it was truly global idea. I noticed that we do not have a Rupee room—that would make us too local.

Yen has a phone, but no computers. Harish is trying to get us laptops. We will soon be connected to the world. In the meantime, I wait for someone to go on a break so that I can check my email. I find myself getting addicted to this email checking business. Every time I hear a ping and see a small white envelope at the corner of my screen, I want to access my email. It is usually a general mail from admin@firstglobal.com, telling us about an impending fire drill, or from systemsec@firstglobal.com, warning us about an impending machine downtime. I sometimes get jokes forwarded by Jimmy or Sumitra. Reading them has so far been the high point of my day.

I hope that now I can finally get to do something meaningful and justify my salary.

Love,
D.

Hi Vic,

I downloaded the information to Jimmy yesterday. Please notice how my lingo has become First-

Globalized. Here, we do not merely pass on information, we download it. If we have to pass on information in less time, we brief people and get debriefed in return. We do not contact people, we touch base with them. We don't get things done quickly, but ASAP. I have my meals in LR (lunchroom) and wait to be noticed by someone from the LT (leadership team) and go to the LOO to answer calls of nature!

Jimmy was not happy with our assignment. I tried echoing Harish's words to him.

Me: 'Jimmy, this is a challenging assignment.'

JD: 'Which means that only the cerebrally challenged would accept it!'

Me: 'It will give us high visibility.'

JD: 'Only if people have night vision goggles to see in the black hole we are banished to.'

Me: 'It's a great learning experience.'

JD: 'So is prison.'

Me: 'Harish said it would be good for our career.'

JD: 'Provided we don't want a promotion or bonus for the next five years. You really are a dummy. Why do you think we have been put on this? To do strategic redesign? To actually help improve workflows?'

Me: 'That is what Harish said.'

JD: 'Dummy, you are so silly.'

Me: 'Don't call me that.'

JD: 'Dumb Balls.'

Me: 'Jamshed, don't call me that!'

JD: 'Who told you about that?'

Me: 'Hah! I saw the cover of your personal file when I went to submit a form to HR, Jamshedji.' We were behaving like kids, not two responsible bankers. We needed to be gainfully occupied soon.

By this time, I was feeling depressed too. Apparently, this project has been going on for six months and nothing has happened. So, after feeling some pressure from the head office in the US, the consulting firm of ASTC had been engaged to do some process re-engineering. I didn't understand why Jimmy was so against our assignment. Then we met a couple of other bankers at LR. Ajay and Lalit exchanged knowing looks when Jimmy spoke about the task force.

'Oh, you both are going to be on Harish's project,' Lalit smirked. 'All the best!' Lalit is a fair, clean-shaven product manager. He is superficially nice-looking, but there is something slimy and shifty about him. He is the type who appears to be patting you on the back, but is actually looking for a good spot to stab you with a sharp knife. I believe he is a success story in the bank. He has been promoted to manager within a year—it normally takes about two to three years for the normal worker ant to move up the ladder. According to him, Harish is a 'loser'. They didn't want to promote him to vice president, so they have handed him this project to keep him quiet. So anyone who gets attached to Harish is also a 'loser'.

So, I am on a 'losing' project. Vic, I don't care. I have to make it work. I can't go back to SSV after a month.

Sincerely,
Damayanthi.

Dear Vic,

While you have been busy trying to rehabilitate a hooker (too bad the horse kicked her teeth in on the first day) in your father's stables, I have been hard at work. We have spent the last few days in Yen, trudging through process manuals and trying to figure out what goes on in the bank. We have three more days before the ASTC team comes in and we need to be knowledgeable by then. There are global processes for counting money, putting away money in the vault, taking out money from the vault, recounting money, handing over money and searching for lost money. The most interesting one was a note on the process for handling a hold-up at the teller counter.

    1.1. The teller should stay calm and not panic.

    1.2. The teller should memorize the features of the perpetrator.

    1.3. The teller should notice the size, make and nature of weapon in the possession of the perpetrator.

I wonder who wrote all this. I wonder if the poor teller will remember the steps with a gun pointed to his head—'Point number 1.1. from my process manual said I shouldn't panic.'

I woke up this morning with arrows and boxes floating in front of me after peering at a hundred and fifty flowcharts. I even had a dream where I was designing a process for brushing teeth and was making a presentation to Big B. There was a PowerPoint presentation with a huge mouth and thirty-two teeth, and I was saying something like, 'Squeezing the toothpaste with your left hand directly onto your teeth and keeping the brush poised at an angle of 135 degrees can save twenty seconds of brushing time. Drinking the gargling water instead of spitting it out will not only help save water, but also provide your body with valuable nutrients in the form of fluoride and peppermint.' Good thing I woke up, else I would have missed the 8.42 local and would have been late for an important meeting.

The important meeting turned out to be a gyan session. Gyan, meaning knowledge in Hindi, actually means boring general stuff you are better off not knowing. Today, Harish despatched us to Kroner to listen to some AVP giving a talk on some process re-engineering he had done in the branch. This guy, Rohit, went on ad nauseum about cycle times, quality tools he had used and statistical measures he had devised, how his keen analytical ability had helped him spot process inefficiencies and his sheer genius had immediately led him to identify areas for improvement. I was bored and sleepy and doodled in my notebook instead of taking down notes. It sounded important, but I was just not in the mood.

Jimmy looked dazed. 'This guy is so full of shit,' he muttered. The total output at the end of the session was this:

A young banker called Rohit
Was completely full of bullshit
A single blast of gas
Shot out from his ass
Could stun the audience in a minute

I can't take it any longer. My fingers are numb from turning pages and my eyes glazed from staring at the computer screen. I will quit. There isn't anything worthwhile to do. I can't believe I left SSV to read process manuals.

Warm regards,
Damayanthi.

Dear Vic,

No, Vic, I don't think I will quit after all. I spoke to my friend Sumi after a long time and asked her for some advice. Sumi heard me crib and laughed.

'Welcome to the corporate world, D,' she said.

'I didn't think it would be so boring. It is just as bad as SSV sometimes,' I moaned.

'So what did you think? That you would be doing some heavy-duty strategic M&A stuff, advising CFOs where to put their-ill gotten gains? It is all bullshit, D. The whole system survives on it. You know that, right? Life is a bitch and then you get passed over for promotion. Ha ha ha!'

'At least you are doing some good work,' I said wistfully. 'You went to Paris sometime back and then to Manila.'

'And do you know what I have been doing for the past three weeks? D, I am reading reports on the bio fuel industry in India. Some client of ours wants to enter the biogas business and we are evaluating the business plan. Now my asshole boss wants me to do field research in some obscure village in eastern UP. Next thing I know, I will be squatting like those village women and putting cow dung cakes on the walls of our cubicles. So you don't complain!'

'I don't know, Sumi. It is so mind-numbing. I don't know what to do!'

'Find a hot guy, D. I heard some of these banker types are quite cute, tie-vie and all? That will take your mind off work.'

'No such luck there, Sumi. I can't see anyone remotely eligible here.'

'D, forget all this eligible Tam Brahm business. Just find a nice guy with average intelligence, a good body, no BO and preferably no parents.' For a change, Sumi sounded a little irritated.

'Why, Sumi? What happened?'

'It is Deb's parents,' sighed Sumi. 'We thought they would be easier to handle than Appa and Amma, so Deb broke the news to them first thinking that they will be okay. According to him, they are quite liberal, modern Bongs. Unfortunately, that does not extend to their only darling son who is supposed to marry this

Bengali bou type. There is this daughter of a family friend who is an accompleeshed cooker of phive types of pheesh and she warbles Robindroshongeet like a Bong nightingale. According to Deb, she looks like an anaemic roshogolla, which means she is fair and thin on top of being accompleeshed.' She mimicked a Bengali accent and, though I sympathized with her, I couldn't help laughing.

'Don't worry, Sumi. It will work out. At least you have a man.'

'I don't know, D. I thought I knew Deb, but he acts as though it's not a big deal. In the end, I will be the one who has to adjust. Catch *him* learning to make rasam,' she snorted.

'The path of true love does not run smooth,' I quoted, trying to sound wise.

'Bah! Forget this love-shove marriage business, D. Just go out there and have a good time with as many guys as you can and settle down into a good arranged marriage only by the age of thirty-five.'

'I wish. Where are all the guys?'

'They won't fall into your lap like a laddoo from heaven. You have to hunt for them. Hang in there. But don't complain to your boss about how your job sucks. That definitely means bad marks in your report card. The first time I did it, my boss marked me down on "Motivation and Proactive Approach". My jerk likes to say, "Don't come to me with your problems, come to me with your solution." You idliface, I want to tell him, why the hell are they paying you a fat salary? To solve problems or to listen to other people's solutions and pass them off as your own? D, you can go talk to your HR person about your job role and a career development plan and all that. It's good to shake those buggers out of their stupor once in a while.'

It sounded like good advice, so I went with my mixed feelings to HR. We have this warm, fuzzy-feeling activity called FAF (Frank and Friendly) discussions, where employees are encouraged to tell their Friendly Neighbourhood Human Resource Manager about stuff that is bugging them. Obviously, you can't tell your boss a lot of things, especially if you think he is Jerk No. 1, because he can really screw you during your PEP (Performance Enhancement Programme). That is the annual review and your career depends on how much your boss hates or loves you. I think PEP is supposed to pep up employees, but from what I hear, it is the shittiest part of the year. I'm learning how the wheels turn here and am also learning how to casually use words like screw and shit in daily conversation. I can't say f*** yet.

I called Madhurima and made my way for FAF time with her. I told her about being demotivated and depressed. That I think that the job is not satisfying.

I ought to be doing something more productive and enriching. Madhurima listened with an encouraging look and gave me a return spiel about how we all have these cycles. She made it sound like I was going through PMS instead of genuine job anxiety. Then she handed me a small book called *FISH!* I was supposed to read it to recharge and motivate myself. I flipped through it—it was about these guys who self-actualize by throwing large, smelly, bloody pieces of fish around the place and have a party doing it. It's all about attitude, I said to myself. I will have a good time reading process manuals. Even if it kills me.

Anyway, I felt better after talking to someone. So it was with a light and almost jaunty step that I entered Dirham for the first meeting with ASTC.

ASTC stands for Always Screw The Client.

No, Vic, just joking. That is Jimmy's version. Apparently, this is a top-notch consulting outfit like McKinsey and BCG, only more niche and finance focused. I think ASTC stands for Always Satisfy The Customer. No—that sounds too much like an escorts services agency. I think ASTC originally stood for the names of the original partners of the firm, sort of like KPMG, but now no one remembers who those guys were.

The ASTC consultant was already there. He was a tall, lean man wearing gold-rimmed spectacles and a world-weary look on his face. He wore a dark suit with a warm red tie that lay on a crisp white shirt. He was reading the day's *Economic Times* and looked up when I entered. We looked at each other for a few seconds. I thought he looked insufferably superior. His expression seemed to say—'I know everything and what I don't know is not worth knowing.'

'Hi, I am Gigi. I am the senior consultant with ASTC,' he said and extended a languid hand.

'Geegee!' I exclaimed. Men obviously did not have names like Gigi.

'No! CG. As in C for calculus and G for geometry.' CG looked annoyed.

LV: 'Like, not C for charmer or G for gorgeous.'

'I am Damayanthi. I work with the special project team and am going to be working on the process improvement project,' I said in a brisk, professional manner.

He just gave me a cool, appraising nod, which made me wonder if my minimal make-up was smudged or my kurta was crumpled or my tongue was hanging out like a thirsty dog's. We shared a brief, uncomfortable pause.

'So you are going fishing?' CG said, looking at the book in my hand.

Okay, he was trying to make conversation. Think, D, think.

LV: 'Yeah! I am trying to hook a great catch, but I will let you be the one that got away.'

'Yes,' I said. 'HR handed me this after a FAF. I was hoping for something better, but guess I fell for it.'

'Hook, line and sinker,' CG responded with a condescending curl of the lips.

LV: I was angling for a raise, but ended up taking the bait.'

Me: 'Uh-uh.'

Whatever happened to my witty repartee? Instead of having an intelligent exchange of words, I was just standing there, gaping like a cod.

I had this terrible urge to say something smart to make up for my lapse. So I blurted out, 'So you are reading the *ET*.'

Great! Even a complete moron could see that.

CG nodded. 'So what do you think of the proposed loan waiver for farmers that has just been announced?'

Whaaat! I had not glanced at a paper for the past two weeks. Clearly this was compulsory reading in banking circles. I was kind of getting hooked to the *Times of India* supplement with pictures of beautiful people blowing air kisses to each other.

'I guess the farmers will be happy to get the loans waived off,' I said. That was safe. Surely anybody would, be happy if they didn't have to pay back a loan? I know I would if I had a loan! Poor farmers would love that.

Amused and superior look from CG. 'On one hand, it is a populist measure which could boost the sagging image of the current government, but on the other, the sizeable cost to the exchequer will have a significant negative impact on our fiscal deficit.'

'Uh-uh.' I tried to keep an intelligent look on my face so that I didn't look completely ignorant. Did real people actually talk like that? And about fiscal deficit? Who really, truly cared about fiscal deficit?

Another uncomfortable silence while CG thinks Damayanthi is a complete moron with a hearing problem and Damayanthi thinks CG is a pompous ass and wishes she had read widely and formed opinions about news items of national importance.

I was saved by the entry of Jimmy and Harish. We will be working with CG on the re-engineering project. CG did not look too happy when he heard that. I could hear the little cogs in his mind going, 'I am stuck with a child and a retard. Help!'

Jimmy and I just have to show him. I am now going to read the last three days' *ET*. The headlines, at least.

Vision of myself asking CG, 'So what do you feel about the proposed takeover of Yahoo by Microsoft?' *'What?' CG is stunned. He has been out of touch.*

Damayanthi continues with a confident, knowledgeable look on her beautiful face, 'On one hand, the synergies from this merger will obviously benefit the consumer especially in the middle of the spectrum. However, such a consolidation raises serious questions about the symbiotic relationship between media and technology, which has serious indications of an oligarchic business model.' CG gazes at Damayanthi with awe and reverence.'That is an intelligent and refreshing point of view, Damayanthi. You are an amazing combination of beauty and brains.'

It will happen. Some day.

Goodnight, Vic.
Damayanthi.

❦

Dear Vic,

I believe I am getting a flatmate. Shinde from admin told me a couple of days back that another girl is moving in here. She is joining us from the Delhi retail branch. She is a relationship manager with private banking. Sounds like a respectable lady, but I have got used to living alone for the past month. I don't want anyone intruding into my space.

I had an interesting weekend. I have decided to add a few personal touches to the house and give it a nice, cosy feeling. I can't have my humble abode looking like a dump when my flatmate walks in.

Essentials purchased include:

1 pair of kitchen scissors—to open the chips packets; teeth don't work too well.
1 Vim bar and scrubber—maid complained about washing vessels with detergent.
1 small table lamp—to read in bed and snooze without getting up to switch off the light.
1 shower curtain—grey with pink roses to match the bathroom tiles.

I think this place is beginning to look better. Shower curtains make a huge difference. I feel almost married now and can see myself buying matching His-and-Her hand towels next.

I also indulged in a bout of spring cleaning. The bai and I scrubbed the windows with Colin and I dusted the fans. We applied a dash of lime to the greasy cooking range and hosed down the fridge with a mixture of two parts Surf and one part water. Soon I will be ready to contribute to *Femina*'s 'Housekeeping Hints' and be a potential winner of Sumeet Oven-

Toaster-Grill. I think there is a housewife lurking beneath the tough banker exterior. Amma would have been proud to see my house-proud avatar. Maybe my latent cleaning genes have only now bubbled to the surface.

Jimmy and I had been invited by Ajay Mahtani for dinner. Ajay has been with FG for almost a year. I had just been introduced to him last week at LR. I took a train to Andheri, met Jimmy at the station and landed up at Ajay's apartment. It's in a place called Lokhandvala. It is supposed to be the haunt of minor cine stars and TV personalities, but I did not see a single one. I fact, I have not spotted any celebrity so far. The closest I came was sighting a vague blur on the balcony of Shahrukh Khan's house in Bandstand.

There was a motley gathering at Ajay's place. It was a teenager's room, bloated up into a house. Mattresses were carelessly thrown on the floor and cartons of clothes sat in the bedroom. There were two large posters of Aishwarya Rai and Sachin Tendulkar on the wall, along with one which had Garfield saying, 'This is my mess and I love it.' Ajay shared this mess with two of his friends from two other companies. Apparently, they had lived in the same dorm in IIM and wanted to recreate the experience.

Dinner was a biryani-and-beer affair. Ajay had fixed up a Hi-Fi music system, complete with Bose speakers (that's where his first year's savings had gone) and a bar whose contents were restricted to bottles of Fosters beer. I met Ajay's friends, Vyom and Salil, and another guy called KP who looked half-asleep. He didn't say anything, except something like 'Motherchod' every now and then. Maybe he didn't want to leave his mother and come here. I couldn't follow everything they said. A lot of it was in colloquial Hindi. So I was this quiet fly on the wall and listened to five grown men talking. Yes, Vic, there was Damayanthi, alone in a room with four strange men and none of them fell on her young person like starved wolfhounds. No alcohol was offered to her after the refusal of beer. Nothing was mixed in her veg biryani. Her honour remained intact, but her self-esteem took a beating.

At the end of our dinner, however, I was glad that I had not caught their attention or fancy. Damayanthi is discovering men and not liking them too much.

Vyom is apparently engaged to some homely girl handpicked by his parents. He was going on about how he didn't want a career woman for a wife. They were so aggressive, demanding and selfish!

'After I come back home late in the evening, I need someone to give me a hot cup of tea and massage my head,' he said.

'Not just that,' said Ajay. 'Who wants to come home and argue about whose turn it is to make dinner and who should have paid the bills? Too much jhanjhat. And she'll have nakhras about her job and her promotion.'

Surprisingly, the other guys agreed with him. 'Yaar, if she looks remotely like Katrina, I don't care what she does,' added Jimmy. He was a huge fan of Katrina Kaif and had a really oomphy picture of her as his screensaver. He replaced it frequently with oomphier pictures of her in various skimpy outfits. I gave him a dirty look.

'She can teach in a school or do some work from home,' added Vyom generously.

'Otherwise she'll be spending all our hard-earned money on shopping or kitty parties,' guffawed Ajay.

I wanted to brain them with a beer bottle, but it wasn't worth the trouble. I hoped their wives would run away with the plumber or become the next Shahnaz Hussain and control a million-dollar empire. Clearly, the male IQ was on the wane. After that, they all talked about work and recounted stories of bizarre bosses and bumbling subordinates. Jimmy made an occasional contribution to the discussion, but I listened quietly and soaked in the office gossip.

I was suddenly homesick when I returned. So I called home. Appa was already asleep and Amma had just switched off the TV after the last serial.

We had the same conversation we had the day after I landed. I answered my usual six questions with my usual six answers.

'Are you eating properly?'

'YES.'

'Are you getting your meals on time?

'YES.'

'Is it safe?'

'YES.'

'Is the maid coming regularly?'

'YES.'

'Have you met anybody?'

'NO.'

'Are you fine?'

'YES.' Meaning, I have been good—very good— and therefore not fine.

Then I got to hear about what was happening in Chennai. How many more girls have managed to get married, how many have got engaged, how many are in advanced stages of closure, how difficult it is getting to find nice boys and how everybody longs for the patter of little feet in the house. Vic, you are so lucky your parents are not bugging you to get hitched.

Good night,
Damayanthi.

6

Hi Vic,

Like you, I had no idea what goes on in the dark dungeons of a bank. You probably have a picture of me raking piles of cash and valuables into large cavernous lockers and slipping a secret key into my salwar pocket. That sounds more like Gringotts than First Global. Unfortunately, we do not have goblins guarding gold. Nor are there secret numbered accounts presided over by suave Swiss bankers.

I now have a good understanding of the inner cogs of First Global. So let me enlighten you. At the lowest rungs are the operations guys, who are the galley slaves. They work in the big centralized operations (COps) centre at Powai, where human robots process cheques, pass data entries and keep the wheels of the bank turning. Then you have the people at the various branches—FG has about twenty of them across the country, mostly in the bigger cities. These all customer touch point roles, which puts them one step above their non-customer touch point counterparts. Then there are the retail guys, who peddle credit cards and car loans—the only two products that FG currently offers to the Indian retail customer. These are a bunch of perpetually harassed guys, who run after more perpetually harassed guys, our agents, who perpetually harass innocent bystanders and bully them into signing up for our products. The other, corporate part of the bank deals with corporate customers through relationship managers, who wine and dine corporate honchos in companies like Reliance and Ranbaxy. They are ably assisted by product managers, who read the *Economic Times* and RBI bulletins and try to make sense of the new Repo rate and EXIM policy. At the top rung are the hotshots at treasury, who probably wear suspenders and do deals in the (what else?) dealing room. They are supposed to get ulcers by the age of thirty, retire by the age of thirty-five or burn out at forty. I am sure there are still some parts I don't know about but will discover shortly. Then there are the flotsam—like Jimmy and me—who do odd jobs that nobody wants.

I had my first review meeting with Harish on the status update of our project. I remembered Sumi's advice about not complaining to your boss. I had to appear motivated and project a positive attitude. 'The project is going on well,' I said. 'We are on target as per our timelines. The internal focus group discussions have been completed and we are gathering the voice of customer data from clients who deal with us for both retail and wholesale products. We have a presentation next week with ASTC on next steps.' I am learning, Vic, the art of gyan-giving.

He asked if there was any interesting information we found in the preliminary analyses. I couldn't recall anything of significance, but we obviously cannot disappoint senior management. I remembered someone talking about the time it took to get a simple query resolved and another one saying that it took too bloody long to get a letter of credit opened.

'There were some issues on turnaround times,' I remarked. 'These were more evident for certain processes like complaint resolution. Some of these areas are not directly related to our project since we are looking primarily at front-end solutions.'

I noticed Harish beginning to look animated. 'That is what I have been saying all along. We need to re-evaluate the processes we have put in place across all operations. We have grown a lot since we centralized operations a year ago and we have not seen how well the process has worked for us.'

I nodded encouragingly and added my two bits. 'I have seen what we do in COps and can see a lot of areas where we can do better with a little re-engineering.'

'Excellent,' squeaked Harsh. 'This is the kind of thinking we need.' I felt a warm glow of happiness.

'How are you enjoying the assignment so far?' he asked

'It's a great experience. I am learning so much about the different parts of the bank,' I said cheerfully. Actually, we were not doing much, except still looking at process manuals.

'Good, good,' he continued to squeak. 'I hope you are not working too hard. It can be difficult getting the hang of so many new things.'

'No, no,' I hastened to assure him. I was quite capable of understanding everything quickly—thank you very much! I didn't want him thinking that I wasn't smart enough or shirked work.

'It's interesting, but not very difficult,' I said coolly, with an all-in-a-day's-work air. More marks on 'Capable of taking on more responsibility'.

'Then we must give you something really challenging to do,' Harish said with a smile. In retrospect, I can see that it was the smile of the evil

Mogambo about to throw the heroine into a pit of fiery acid.

'It would be a great idea if you could work on a project to map all COps processes and identify inefficiencies. I am sure we can do better in terms of cycle times and costs. It is critical for the bank at this time, and I have been looking for someone to handle this.'

'But... but...' I stuttered. Too late. I had fallen into the trap. There was no way out.

Young Ms Damayanthi Balachandran, being only one month in the corporate system, succumbed to a clear case of managementitis. Managementitis, spread by senior management members, starts out as an innocuous compliment on the victim's abilities and mutates into a dull, career-limiting assignment, which will lead to long working hours with no prospect of increased pay. There is no known remedy for those afflicted with this disease, though prolonged exposure produces thicker skin and greater ability to spot the virus in its initial stages.

I hesitated. Harish then spoke the magic words that sealed my decision. 'This project will be critical for your career. If you can show areas for definite improvement, it will go all the way up to the ManCom. AB is personally interested in any improvement measures in COps. If this goes off well, you can probably have your choice of your next assignment.'

Increased exposure to sustained managementitis causes victim to believe that the side effects are actually positive and surviving the dull, career-limiting move will lead to long-term immunity from the disease.

Vision of Big B shaking my hand. 'Damayanthi, you have done excellent work on this project. We are promoting you to assistant vice president and transferring you to our London office.' Damayanthi is received in London by the local vice president who looks like Daniel Craig. He murmurs, 'I have heard so much about you.'

Victim of managementitis suffers from delusions of grandeur and has visions of her own greatness and indispensability to the system.

'You can start by looking at the process manuals and spend some time at COps examining each process,' Harish went on. 'We want this to be done in a month.'

'A month!' It would take me three months to figure out all the processes in the first place.

'Yes. Since you can grasp new things quickly, it won't be much of a problem. You have already met the ASTC guys. CG will be focusing specially on this project and I need you both to work closely with him. I believe these guys have done some good work with some other banks like ours.'

We are in for it. The prospect of working closely with CG was not exciting. I would probably have to be thoroughly prepared and mug up the *ET* headlines every day. I had to download this to Jimmy.

'We have this great opportunity for another project in COps, Jimmy,' I started. He looked suspiciously at me.

'It's really good for your career and AB is personally interested in any process improvement measures in COps. If this goes off well, you can probably have your choice of your next assignment,' I went on.

'Cut the crap, Damayanthi,' he said. 'Now we've got some more shit work to do. No more Juice Corner.'

We have spent the last week trudging through process manuals and trying to figure out what goes on in the big operations factory in Powai. We have no other trainee assigned to us. Senior management is doing resource optimization!

Bye,
D.

Hello Vic,

It looks as though our project is going to be a loser project after all. CG is very clear about how he wants to approach the issue—follow the ASTC model, which involves making lots of flowcharts and collecting data and analysing it on complex-looking Excel spreadsheets. Jimmy prefers the Jimmy model, which involves doing nothing and looking busy while surfing the internet. Harish adheres to the First Global model, which involves holding endless meetings and taking minutes with action plans and discussing the minutes in the next meeting and so on. Damayanthi is stuck between models.

We have spent the first three days trying to decide our approach to the project. Here is a snapshot of one of our meetings.

CG begins. 'I think we can start off by analysing the data collected so far. The best way would be to prepare an Excel spreadsheet. Damayanthi, can you write a macro which will segregate the data as per cycle times and operating costs?'

LV: 'Duh-uh? What language are you speaking? Can I get an interpreter, please?'

Me: 'I can try.'

CG frowns. He will become like that jerk boss of Sumi, asking for solutions instead of listening to problems. He probably thinks I am the kind who believes that XL is my kurta size and spreadsheets have something to do with bed linen. My exposure to technology is based on the need-to-know principle propounded by my former employers, who still love the old-fashioned pencil-and-paper method. I am slowly picking things up at FG, but have a long way to go before I can write a macro.

CG continues. 'We need to approach this in a systematic manner, failing which the recommendations we make may be completely unsubstantiated.'

Harish: 'Absolutely. Jimmy, Damayanthi, you guys get on to it right away. We need quick results.'

Jimmy: 'Right. Sure.' He has just woken up from some pleasant reverie.

'Once we are able to map each process out, we should do a fishbone analysis to identify the root cause of any problems that come up during the analysis. While on one hand, it is imperative to meet our deadline and get quick results, on the other, the benefit of ASTC's rigorous and meticulous approach is the guarantee that our recommendations will fulfil the value proposition that we promise our clients,' CG goes on. He sounds sincere, serious.

I am sure he is a dedicated consultant, but I do wish he would lighten up sometimes.

'What do you think, Damayanthi?' His voice bores into my consciousness.

LV: 'I can't think any more, CG. My brain stops functioning when you say, "On one hand..."'

'That sounds logical,' I say slowly. 'Maybe I can visit COps and take detailed notes on the processes there.' At least that will get me away from CG and his spreadsheets.

'Great! So Damayanthi, why don't you send out a mail with the minutes of this meeting and action items and we will review it during the next meeting.'

Harish leaves and the meeting is officially over.

We hung around as Jimmy tried to postpone getting to work for as long as possible.

'So CG, did you catch the match last night?' Jimmy asked.

CG paused for a minute, wondering if it was part of his rigorous and meticulous approach to discuss cricket matches with clients. Then his face broke into a slight smile and he said, 'Awesome, wasn't it?' I think it was the first time I saw him smile. It made him look younger, almost boyish, less intimidating. For the next few minutes, they animatedly discussed cricket and then moved on to Formula One racing.

Jimmy and CG now seem to get along together. I still have to break the ice, a possibility that seems remote. Not that I want anything more than a professional, working relationship with CG.

Love,
D.

7

~~

Hey Vic,

Woe and behold! Sonya Sood, my new flatmate, moved in today. I was expecting a respectable lady and hoping for a kindred soul, but I am stuck with a size-zero social butterfly. I have never seen anyone like her before, not in real life. She has legs that go on for miles, smooth, fair skin without a single blot, blotch or blemish, silky brown hair and pearly white teeth which can only be the result of the loving ministrations of a skilled orthodontist. Her butt looks like a pair of taut Chinese apples, which immediately makes me feel like I have two watermelons strapped to my derriere.

She was dressed in tight jeans and a short, strappy top which I would never be able to carry off in my wildest dreams. Looking at her polished nails and platform heels, I felt quite frumpy. Sometimes, you look at a person and know that you will get along with them really well and the air is abuzz with positive vibes. This absolutely did not happen with my new flatmate. In fact, in our past lives, we were probably the snake and snake charmer who shared a hate-hate relationship but were irrevocably linked together by occupational choices.

After looking around the flat with a disdainful air, she said, 'I suppose it's okay, though I would have preferred staying somewhere in town. It takes so long to commute in this stupid city. In Delhi, I used my Lancer, and our bungalow was just a few minutes from Connaught Place.'

LV: 'Yes, m'lady. I note that you are rich too and probably don't have to work for a living. You are only doing this job to pass the time till you find a richer guy and can quit to spend his millions.'

Me: 'The trains are quite convenient.'

'You travel by the local train!' she exclaimed in horror, as though I had admitted to having caught a venereal disease after frolicking in the Mumbai slums. 'I can't bear the thought.'

LV: 'Maybe you can have your private helicopter pick you up and transport you to office every morning or sprout wings and fly away.'

Me: 'Maybe you can get a place closer to office and move there.' Please do.

She shrugged her skinny shoulders and said, 'I have to manage for now.' She didn't look too happy about it.

'We'll have to change all the furnishings, of course,' she went on, scrutinizing the surroundings. 'This sofa colour is so drab and the upholstery is fraying. I can't believe we don't have wall-to-wall carpeting. The curtains in the bedroom don't go with the bedspread at all.' Within ten minutes, she managed to make me feel as though I had been living in a pigsty. Suddenly, I was aware of the dirt on the ceiling fans, a stray cobweb and a tea cup ring on the coffee table. She was about to convert the pigsty into a model house to be featured in the next edition of *Society Homes*, with Ms Sonya Sood posing languidly on a 10x10 silk-on-silk handwoven Persian carpet.

'I don't think the bank will pay for all that,' I ventured.

The *Good Housekeeping* graduate brushed off this comment like a pesky fly.

'Rubbish. I'll talk to Shinde. We can't live like this. They spend millions to send VPs to Tahiti and Honolulu for conferences. This is nothing.'

She breezed into the kitchen. 'I suppose there is a housekeeper or cook?' she enquired while inspecting the glasses. Next she'll be expecting Jeeves to run the bath for her and hand the mail on a silver salver.

'No cook,' I said. 'I make cornflakes and toast for breakfast and a dabba is delivered for dinner every night.'

Shock and horror. Maybe Little Miss Muffet was used to Mama's hot parathas and freshly squeezed orange juice in the morning.

'I will arrange for a cook soon,' she said, as though cooks dropped from the sky like birdshit. 'Mamma will send one from Delhi if required.'

I cribbed to Jimmy about her over dinner and he agreed that she sounded really horrible. He stays in town with his parents in some swank Malabar Hill penthouse. His family is into some shipping and textile business, but Jimmy didn't want to join it. He wanted to make it on his own. I thought it was really brave. This was one of my promised dinners, so I persuaded him to come over to the suburbs. I have found this place called Juicy Tomatoes in Bandra, with a well-stocked salad bar where you can pile on as much as you want. Eating salads makes me feel really virtuous, like contributing to a just cause—in this case, 'Save Damayanthi's Hips'. But Jimmy insisted on ordering a huge gooey brownie (how can you resist one of those?) and then struggled to eat it all. I was forced to help him finish it.

Normally, I would not have given a brownie a second thought. Brownies are meant to be eaten and I never deny them their purpose in life. It must have been the sight of Sonya's lissom figure that made me more conscious of my own pear-shaped body.

Now I am bloated with guilty calories.

Yours fatly,
Damayanthi.

Hey Vic,

It has been a week, and my apartment has been taken over by a manic interior decorator. Madras minimalism has given way to Punjabi baroque. Sonya has extended her skinny arms to every room in the house. Only my bathroom remains truly mine.

She has put up a painting in the large wall space in our dining room. Our drawing room in Chennai had a rather old Tanjore painting given by some relative, two of Amma's framed flowered embroidery pieces and a mounted poster saying, 'Cleanliness is next to Godliness.' Now I have a fake oil-on-canvas version of Van Gogh's *Sunflowers*. It does throw a cheerful yellow glow in the room, but it was *my* blank wall earlier. A lava lamp has been placed in one corner of the living room. She has arranged silver-framed photographs of her family on the side table. There is Designer Mom, a stylish lady who looks as though each body part has been carefully designed by a talented plastic surgeon as per the latest measurements from *Vogue*; Golfing Dad, with some trophy, surrounded by some corporate bigwig types; younger brother hugging adoring sis at some party, both holding tankards of beer like poster children for sibling revelry. Another happy family photo taken at exotic family vacation at some Mauritius-like place—blue sea and picture-postcard sky and tropical-style hotel in the background.

Sonya has taken over the clothesline as well. My solid cotton Libertina bra hangs next to her little lacy confections like a spinster glaring at the debutantes at a ball. My little cotton washcloth has been completely smothered by a large, fluffy, pink terry towel. Even Gangabai seems to have transferred her affections to Sonya, if the clothesline space allocation is anything to go by.

A rather ugly statue of a generously proportioned semi-nude maiden in a bilious green shade and a First Global calendar which were in the foyer have magically found their way to my room, the last bastion of poor taste in 124 Pine Crest. I happened to peek into her bathroom and saw it transformed into a glamouroom. In our house, the bathroom was just a place where you did your business quickly and went on your way. It was clean, spartan and functional, like all the other rooms in our home. If at all one cared to take a whiff, it smelt of a strong disinfectant and Baygon spray. This one enveloped the casual visitor in a lime and lemony fragrance, courtesy small bowls of potpourri and room freshener placed and sprayed across the boudoir. Bottles, vials, pots, tubs, tubes and jars of cosmetics I had only seen in the pages of *Cosmo* and *Elle* were displayed near the washbasin. She uses three different types of shampoo and four types of conditioner! To top it all, there was a pink bath mat, along with matching pink shower curtains with 'Princess' scrawled inside a fuchsia heart. Legally, she should have been a blonde.

In fact, she dresses as though she is going for a fashion show. Her shoes, handbag and clothes are carefully coordinated. She clearly has not heard of the LBH—the Little Black Handbag that goes with everything, like the one I have. She either wears these chic trousers and short stylish shirts with the top button open, tailored to fit her curves, or straight skirts just short of being micro-minis that show off her long legs. She might very well be a model for Chanel's Office Couture for Young Ladies collection.

Her perfume lingers long after she has gone, her lipstick is intact till late evening and her coif looks like it has never seen a bad hair day. She calls herself a private banker for platinum customers. Those are the high net worth individuals who have too much money and don't know what to with it. So the Sonya types try to wheedle as much as they can for the bank while offering so-called advice on gold bonds and hedge funds, which are provided by hard-working product managers. I can just imagine her having very private discussions, holding hands and cooing to pot-bellied platinum types in five-star hotels, over vials of wine. Customers probably take back their complaints and shower her with compliments instead.

Her tentacles have extended to the kitchen now. Yesterday, she threw away the pulikachhal which Amma had made for me, claiming that it was some old, spoilt thing. Okay, so I had used it just once in the last two months, but she could at least have asked me.

When confronted, she gave me a disdainful look and said, 'There was some old oily stuff or something in a bottle. It was like so gross that I chucked it out.'

'It was tamarind paste,' I said coldly.

'To make chutney or something?'

'No, you mix it with rice and eat it.'

'Whatever.' She made a face to indicate that only the gastronomically challenged would consider tamarind rice food.

I have adopted an I-don't-really-care-for-these-materialistic-trappings attitude. We Balachandrans believe in simple living and high thinking. Intellect has been traditionally more valued than interior decoration. I have grown up among plastic chairs and unmatched draperies. I will not be swayed by these crude, exhibitionistic displays of sophistication.

I have turned my bedsheets inside out. They look newer like this and match better with the curtains.

Bye,
D.

Dear Victoria,

The only thing that smells better than Sonya's bathroom is the sweet fragrance of revenge. Today, I threw out the pieces of chicken or something she had stored in our freezer. Can you imagine my chocolate ice cream rubbing shoulders or breast with some dead creature? What would Amma say to see my pure, Brahmin kitchen turned into an animal graveyard? It was time to act.

She hunted around for it before dinner and asked me, 'Have you seen my chicken?'

LV: 'Maybe it went to cross the road.'

Me: 'No, is it lost?' I tried to sport a look of innocence mixed with indifference.

'I am sure I put it in the freezer.'

LV: 'There were only some scraps of dead, decaying flesh in the freezer. It looked so gross that I chucked it out. Ha! Ha! Ha!'

'Oh.' Damayanthi feigns ignorance and gets back to reading *The Collected Works of M.K. Gandhi*, which she had bought as protection. It is a good, fat book—hardbound. Damayanthi is a non-violent woman of peace who dislikes conflicts, but she understands the importance of having deterrents.

'Did you take it?' Sonya was not giving up. She was in the mood to fight.

'Me! I am a pure vegetarian. I couldn't even bear to touch it.' All true. Luckily, it was in a plastic bag and I used the ice tongs to lift it.

Sonya looked suspicious, but one cannot accuse a girl earnestly reading *The Collected Works of M.K. Gandhi* of stealing or telling lies. So Sonya goes without her grilled chicken and puts on calories by eating two slices of white bread. Carbs galore! Hurrah! I know it was a mean thing to do, but worth every minute of it. I happily ate my curd rice and mango pickle. Sonya does not know what she is missing.

Your evil friend,
Damayanthi.

✿

Vic,

Sonya continues to shock me. I know you are the sexually active, strawberry daiquiri-swigging, ciggie-smoking chick about town, but for me it was a little shocking to discover bits of ash in a glass bowl on our drawing room table. I think Sonya smokes. That would explain the strange odour I smelt yesterday, as though old clothes had been taken out of mothballs and burnt.

I also saw a few empty bottles of Bacardi Breezer by our dustbin. They are alcoholic drinks and not fruit juices as I had first thought. She drinks too, or consorts with alcoholics.

I am sure she is entertaining men in her room. Last night, I was looking for the newspaper to do the crossword. I thought Sonya had taken it into her room and was about to knock on her door and ask for it when I heard voices. One was definitely male. And they were definitely not doing the crossword, unless the words were 'ummm', 'oooh' and 'unhnnn'. I went back into my room and did not emerge from it for the rest of the night.

I live in a den of vice, with a girl whose clothes are tight and morals are loose. Despite that, or because of that, she seems to be having a great time.

I hate her.

Help!
Damayanthi.

8

Dear Vic,

I have been so preoccupied with my new flatmate that I have not briefed you on the latest at the work front. I have been travelling to Powai to COps and have the luxury of leaving fifteen minutes later than Sonya, who actually hires a taxi to drive her to office every day. She cannot pollute her perfect little self by consorting with the hoi polloi on public transport.

At COps, I conduct group discussions. This consists of getting a group of people together and forcing them to discuss three questions.

1. What are some of the areas for improvement in COps?
2. How can we implement these suggestions?

3. What could be some challenges in implementation?

After a few days of listening to such discussions, I still have no clue about what really happens here, but I have become some kind of an expert on human behaviour. In any group discussion, you will find four distinct types.

The Cynics believe that the whole discussion is a waste of time. They know that nothing will really happen after all this. They have been around for years and nothing has happened to improve anything in their lives. The kinder ones will pity you and the meaner ones will pass nasty comments about how they could be better occupied twiddling their thumbs.

The Critics will vociferously launch into attacks on the system. Ha, they say, you ask about process improvements—we don't know where to begin. They will usually start with the canteen food, the poor functioning of the air conditioners, the lack of parking space outside the COps facility, the mean management which does not promote COps people on time. Any change proposed by the others will also be criticized and shot down.

A small minority are Idealists. You usually get about one or two in a group. These folks believe that improvements can be made to the process, but their suggestions have no connection with reality. One remarked that sending all COps people on an offsite assignment to Mauritius will have a remarkable, positive impact on their performance. Another suggested we gift our customers a basic computer so that we can send account statements by email to those who didn't have computers.

The Bystanders don't really care one way or another. They sit still with a glazed, faraway look in their eyes and come to life when you ask them pointedly for their inputs. Depending upon their mood, they will agree with the Critic, Cynic or Idealist, often contradicting themselves.

I spend most of the time brokering peace between the different factions and trying to take notes of what I can understand. Jimmy came for a few sessions and then started on some other work. Another day, and I will be done or done for.

Bye,
D.

Dear Victoria,

Can you please make a presentation on the process improvements at COps and email it to me ASAP? Please. Please!

Harish has asked me to make a presentation on what all I have learnt at COps day after tomorrow. Jimmy and CG and Harish will be there, along with a couple of people from COps. I am doomed. I have only two more days. I have no idea how to make a PowerPoint presentation. I have to burn the fluorescent lamps and give myself a PowerPoint tutorial.

Help.
D.

Dearest Vic,

Thankfully, reinforcement has come. After I almost cried to Jimmy, he agreed to help me. The sight of Sonya romping around in her lacy shorts is also an incentive. She was all sweetness and light when introduced to Jimmy. They discovered some mutual acquaintance and started chatting. I had to break up the party and remind Jimmy why he was really here.

'She seems quite okay,' Jimmy said later, when we were alone.

'Traitor!' I glared at him. 'You don't have to live with her.'

'Want to swap?' he asked, grinning.

I am not going to let Sonya chase me out of Pine Crest. I have right of first occupancy. Our cold war will continue. The cook has not materialized and Sonya probably fixes her own dinner while I eat out of the dabba or enjoy my curd rice. Our dinner timings are different and I do not ever see her eat. Maybe that accounts for her stick-insect figure.

Jimmy managed to work after the distractor retired to her room. Somehow, I got some points to put up on the slides that Jimmy was preparing. I also got to know that we need to use the First Global Template for all presentations. I now have four slides with headings and bullets and a graph to show the increase in customer complaints over the years. It looks quite professional.

Vision of Damayanthi making a power-packed point with the presentation. I say, 'As you can see from the graph, the number of complaints has increased steadily over the past twelve-month period, with the maximum increase being in complaints related to late delivery of account statements. Therefore, gentlemen, the recommendation is…' Harish and CG listen with rapt attention. CG looks impressed. The vice president from COps compliments me on my remarkable analysis and incisive insights.

I don't have time to really practise, but I guess I have to manage.

Your power-packed PowerPoint expert,
Damayanthi.

Dear Vic,

I am a corporate misfit. Perhaps I am fit only for the dingy dump of SSV & Sons. At the end of my presentation, there were more holes in it than a piece of Swiss cheese gnawed at by rats. The credit for demolishing Damayanthi must go to the honourable gentleman from ASTC.

CG had been listening to my introduction with a grim look on his face. He wore the same dark suit, red tie and crisp white shirt—it seems to be some kind of a uniform. I hadn't seen him for some time and, for some strange reason, he made me nervous. He subjects you to an intense scrutiny, as though he is looking for the slightest fault to nail you down.

I had not even gone past the first slide when CG asked a question. The scrutiny was replaced by a predatory glare, sort of like one a tiger might have while eyeing a little deer grazing blissfully amidst tall savannah grass.

'How many people did you interview to get this information?' the tiger in the tie growled.

'About twenty-five or so, through the focus group methodology,' I answered confidently.

'Exactly how many?'

'Er… uh…'

'There are two hundred and twenty-seven people working in COps. Do you think twenty-five is a significant sample size?'

'Er… those were the only people who turned up.'

'Why do you think there were errors in processing the fixed deposit redemption requests?'

'Why will giving pre-printed forms to the customer help this issue? Hasn't this been done before?'

'You are recommending returning cheques that have not been deposited along with the deposit slip. What impact will it have on customer satisfaction?'

I had the same response to all of these. 'I will get back to you later on that.'

I could see that no one was very impressed. Only Jimmy gave me sympathetic looks and asked me an easy question that I could answer.

Harish also managed to point out that the font used in First Global presentations is Times New Roman 12 and not the flowing freestyle script I had used to enhance the aesthetic appeal of my slides.

I have said I will gather more data and get back after two days.

Do they demote people in First Global? Clearly my career is over. I will never be confirmed. I spoke to Amma a few minutes ago and pretended that all was well in the corporate world, but I have a horrible, sinking feeling that I have to crawl back to SSV and beg Iyer Sir to take me back.

Despondently yours,
Damayanthi.

❀

Vic,

I had a dream last night—more of a nightmare. I was in a large kitchen, the kind you might find in a medieval English castle. There were huge black pots and pans, knifes and spoons, plates and bowls, all gleaming with dull menace. Something was boiling in an enormous cauldron. A chef was sprinkling chilli powder into the cauldron and I could feel it starting to burn. Then I realized that I was in the pot and the chef looking down at me was CG. 'A dash of red chillies,' he said with an evil laugh. Thankfully, I woke up.

Today is Saturday and I have to spend my weekend getting my presentation into shape. COps works on Saturdays, so I have to move my behind there and fill in the blanks for the next presentation.

Rest at night.
D.

Vic,

There will be little rest tonight. I am working on the presentation. Sonya is out partying somewhere while Damayanthi is sitting with her laptop, trying to make a professional presentation. I don't feel so despondent any longer. Strangely enough, the credit goes to CG.

He was there at COps when I reached. I couldn't recognize him at first because he no longer wore the blue suit and tie he sported in office. Instead, he wore a pair of faded blue jeans and a white cotton shirt and looked almost human. His hair, released from the gel coating, was really a little curly and he looked a more relaxed. Saturday is casual day at First Global and most employees were also in jeans and sneakers. Why had I chosen this day to wear my old grey salwar kameez?

I was about to duck behind a cubicle to avoid meeting him. Maybe my grey salwar kameez would blend with the grey upholstery and he would pass me by. But he noticed me and waved a hand. I gave him a cool, stiff greeting and tried to sport a I-have-tons-of-things-to-do air. He didn't take the hint and came striding purposefully towards me.

'So are you doing some more research?' he asked.

Me: 'Yes.'

CG: 'So what progress have you made?'

Me: 'Not much.'

CG: 'I think we need to get some more data to support your recommendations and do a cost-benefit analysis for some of the suggested improvements. On one hand, we need to consider the productivity enhancements that can be implemented internally, and on the other, look at possible ways of educating customers so that we reduce cycle times of certain transactions.'

LV: 'Duh-uh?'

Me: 'Yes.'

Maybe he sensed that I was not exactly in a chatty mood. For a minute, I thought he was almost discomfited. The superior mask slipped a bit.

'Look, I didn't mean to make it uncomfortable for you at the presentation. It is my job to see that we do a complete, in-depth analysis for this project. If you want, I can work with you a bit to put some more stuff together.'

LV: 'So you think I am incapable of doing this? I don't need your help, you superior boor.'

Me: 'Thanks.'

Luckily, this time, my senses won over my spirit. Obviously, if CG helps to make a presentation, he can't blast it to smithereens later. I have to admit he made sense. My initial presentation seemed like a shoddy affair, a hot-air balloon adrift in the corporate air without any data to ballast it. I managed to nail down about five workable recommendations with a potential cost-benefit estimate, along with possible impact on customer satisfaction. First Global measures CSat very seriously. The quarterly results go to the Big B and any significant decline calls for heads to roll.

We worked for two hours, sincerely and seriously. At lunchtime, we headed together to the COps cafeteria. The crowd at COps is quite different from the bank. These are young guys and the place is more like a BPO. The food is at any rate better than what we get at FG. We got our food in plastic trays and even had a choice of a Healthy Meal lunch, fruits and a salad, which I avoided. Surprisingly, CG opted for it. He didn't seem fat or even pleasantly plump. In fact, he was quite lean. There was no bulging six-pack, but he looked fit and solid. Not that I was looking at his body or anything—I just happened to notice because of the Healthy Meal lunch order.

We started on our food. I was a little more comfortable with him and it seemed as though the ice had melted marginally since morning.

Now is the time to make scintillating conversation and impress him. He will no longer look at you as though you are an IQ-challenged specimen.

'Are you dieting?' I asked. God, what a silly thing to ask a man!

'No, no, nothing like that. I just believe in eating healthy,' he hastened to clarify. Of course, men never diet. They only work out.

Suddenly I felt greedy, unhealthy and fat. I had to pass up the chance of a second helping of the gulab jamun. I don't care. I will never get a figure like Sonya's. And it is not like I want to impress CG with my vital statistics. It is not like I want to impress him at all.

CG seemed to unwind a little over lunch. I realized that he could sound normal and not like an RBI bulletin announcing the monetary policy all the time.

'So tell me about yourself,' he said. I was surprised he even wanted to know anything about me. Maybe he has a 'Builds Effective Relationships with Clients' column on his performance appraisal sheet.

'Er... there is nothing much to tell,' I mumbled, suddenly feeling self-conscious.

Where was Little Voice when I needed it? In retrospect, I realize I couldn't have sounded more boring.

CG raised an eyebrow. 'That sounds mysterious. Does that mean you have some secrets you are hiding?'

LV: 'My life is an open book, but all the pages are blank.'

Me: 'I don't have any secrets.'

CG: 'No?'

Me: 'My life is an open book but, all the pages are blank.'

Yes, I actually said that!

A hint of a grin flickered on his face for an instant. 'Come on. I am sure you have done some silly things you regret?' he probed.

LV: 'Actually, my biggest regret is that I haven't done silly things that I can regret.'

'I have led a pretty boring, straightforward life. What about you? What is the silliest thing you have ever done?' I quickly deflected the question to him.

'You know, I've led a pretty straightforward life too. More focused on studies and winning all possible competitions in school and college.'

'Exactly.' I knew what he meant. 'But I am sure you have had some interesting experiences...' I was getting to see a little more than the tip of the iceberg.

'But... I guess the time I overdosed on bhaang on my first campus Holi was probably the silliest.' Okay, he did do things apart from being class-topper and all-round champ.

Bhaang, I discovered later, is this potent, intoxicating drink that people in the north swig during Holi.

'What happened?'

'I can't recall clearly, but my friends claim that apart from laughing and crying for a few hours, I tried to climb the flagpole, pretending to be Spiderman trying to save Amrapali Bhandarkar. She was this gorgeous girl who was sort of our campus goddess. But I got stuck halfway and couldn't come down. My friends got a ladder and had to help me down after an hour.'

We laughed together. I just couldn't imagine CG doing a thing like that. There was clearly much more behind that stuffed white shirt of his than it appeared.

'And Amrapali?'

'She never looked at me again.' He smiled ruefully. 'Now, your turn.' He was being rather persistent and I felt that I should share something with him. Either this was his way of amusing himself or he was genuinely interested. Somehow, his candour seemed to rub off on me.

All of a sudden, I could recall vividly the most embarrassing moment of my early childhood. I had never told anyone about this blot on my otherwise unblemished record of non-silly behaviour.

'Umm… I always used to come first in class, all through school. But in class five, I fell ill with chickenpox and missed school for a while. Well, at the end of the term, we used to have this prize distribution ceremony in our auditorium, where the toppers would get a gold medal. That year, when the principal announced the first rank in class five, I just got up and started walking to the stage even before she called out my name. I guess I was very used to it. Then, halfway to the stage, I heard everyone laughing and realized that she was calling my classmate PP, who had actually got the first rank. I felt so silly that I ran out of the auditorium and cried for a whole day.'

'Poor little Damayanthi,' sighed CG sympathetically, trying to hide the little smile that threatened to overtake his face. 'So what rank did you get?'

'Second, of course.'

'Of course.' He nodded.

'That horrible Padmapriya never let me forget it. The only time she managed to get the first rank.'

'That wasn't really silly.' CG chuckled.

'It was silly to me. But you win. I can't imagine getting intoxicated and climbing a flagpole like Spiderman.'

After that, lunch got over and CG left for some personal work.

I am halfway through the new, improved presentation and will finish it tomorrow. It is not as though I have a list of social engagements on Sunday.

I don't know why I told him all that, Vic.

Good night,
D.

Dear Vic,

I am happy to report that my second presentation went off well. This one was a teleconference since the COps folks couldn't make it to our main office. I emailed the stuff to them earlier and they dialled in at the given time. It can't get more corporate than this.

This time, CG was not present and I was much more confident. He had to go for a day to the Delhi branch to do some work for us.

The COps VP had a question on the new process for sending account statements by email and security issues.

I said, 'On one hand, email provides a convenient and cost-effective method of sending account statements to customers. On the other, many of our customers do have concerns about the security aspects of such a service. The solution for this is to get customers to sign up for this service voluntarily and provide them with adequate password protection. The password for opening the statement will be the customer's confidential PIN generated by the customer himself through our phone banking service.'

The VP bought this solution. Even Harish looked pleased after the presentation. He asked for some more data to get a better fix on the cost saving estimate of half a million dollars and said he would send it across to Big B. Today, I felt that I had actually done something useful. I was feeling like celebrating tonight, but there was no one I could actually call for dinner. Jimmy was busy with some family function. There was no one else I wanted to celebrate with. Or could call my friend.

Finally, I called CG. I felt that I should thank him for his help. His phone rang for what seemed like hours and there was no response. I guessed he was busy.

So, instead of feeling upbeat, I was down in the dumps and decided I would zone out in front of the TV for a while, maybe even catch an episode of *SATC* late at night. I finished my dinner, positioned myself in the living room in front of the TV with a (very small) cup of chocolate ice cream and started surfing channels. Just then Sonya walked and demanded that I turn over the remote and all control to her. What she said was, 'Can you pass me the remote?' but her tone was so demanding that it sounded like a royal command. I ignored her the first time, appearing to be engrossed in the antics of a pair of wild hyenas in the wildlife documentary on Nat Geo where I had paused for a moment. I grudgingly fished the remote from under the sofa cushion and passed it to her when she asked again.

'I am watching something,' I said. The hyenas chose that minute to perform a procreative act on international television. Sonya looked disgusted. She obviously had no interest in the wonders of nature. The hyenas finished their thing and took a commercial break. She flipped through the channels and stopped at MTV. We both sat silently for a few minutes as some rappers rapped their stuff. Call me old-fashioned, but I cannot consider rap music. Hip-hop may be hip, but I like my songs with some melody and meaning. I lunged for the remote and tuned in to Channel V which was playing Bollywood chartbusters and we watched Shahrukh Khan prance around with Kajol.

'I have to watch something at ten-thirty,' she said. Notice the words, Vic. 'Have to', as though it was a matter of life and death.

'So do I,' I replied. No way I was giving up *SATC* for Sonya to fawn over some unintelligible noise.

It was almost 10.30. The remote lay on neutral ground and we circled it with our eyes. It reminded me of a game we used to play as kids—'The Dog and the Bone'.

Just as I had expected, she edged towards the remote. Suddenly her mobile phone rang and she was distracted for a second. Damayanthi's hands moved faster than a cobra striking and she grabbed the remote and immediately switched to HBO.

Sonya disconnected the call and turned to me with a surprised look. How come *you* watch *Sex and the City*, she seemed to ask. Maybe she thinks I've come from a planet where they do not know the meaning of sex.

So, Vic, we both sat and watched Carrie and her friends do a lot of girlfriend bonding. I wish Sonya were different. It would have been great to watch TV together, laughing at the antics of the characters, eating chocolate ice cream out of a large tub, discussing men and movies and giggling over nothing at all. Instead, we resumed our silent viewing and retired to our rooms after the serial was over.

Just when I was about to turn in, I got a call. It was CG.

'Hi Damayanthi. I got a missed call from you. I hope it is not too late? I had a review meeting at the office and couldn't take your call.' He sounded polite, distant—somewhat different from the person with whom I had discussed the silliest thing I had done in my life. There was a lot of noise in the background— sounds of music, people talking, a girl laughing.

'No, it's okay. I just wanted to tell you about the presentation today, considering you did help me put it together.' I tried to sound as polite as I could.

'Oh! So how did it go?'

'Quite well. There were no awkward questions this time.'

' Great. Er… good. So it went off well.' The rest of what he might have said was lost. Clearly he was out with other people and enjoying himself.

'Yes. Thank you for your help. It really helped.' There I went, sounding like a moron again. Better sign off, D.

'That's okay. It is a part of the job.'

Of course, he only saw it as a job. He wasn't doing any selfless social service by helping me. Nor was it because of any ulterior, personal motive. I guess there really is a 'Build Effective Relationships with Clients' component in his job description.

'Yes. You seem to be busy somewhere. So good night and thanks.'

'No, no... it's okay. But if you need to go...'

'No... You seem to be out, so...er... good night.'

'Oh? Okay, good night. See you.'

'Yes. Bye.'

Suddenly, I don't feel sleepy any more. But I suppose I had better try to sleep. Have to wake up to the routine again.

Good night, Vic,
Damayanthi.

9

⮑

Dear Vic,

I believe you are joining Crochet for Calmness classes to achieve inner peace and spiritual equilibrium. This seems to be some form of new-age meditation. They seem to be doing all sorts of things in the name of meditation and stress relief these days. But Crochet for Calmness seems a bit more appealing than Potato Peeling for Peace or Divine Dish Washing.

I could actually do with some divine intervention myself. Work and life have been quite boring so far. But now I think there is some light at the end of the corporate tunnel. Harish has nominated me for a training programme. There is a three-day programme called First Global Essentials (FGE) for people who have joined recently. Normally, one has to put in six months in the bank and get confirmed before being sent for these programmes. But one of the participants quit and they wanted a replacement. Harish (god bless his kind soul) suggested that I would find it useful since I was new to the corporate world. SSV is not counted as a true corporate. This indicates that I will be confirmed after all. Jimmy will attend the next session in December since both of us cannot be spared at the same time. Hurrah! I am glad I am more dispensable. Three days out of office, being groomed for life at First Global! The best thing of all is that the programme is in Goa. Yes, Vic, I shall be heading to that haven of hedonism.

I had always wanted to go to Goa, but it was far, far away from Amman Kovil Street. Goa never figured on the list of holiday destinations for our family. We have been to Ooty and Kodaikanal and I have ventured as far as Delhi to visit cousins. Most summers were spent at Thanjavur, when we made our annual family visit to my paternal grandparents who still live there. My cousins Ramesh and Radha from Delhi and Mohini from Coimbatore would also converge there. The grandparents didn't have a TV in those days, though now Patti would never miss her serials on Sun TV. The gang of cousins would roam around the nearby countryside, walking across rice fields, playing in the mango grove and praying at the neighbourhood temple. We graduated from hide-and-seek and catch-catch to cards and carrom as we grew older. I remember the girls would gang up on poor Ramesh, who used to be a chubby, studious boy with his nose in science textbooks, diligently doing his holiday homework. Radha, who is a few years older than me, would bring her dolls and Mohini, the youngest, would be made the baby in our little games. Patti had bought a set of tiny cooking utensils made of clay, painted in all kinds of bright colours, and we would spend many hours creating our own little kitchen and doing make-believe cooking. Once, we pretended to make payasam and Ramesh almost drank a vile concoction of talcum powder and water. Now he is a prosperous NRI, an academic at MIT who makes the occasional trip to our dusty shores. Radha is completing her PhD in economics at Yale. Both are married to other respectable Tam Brahms. According to Amma, even Mohini, who is just completing her undergraduate studies, will get married before me. My uncle has started looking out for her already. I am the black fruit in our family tree.

Well, Vic, at least I have Goa to look forward to. We will be off next week. Our travel desk will make all arrangements. I looked at the invitation email at office and was so excited that I couldn't do anything all day. There are about six of us from Mumbai, only two other girls in a group of twenty. I don't know any of them. At least the male-female ratio is favourable. We are staying at the Dona Pilar Resort which has its own private beach. The agenda looks action-packed. We will watch videos of eminent First Global personalities talking about life and careers at FG, understand the First Global values, the essentials of office etiquette. One of the days is supposed to be about communication and presentation, another about team building essentials. I had feared that there would be a heavy dose of finance and compliance stuff, but this seems cool. A breeze. I can almost smell the sea breeze…

Vision of myself on the beaches of Goa. I am wearing a daring bikini top and a black sarong and dancing like a bohemian hippie under the moonlit sky, on the ocean shore. I hold a glass of wine and sway to funky, pulsating music and the sound of the waves. Handsome, well-muscled, bare-bodied man dances with me. He puts his hand through my silken tresses, pulls me closer and says—

'Oh, so you are off for FGE?'

Jimmy was peering over my shoulder at my email. I hate it when he does that. When I requested him to cease this intrusive practice, he had the gall to say, 'Not that you get any interesting emails.' Which is, unfortunately, true. But at least I can pretend that I have emails that no one should know about.

Jimmy has been to Goa many times. A family friend even owns a villa there. Apparently, the location of FGE keeps changing. He hopes that it will be held in some exotic location the next time, when he is scheduled to attend. Goa is exotic enough for *me*! I was quite excited about my Goa trip and called the parents to inform them about my impending departure.

Amma said, 'Goa? I believe Goa is not safe these days. I heard tourists are getting killed.'

LV: 'Goa is as safe as Mount Road on a Monday morning, Amma.'

Me: 'No, no, it is quite safe.'

Amma: 'I have heard that they drink a lot in Goa. You don't take any drinks or anything...'

LV: 'Sorry, Amma. I have to sample the local fare. I plan to replace my morning coffee with a glass of feni.'

Me: 'Okay.'

Amma: 'And be careful who you talk to outside. Some of the people sell all kinds of things. It is very dangerous.'

LV: 'What you mean is "Don't do drugs!" I am not going to turn into a dope addict after three days in Goa.'

Me: 'I won't.'

Amma: 'What!'

Me: 'I mean I will. I will be careful.'

Amma: 'And Damayanthi, don't do anything silly. In office it is safe, but…'

LV: 'I will lose my head in Goa and jump into bed with the first beach bum I see!'

Me: 'Okay. Good night.'

Sorry, Amma. This is going to be my first real holiday and I am not going to ruin it by not doing things I have always wanted to do.

Love,
Damayanthi.

❧

Vic,

I am sorry that the crocheting classes did not calm you down. But it is great that you made a new friend while uncrossing your spools of thread. Algernon does sound nice. Any man who is handy with needle and thread is a treasure. At least he will never ask you to sew his buttons or darn his socks.

Vic, I might need some help. I am now consumed with the thought of what to pack for my training. The dress code says business casuals. I can't figure out what that means. And I wish I had taken swimming lessons as a kid. Now I shall not be able to frolic in the Arabian Sea, on a beach that does not double up as a public park.

I suppose it is good in a way, since my body cannot be seen in public in a swimsuit. Not that I am fat. Curvaceous will be the best word to describe my hips and generous will be apt for my bosom. I would have been a contender for a Tamil film heroine had we lived in another era. These days, I am overweight. It wouldn't be so bad if I am not confronted by perfect specimens of femininity every time I open a magazine or switch on the TV. Lithe teenagers with IQs that match their waist size, prancing about in clothes that would adequately cover only a two-year-old. Model mothers talking proudly about how they got back their perfectly toned thighs before you could say 'Liposuction'. It seems that there is no longer any normal figure. Our beauty ideal today has been influenced by western norms and everyone wants to look like a toothpick and have less body fat than a bell pin. The message is clear—if you don't look like a beauty pageant contestant, you should be prepared to live the life of a social outcast with a paper bag (XXL) over your head.

On top of it all, I have a probable beauty pageant contestant for a flatmate, who flaunts her ribcage in my face all the time. I shall skip dinner tonight to prepare my body.

D.

🌼

Hey Vic,

I don't think Goa is quite like that. Going topless in Ibiza or skinny-dipping in the Riviera is definitely different. I know you don't have to worry about your swimsuit or knowing how to swim in such a situation—the whole point is to flaunt your beachwear. I do not own any beachwear. Swimsuit in Chennai means a salwar kameez which can be rolled up to your knees when you get your feet wet. Many maamis wear saris to the beach and tuck it up at the waist when they wade into the Marina waters. Anyone wearing beachwear to the beach will cause a public riot.

However, I have bought myself a daring black top. There was a sale going on at Globus and I darted into it on the way back from office. It is daring because the amount of skin shown seems more than the amount concealed. It is a sleeveless, backless (okay, not entirely backless but cut a bit deeply) top in some knit material, which clings to my generous bosom, and I would like to believe that it flatters my figure. I tried and retried it about seven times, wishing I had another body, some other set of hips and someone else's waist. There is something about the mirrors they keep in trial rooms—you would think that shop mirrors would flatter you by making you look good in the clothes you try, but for shape-challenged people like me, it is like a visit to the Chamber of Horrors. I finally took a plunge just like my top's neckline and invested in it. Any top that costs more than Rs 1,000 has to be an investment. I have a long black-and-white skirt to go with it. If, by some remote chance, I get invited to a rave party on the beach, I will at least have clothes to wear.

I have heard that participants at FGE usually share rooms. Now I also have to get appropriate nightwear so that my roommate does not think that I have come from the dark ages. I have managed to get by in those shapeless nighties for all these years, but of late I realize that it makes me look as though I have jumped into a carpet bag. With Sonya strutting about in her shorts, I have actually begun to look and feel like a granny with my ankle-length gunnysack. So I was forced to buy a silky, strappy baby doll-type nightie in pale yellow. It flows easily and lovingly caresses my curves, providing more than a glimpse of cleavage. I loved it the moment I tried it on and didn't think about spending a fortune on something not more than one person would see.

Next on the list was make-up. I have always had ambivalent feelings about the usage of cosmetics. Amma still does not wear lipstick, has never owned a blusher, has never seen mascara and believes in the wonderful cosmetic properties of turmeric and sandalwood paste. I have grown up getting an exfoliating gram flour body scrub every Sunday and have eschewed all hair products in favour of good old coconut oil. I read Naomi Wolf's *The Beauty Myth* in college and stayed away from wicked chemical products that demeaned our self-esteem and promoted the evil agenda of multinational companies. It is only on special occasions, like a cousin's wedding, that I succumb to the transforming power of a well-applied line of kohl and a coating of face powder.

These days, my make-up is restricted to a quick dash from a kajal stick and a smear of lip gloss so that I look more professional. I use lipstick only for special occasions—it is always 'Simply Natural', a colour that really doesn't look too lipsticky. Vanity was always a deadly sin in the Balachandran household and Restraint in All Things was a virtue one aspired to.

Now I wished I could have a makeover. The genuine natural look would obviously not be welcomed or useful in any rave party I might attend on the beach—other girls would slather on the mascara and bat their eyelids at suitable males. The agenda mentioned a team dinner on the last evening and it is professionally critical for me to look good. So I have invested in eyeliner, mascara and three shades of lipstick. It is not much of a cosmetic collection compared to Sonya's salon, but it is a start.

After my purchases, I feel better prepared for Goa. I also have to read the contents of a thick file for the training programme, but have left that for later. Yes, this is the same Damayanthi who finished all her weekend homework on Friday afternoon.

Goa, here I come.

Good night,
D.

10

~⁓

Hola Victorrya,

I am here. Finally, the first holiday I have had in years! I know there is a training programme to attend somewhere, sometime, but right now I am in the holiday mood. I took the last flight out of Mumbai and landed here at 9.00 p.m. I think all the others attending the programme arrived earlier. I was a little apprehensive about getting to the hotel from the airport by myself, but luckily the good folks at Dona Pilar had sent a car for me. I almost missed it since the driver held a placard welcoming Mr D. Balachandran to Goa. He was reassured that the mistake was on their part only after I showed him my First Global ID card and my email confirming the hotel booking and agenda.

Dona Pilar is a lovely resort done up in white and blue—white walls, blue furnishings, white uniforms with blue trimmings for staff. Very Mediterranean, very lazy. The front desk people took a long time to check me in and I had to repeatedly insist that there was only one D. Balachandran in First Global and she was a girl.

Vic, the room is really nice. There is a TV in front of the bed, a real bathtub in the bathroom and a mini bar well stocked with spirits and chocolates. There are double beds with blue bedspreads, so I suppose I shall be sharing the room with someone. I am tired now and a little buzzed with all the excitement so I will retire for the night. I have changed into my new night dress—sorry, negligee—just in case there is someone…

Someone *is* knocking at the door.

D.

Vic, dear Vic,

You are not going to believe what just happened. I got up to open the door thinking it was probably room service to clear my dinner. It was too late for my roommate to come in, so I wasn't expecting anyone.

The door opened to reveal a man. Not just any ordinary man but a very good-looking man wearing blue jeans and a tight red T-shirt. He had crisp black hair, warm brown eyes, a tanned brown face, even white teeth and a well-muscled torso that hinted at six-pack abs. The quality of room service had either dramatically improved or I was dreaming.

'Hi, er... er... I think there has been a mistake,' said the man. He looked surprised, as though he had been expecting someone else. My heart, which had been doing rapid double somersaults, flip-flopped back into its usual place.

'Mistake?' I said weakly. A seriously good-looking man turning up at my door had to be a mistake.

'Are you with First Global?' he asked.

I nodded.

'So am I.' Wow! A colleague. Was I going to spend three days with him in the same training session?

Steady, Damayanthi. Stop drooling like you have never seen a good-looking man before. Actually, I hadn't. Not so close. Not at touchable distance. This was movie star good-looking, the kind a girl like me could only dream about and hanker after from a distance.

'I am supposed to be sharing a room with a D. Balachandran.' The man looked a little doubtful. He looked cute even with a frown. *Sigh...*

Wait a minute. Was that me? What is First Global doing? Is this some kind of test? How do I pass it? How do I pass it up?

Of course, the hotel guys had D. Balachandran in their records as a male. That explained the guy with the placard. But D. Balachandran is not a man, you bozos, but a beautiful young woman, who is looking into the eyes of a handsome young man.

The handsome young man was looking at me with a puzzled expression. Was I really drooling? Was my hair okay? Why didn't I put on some perfume before going to bed? Was it me having these inane thoughts?

Damayanthi, act like a mature young woman and say something sensible, I admonished myself.

'But I am not a man,' I blurted out.

'I can see that.' The man smiled. A lazy, appraising smile that made me feel a little wobbly. Suddenly I was conscious of my new nightwear, the fact that I was not wearing a bra, and a tight, warm feeling spread through my body.

He held out a hand. 'Hi, I am Rahul,' he said. 'I am with treasury at Mumbai.' That explained why I had never seen him before. The treasury guys' natural habitat was the dealing room on the fourth floor and they seldom descended to join other mortals. Thanks to my stint at COps, I had had no chance of bumping into him even in the elevator or at the gate.

'I am Damayanthi. I work with the special projects team. I am Miss D. Balachandran,' I said, shaking his hand. I hope he noticed the emphasis on the 'Miss'. His grip was firm, warm, and he held my hand in a tight clasp. I didn't want him to stop, but somewhere in the still sane part of my mind, a warning whistle blew and I removed my fingers from his.

'We need to get this sorted out,' said Rahul. He seemed to be the kind of man who sorted stuff out, took charge of things and made them happen. I would have been happy to follow him around anywhere.

'Yes, let us talk to the manager,' I said. There seemed to be a tacit understanding that we would not be sharing rooms. Shit! The closest I have been to sleeping with a man. Not *sleeping* sleeping... well, you know what I mean.

I was ready to march resolutely to the lobby when I heard a gentle swishing sound, the sound made by a hotel door shutting itself quietly. My key card was inside. So there I was, in the middle of the night, in the middle of a hotel corridor, barefoot, clad in a clingy negligee that showed more than a hint of cleavage. I was at the same time thankful that I wasn't in my granny nightie and embarrassed that I was showing my lungs to a total stranger. I felt my ears turn red and arranged my hair over them, hoping Rahul wouldn't notice. The door would not budge despite my pulling and pushing. So I just stood there feeling really foolish.

'Why don't you stay here while I go and speak to the manager? I will also ask housekeeping to get the spare key,' said Rahul.

'Yes. That is probably better,' I agreed. A part of me wanted to walk with him, but another said, 'Damayanthi, you don't want the whole world to see you in that attire!'

'I am sorry,' he said, flashing a wry grin. 'I biked here from Mumbai and didn't think it would get so late. I am really sorry to wake you up and get you into this mess.'

'It is not your fault,' I said. If he kept smiling at me like that, I would forgive him anything.

Vic, things got sorted out. There are three girls and seventeen guys in the group. Some smart hotel flunky had assumed that D. Balachandran was a man and assigned to the same room Rahul and me. Luckily, they had a spare room and we were spared a night together. Damn.

Vision of me and Rahul in our own room at night. It is dark. Thunder grumbles loudly, lightning streaks across the sky, the air is heavy with the threat of an impending storm. Suddenly, there is a loud sound, as though the

earth itself is shaking, and I jump out of bed screaming.
Rahul wakes up and comes across. He takes me in his
arms and murmurs, 'Hush, it is all right.' His arms feel
strong, safe, and he holds me as though he will never let
me go. I turn to him. He says, 'I…'

'Have to get going. Lucky they had that spare
room.' Rahul was getting ready to go to his room. The
door to mine had been opened and I stepped back into
it a little reluctantly.

'Yes, you must be tired,' I murmured.

'Good night.' We shook hands again. I don't
remember, but maybe I put my hand out first. As
a thank you gesture for not getting me kicked out
of my room. 'See you tomorrow.' He disappeared
down the corridor. I stood for a while, gazing at his
retreating back.

Tomorrow is another day. I am really looking
forward to it.

Love,
D.

Dear Vic,

Yes, you should 'do' Goa some day. Maybe you and
Algernon could come over and crochet hammocks all

day long, listening to the sound of waves and basking in the Goan sunshine.

The day began bright and early. We had a team breakfast at 8.30 a.m. at Coral, the banquet hall where our training programme was being held. I saw a lovely Goa morning, the sky a delicate blue streaked with swathes of cirrus clouds. The resort was on the beach and I could almost hear the sounds of the waves as they gently thudded onto the shore. I met the other participants of FGE. Many of them knew each other and formed small groups of three or four at the breakfast tables. The two other girls were from the Kolkata branch. Monideepa and Nobonita chattered away to each other in Bengali, oblivious to the rest of the crowd. I figured that they were sharing the other room, leaving me in solitary splendour. Not that I minded.

Just as I was eating my last slice of watermelon, Rahul walked in. He waved to one of the other guys, looked around and then came and sat down next to me. I am sure the Bengali babes stopped their chattering and looked enviously at me.

'Good morning.' He smiled. 'Hope you slept well.'

'Good morning.' I smiled back and nodded. I hoped I wasn't wearing a wide, goopy grin. I looked around happily. None of the other guys came even close to Rahul in terms of attractiveness. For a change,

I had the alpha male sitting next to me instead of being a stranded wallflower. I was glad I had spent those five extra minutes on my make-up. I had been generous with my kajal stick and the eyeliner made my eyes look larger and more luminous. My lipstick matched the maroon tones of my kurti and I had left my hair open to fall around my shoulders. My hair is thick and wavy, thanks to years of coconut oil and shikakai baths and some Malayali genes from my mother's side. Usually, I do the sensible thing and tie it up in a fat ponytail or a thick braid, but today I was not in a sensible mood.

Rahul and I chatted over cups of coffee. He had his black, with no sugar. I didn't really like the coffee—nothing compared to Amma's filter kaapi made from a fresh decoction—but another cup of it gave me a chance to have a conversation with Rahul.

'How long have you been at First Global?' I asked.

'About eight or nine months. I was with Citi first. That was my campus job.'

I kept up a steady stream of questions. Somehow, I didn't want to divulge the dull details of my life. Working for SSV Iyer & Sons did not seem remotely interesting or glamorous. Compared to Rahul's life, mine was that of a little frog sitting in the Amman Kovil well.

Rahul said that he had worked for a few years before doing his MBA.

'What kind of work were you doing?'

'Well, my first job was as a bartender.'

'Wow!' I had never met a bartender. I had never been in a bar either and immediately thought of Tom Cruise deftly juggling glasses and regaling bystanders with witticisms in *Cocktail*. Rahul must have made a very cute bartender. I bet girls were offering to buy him drinks all the time.

'Yeah, I wanted to make some money, and one of my friends had an uncle who had this cool club called Mojo Rising in Bangkok. We had gone there for a break after college. So I learnt how to mix drinks. I can still fix a mean Margarita.'

He already had me drinking out of his hands.

Vision of me in a red silk dress at a swanky, hip club. Rahul is handing me a tall, cool drink and saying, 'I made this especially for you.' I take a sip, close my eyes and purr like a satisfied kitten.

'Is the coffee that good?' asked Rahul with amusement. I came to my senses and mumbled something innocuous and quickly asked what he had done after that.

'For a year I worked for an online gaming company designing games.'

'Oh! That must have been fascinating.' I knew nothing about gaming—the only games I knew were Snakes and Ladders, Ludo and Monopoly—but I was listening with rapt attention as if to the *Arabian Nights*.

'It was for a while, but the company wasn't making any money.'

'So…?'

'I quit and then worked with a financial services firm for a year. I was doing research and analysing companies for private equity firms.'

'Did you enjoy that?'

'It was okay for a while, then I got bored. So I decided that I might as well do an MBA. Luckily, I got into an IIM and am now a respectable banker.' The twinkle in his eyes, though, was not all that respectable.

I suddenly realized that all the others had already moved into our training room. So Rahul and I hurriedly got up and dashed inside. I couldn't afford to be late for my first training programme. But Rahul seemed quite unconcerned, as though he was used to people waiting for him. The twenty participants were divided into four groups and seated around circular white tables. Unfortunately, Rahul was not in my group. The four others I sat with looked really boring compared to Rahul. One was a chartered accountant who looked about forty-five, two were bankers in their first jobs and the fourth was a nondescript, pimply fellow who wore a pair of thick black-framed glasses. Dull, dull, dull. Monideepa and Nobonita were unhappy at being separated and gesticulated at each other from their tables.

The day was a series of presentations and videos about First Global—'Our Mission, Vision and Values'. After listening to our Global Chief Paul Meyers extolling the virtues of FG as *the* place to be, I felt proud and happy to be a part of 'this amazing group of people'. I even took down notes from his speech in my binder. I was amazed that I, B. Damayanthi, was actually here in this room, watching videos about the greatness of First Global with other smart, banker-type people and one smart, handsome man.

We breaked for lunch soon and I made small talk with some of the others. I saw Rahul standing at the buffet table and subtly made my way there. Obviously, a girl cannot be obvious. Even though I have had no experience with men, I have read enough to know that nothing turns off a man more than a girl who openly chases him. There was no Chasing gene in my Tam Brahm self in any case. Somehow, I found myself standing behind him, waiting to help myself to the salad.

'Wasn't that some spiel?' he asked with an I-don't-know-how-I sat-through-it-all shrug of his shoulders.

'Yes,' I found myself saying. Suddenly, I felt very naïve that I had not seen through the corporate spiel. Rahul, with more experience behind him, had seen through the shallow words that our leaders spouted while I, like a sucker, had bought into all those First Global values of integrity, excellence and customer orientation.

I helped myself to the potato salad and eyed Rahul's food choices. He ignored the fish and chicken and headed to the vegetarian section.

'Are you a vegetarian?' I blurted out. I could hear Amma's voice in my head: 'You cannot be cooking non-vegetarian food.'

'Yeah! I tried pretty much everything that moves, but have given it all up now.'

'Oh! Why?'

'Just like that. I think a vegetarian diet is much healthier and better. Better for the animals as well.'

Not only was he handsome, he was also compassionate and kind to animals. I instinctively felt that he was good with children as well. He probably teaches his naughty nephews cricket and spoils his little niece silly.

Now why did I think of children? Vic, I had barely known him for a day and I was already thinking of cooking a delicious vegetarian meal for us and little Rahul and Rahulla. Considering that I don't cook at all, this was taking things too far. I focused on my salad and avoided the delicious-looking chocolate mousse that was dessert.

We headed back into the room after lunch for another session. It started off with the trainer doing what he called an ice-breaker round so that we could all get to know each other better. We had to write two things we admire and two things we dislike in others and share it with the group. I put down 'boldness' and 'aggression' as qualities I admired. I don't think of myself as the aggressive type who boldly goes where no girl has gone before, scolds auto drivers with impunity and bargains like a fishwife at the market. I think I secretly admired those girls in college who sneaked out of home after lying to parents and got drunk along the East Coast Road with their boyfriends. Girls who Did Things.

I wrote 'lying' and 'cheating' under qualities I disliked. I couldn't wait to hear Rahul's words.

When it came to his turn, he said, 'I don't like people who are jealous and possessive.' Okay, Vic. There is not a single jealous bone in my body. I am a great believer of that 'If you love someone, set them free' philosophy. The qualities Rahul admired were 'adventurous' and 'willing to try new things'. Damayanthi has to work on those qualities. I am getting there. Being here, in Goa, is already turning out to be an adventure.

The session ended at about 6:00 p.m., with some homework for us to do. We needed to prepare a presentation on a flip chart and deliver it to the class tomorrow. I scooped up my stuff and headed to my room. The others were making evening plans. I was hoping that Rahul would invite me to join him for something, but he was busy with a group of guys. The Bengali Babes were reunited and fell into a quick discussion in their language. They didn't seem to need anyone else.

'So, what are you going to do now?' a voice asked as I was walking out. I turned to see one of my fellow participants. It was M.V. Prakash, the weedy-looking fellow with the thick, black glasses. Maybe he had a good heart and was kind to insects, but I was just not interested in furthering my acquaintance with him.

'Oh, I am going to prepare my presentation,' I said like a conscientious student.

'So am I,' said Prakash and we trotted off sadly to our respective rooms. I couldn't think of any topic for the presentation for an hour. I sat with a notepad and pencil, wondering what Rahul was doing and who he was with. My room has a great view of the hotel gardens and the pool and I gazed dully at it.

I could see a bunch of people in the pool laughing and splashing around. A few foreign tourists in bikinis lay on deckchairs, soaking up the last bit of the evening sun. There were two blond women with bodies like swimsuit models, a fat lady who was unconcerned by the rolls of flesh she exposed, a couple of kids, two teenagers and a handsome young man who was hauling himself out of the pool. I stared harder and realized that it was Rahul, wearing only a pair of black swimming trunks. Even from this distance, I could see his well-muscled torso and the sturdy thighs, imagine the droplets of water glistening on his chest. The blond women said something to him and he laughed in reply. I could feel my ears turning red and hot as I continued to stare at him like some perverted, sex-starved woman.

Damayanthi, pull yourself together and think about your presentation, said a distant voice, but Damayanthi's eyes were gazing in a masochistic way at the pool side. How I wish I had learnt swimming. Or at least had a body that looked good in a bikini! Instead of frolicking in the pool, I was reduced to peering at it like a sick Peeping Tomina. I noticed

Rahul looking up and around. Maybe he felt my X-ray stare boring into his body. I quickly ducked behind the curtain and pretended not to exist.

After wrenching my mind away from many other X-rated thoughts, I tried to concentrate on my presentation. Thanks to all the distractions, my brain had atrophied and I could not come up with anything creative or interesting. Finally, I cheated and decided to make a presentation I already had—the one about process improvements at COps. I peeped out of the window once again, checking to see what was happening at the pool. It was already dark and there was hardly anyone by the poolside. Rahul had vanished, and so had the blond women. Maybe they were out having a drink together. The two of them were probably wrapped around Rahul, running their hot, white hands through his dark hair.

A dull, gloomy feeling descended on me, as though someone had thrown a thick, wet blanket on my head. I switched on the TV and grabbed a bar of Snickers from the mini bar. 'I don't care,' I said out loud to the newsreader on Aaj Tak, who seemed to think that a cat stuck on a third-floor terrace was breaking news. 'I really don't care.' I skipped dinner.

After polishing off a packet of salted cashew and three Kit Kats, I feel more like throwing up than shovelling anything in. I am going to try and sleep now.

Good night,
Damayanthi.

❦

Dear Vic,

I know I should 'go for him' like you suggest, but I can't bring myself to do it. I wish I could flirt confidently like you would have done. Talking to Rahul is just not like talking to Jimmy, or even CG, with whom I think I have a certain degree of comfort.

A whole day has passed. And while I have communicated and presented to the group, there seems to be a lull in my communication with Rahul. I know I should be focusing on my learning, my career and picking up important tips for my life in FG—instead I spent half the day waiting for Rahul to talk to me. We were in different groups and didn't get a chance to talk at all.

I made my presentation in a desultory way, trying to whip up enthusiasm for process improvements at COps. Our trainer, a purposefully cheerful gentleman called Thomas, beamed at me encouragingly and told me that it was concise and well structured, but I needed to make it interesting and more appealing to the audience. Right! I should turn it over to one of those newscasters who will talk about a new way to send account statements as though someone had discovered an elixir for immortality and eternal beauty

Rahul spoke about the history of some cocktails and he made it sound so interesting that all the other participants including me were hanging on his every word. He cracked a joke about being in high spirits in Goa and went on to describe how the drink Sherry got its name and told the audience that Daiquiri was actually a river in Cuba. They all lapped it up and the ebullient Thomas extolled his virtues as a presenter. He had a casual, easygoing style and seemed like that man in the Raymond ads—the one who doesn't have to try too hard.

Surprisingly, Rahul approached me at lunchtime. I pretended to be deep in conversation with Prakash who was or pretended to be interested in the process improvements at COps. Rahul joined us and said that I was doing a very important project and my presentation was good. I felt myself blush and murmured a thank you. Thankfully, Prakash finished his lunch soon. After extracting every little bit of flesh from his chicken, he reluctantly went to deposit his plate.

'So what were you doing yesterday evening?' asked Rahul casually. I felt a surge of inexplicable anger. As though he was really interested!

LV: 'Oh, nothing much. I was at a private party on Vijay Mallya's yacht. And then Malini Ramani begged me to attend an exclusive fashion show she had organized at the beach, where the Kingfisher girls modelled the latest swimsuits.'

Me: 'Nothing much.'

Rahul: 'I went for a swim at the pool here. It was great after sitting in one place through the day.'

LV: 'Yeah? Were you swimming or improving international relations?'

Me: 'Oh!'

Then he said, 'I thought I would ask if you wanted to go for a swim, but didn't want to disturb you in case you had other plans.'

My surge of anger was replaced by a surge of abject gratitude. He had not only thought of me but was thoughtful enough to think that I had other plans!

'I didn't have any plans, but I don't swim,' I blurted out.

'Oh! Maybe we can catch up some other time.'

LV: ' Yes, yes, yes. Any time, anywhere, anything.'

Me: 'Sure.'

The rest of the day consisted of some gyan on communication and listening. Unfortunately, I was too distracted to be a good listener. We had a case to study for the next day and my team got together at dinner to read and prepare it. Like a good girl, I sat with my team members and did some calculations and made Excel spreadsheets to determine the value of ABC Ltd. Normally, I would have enjoyed it. I like juggling numbers around and doing cerebral things, but today it seemed boring, boring, BORING.

Vic, I have just one more day to go and there has been no progress in my relationship with Rahul. Wait a minute. I don't have a relationship. I don't have anything. I am just another programme participant to him. He was probably canoodling with the bikini bombshells. Logic and common sense tells me that there is no way that a guy like him is going to like/love/fall for/whatever a girl like me. But all the books and novels I have read have reinforced the theory that handsome, rich, successful men actually like ordinary girls who are good-hearted and simple. Tired of the size-zero supermodels whose plastic smiles match their plastic boobs, the successful man seeks solace in the arms of a real woman with real hair and a really golden heart. Maybe there is hope.

Damayanthi, you have one more day. Carpe diem!

Love,
D.

11

Dear Vic,

I am sitting in the plane from Goa to Mumbai and writing this to you. My mind is in too much of a whirl to make sense, so you will have to forgive me if I get a little incoherent. Yesterday was Saturday, the last day of the session. We wrapped up early afternoon. My team came first in the case study and presentation and they appreciated my insightful analysis. The training was great, but I don't think I remember too much of what happened. All that gyan has been overwritten by what happened after that.

A large gang was going out to see the sights and sounds of Goa. At last the Bong Babes condescended to talk to me and asked if I would join them and five others for a spot of sightseeing. Since I had nothing to do, I agreed. There was no sign of Rahul. I wondered what he was doing and with whom and why he wasn't doing whatever he was doing with me. Since my mind was clogged with these useless thoughts, I couldn't enjoy the sights of Panjim City.

My newfound friends immediately found a market and wandered off to buy local specialities. Another member of the gang went gaga over Goan wine and picked several poly-packs of Vinicola. The Goans are amazing. They sell wine in packets just like the Aaavin milk we get. I just can imagine a wine seller dropping off the daily dose of wine packets in the morning! I picked up a packet of salted cashews and trailed behind the others.

We headed back to the hotel for dinner which was part of the package—being good, middle-class Indians, we were not going to give up a free meal. I was in the bathroom having a nice pre-dinner soak in the tub when the phone rang. Maybe it was Rahul, I thought. I couldn't have him thinking I wasn't in the room. So I rushed out, all foamy and soapy, to grab the phone.

'Hey, hope I didn't disturb you.' It was Rahul! For once, my prayers had been answered.

'Er... no, not at all.'

'You're sounding a little breathless. Are you okay?'

'I am fine… I was just in the bathtub…' Now why did I tell him that?

'Oh… are you okay to talk?'

LV: 'Well, I am completely naked, there is a bit of foam in my eye, my fingers are about to slip off the receiver and I might catch pneumonia if my bare, wet skin is exposed to the air conditioning any longer, but I really am okay to talk.'

'Y-y-yess…' I was shivering. I hoped he didn't think I was shivering with pure lust. I had read in a book that some people did that.

'Do you want to get decent and call me back?' I could hear a teasing smile in his voice. Was he imagining me… er, indecent? God! Could he see me? Did he hear me blush over the phone?

'Okay. Just give me a second.'

I took down his room number and had the quickest shower in the history of showers, then wrapped the soft, white hotel bathrobe around my body and called him back.

'Hi, it's me, Damayanthi,' I said when he picked up with a deep 'Hello'.

'Hey. So, can you talk now?'

'Yes, absolutely.' *I am decent enough, but I cannot vouch for my thoughts.*

'Are you going for the team dinner now?' he enquired.

'Yes, I guess. Aren't you?'

'No, I don't think so. We've been with these guys for three days… So, I was wondering—would you like to come out for dinner? We could explore a bit of Goa and grab a bite at one of the shacks on the beach.'

Vic, I was stunned for a few seconds. Rahul's invitation had a strange, surreal, dream-come-true quality to it. My mind processed it slowly. It was only dinner, after all. The team dinner would be quite boring. They were not taking attendance for it. It was not as though he had invited me to his room. But did this mean that I was tacitly accepting a possible future invitation to his room for…

'Of course, if you'd rather go for the dinner here…'

'No, no. I'm game to go out.' Damayanthi tried to sound cool, nonchalant, like she goes out for dinners with handsome young men every night of her exciting life.

'Great. Maybe if there is a party on at one of the places, we can go there.'

'Sure.' Hallelujah! There is a god!

Vic, I got the chance to wear my daring top after all. I had thought it would remain in its unworn, virginal state until eternity. So, after paying careful attention to my toilette, I emerged from my room fifteen minutes later, feeling quite pleased with the results. My black backless top clung nicely to my generous bosom. The daring quality of the top was compensated for by the long black-and-white skirt which flowed demurely over my hips and covered my legs.

The above outfit was chosen after careful analysis of all options inspired by an article I had once read: 'What does your outfit signal on a date?' Short, tight clothes mean desperation; revealing clothes mean 'I am available'; long-sleeved tops mean 'I am not ready yet'; salwar kameez is like 'I am the traditional type—look but don't touch'; and so on. The correct outfit gives mixed signals to members of the opposite sex so that they are left guessing. It is like wearing a tight, transparent kameez over a salwar and a sequined scarf instead of a dupatta.

So, what was I signalling? No entry? Admit one? Stop, go, just wait?

Relax, Damayanthi, you are not out on a date. This is just dinner with a colleague, like you have dinner with Jimmy.

I walked down to the lobby at the appointed hour. Rahul approached from the other side. The look on his face said that my efforts and expenses were being appreciated.

'You look very pretty,' he said and I glowed like a 1,000-watt bulb and tried hard not to look too pleased.

Who was I kidding? This was certainly not like dinner with Jimmy.

'How are we going?'

'On my bike.'

There is something very intimate about being on a bike with a man, especially if you are wearing a skirt and are forced to sit side saddle. You have to cling to the body in front of you with one hand to keep yourself from falling off and hold down your skirt with the other to keep it from flying up and showing your panties to passers-by. So, there I was on a bike with Rahul, feeling like the queen of the world, the wind in my hair, a smile on my lips and a song in my head.

I didn't want the drive to end, but eventually we pulled up at a beach. There were a few shacks there, some brightly lit, some a little dimmer. There were plastic chairs out in front of them and interesting groups of people of all shapes, sizes and colours talked and laughed and made merry. I could have been anywhere in the world.

We finally found an Italian place called Antonino's. There were red-and-white checked tablecloths on the tables, candles that gleamed in glassy holders and the smell of warm baking in the air.

Rahul ordered wine.

'I will have the Chardonnay,' he said, looking up from the drinks menu. 'What about you?'

'The same,' I said. I was with a man who knew wines and it was better to go with his choice rather than display my ignorance.

'Have you had this wine before?' asked Rahul.

'No, I like trying new things,' I said brightly. I was also planning to be adventurous.

Yes, Vic, I faintly hear Amma's voice saying 'Don't take any drinks', but wine is really fruit juice. Old, fermented grape juice. And no one gets drunk on wine. Right?

Wrong! After a couple of glasses of the Chardonnay or whatever that potent mixture was, I felt different. Maybe I quaffed off the glasses too quickly. I could see Rahul look a bit surprised when I giggled happily and asked for another one. I can't remember what we talked about, but the conversation, along with the wine, flowed freely. Rahul had travelled to different places and compared the Australian beaches to those of Thailand and street food he had sampled in Vietnam to the hawker stalls in Singapore. I gazed beatifically at him like a smitten Desdemona and made appropriate paying-attention noises. The pasta was delicious, the garlic bread was warm and soft, and the chocolate thingy that we had for dessert was really chocolatey. Then I had the post-dinner wine as well and staggered when we got up to leave.

'Oops,' I said when I kind of stumbled. Not that I was drunk, but something seemed to have got hold of my foot.

Rahul put a hand on my shoulder and asked, 'Are you all right?'

'Great! Smashed! I mean, smashing,' I replied. I was feeling great, a happy little song was humming itself in my head and my heart was drumming in accompaniment. The hand on my shoulder moved to my waist as we walked over the sands. It felt good. I let it stay there.

From the distance I heard the sound of music. 'Hey, there seems to be some kind of party going on there. Want to check it out?' asked Rahul.

Adventurous Damayanthi said, 'Sure.' Another Damayanthi was saying, 'Be careful, they could be selling drugs. They could be putting things in your drink. What will Amma say?' But I couldn't hear her too clearly.

Before I knew it, I was in the middle of a group of multinational strangers gyrating to some lounge-type music. Nobody looked at me as though I didn't belong there. I was reassured by Rahul's solid presence. His hand on me felt protective, like I was in a safe circle, and yet, one part of me felt unsafe and reckless.

'Mind if I smoke?' he asked. Usually, I hate cigarette smoke and make it a point to avoid or sit far away from smokers. But with Rahul, I really didn't mind. He moved with feline grace, all limbs coordinated smoothly, a cigarette dangling from one hand. I held a glass of some other drink in my hand and swayed to the same rhythm. I was thankful for the Bharatnatyam classes under the accomplished Kalavati Ramachandran. At least I was comfortable moving my body to music, though this was a far cry from the 'Thaiya thaiya' steps I used to practise.

Rahul stubbed his cigarette out on the sand. He looked at me, into me and I opened up like a flower in the sun. I remember smiling up at him. His hand reached for my silky hair and pulled me a little closer. I had a strange sense of déjà vu, as though I had seen this somewhere before, of knowing him earlier.

'You look beautiful tonight,' he whispered into my hair, his breath warm on my neck. He seemed to know just what to say.

'You make me feel beautiful,' I thought or maybe said. My little voice and other voice were all tangled up. I felt like I was going to do something silly. And then it happened.

He kissed me. Maybe I kissed him. Somehow, we ended up kissing.

I can still taste the harsh yet smooth flavour of his cigarette mingled with the wine, smell the musky aftershave and feel his cool, smooth skin next to my warm, flushed cheeks, the heat spreading from his hand on my bare back into my body. Maybe we all have an inbuilt kissing mechanism that starts working at the right time, with the right person. It felt so natural, so right that I wondered why I hadn't done it before. What a waste of twenty-six years! I have a lot of catching up to do. Though what happened after that is a little blurry, I can replay that kiss a thousand times in my mind—and it feels just as good. No bells ringing or birds singing or earth moving, but just a joyous, melting feeling that spread all through my body.

Then I remember being on the bike, our bodies touching, the wind cool on my back as we rushed back to the hotel. We walked through the lobby and into the lift in silence, Rahul's hand caressing mine softly. We stopped in front of my room. Rahul seemed to expect me to say something, but I was quiet. One part—the logical, analytical part—of my mind was busy drawing up a flowchart, and the other part was saying, 'Damayanthi, kiss him. What feels so good can't be bad.'

The flowchart was like this:

INVITE RAHUL IN/ ACCEPT HIS INVITATION	DO NOT PROCEED FURTHER
	Because you are not wearing sexy, black lingerie, but ugly, brown old underwear that will turn off the most ardent suitor.
BECAUSE YOU WILL HAVE A WILD NIGHT OF PASSION AND NOT DIE A VIRGIN	Because the moment he touches you, you will give in to your carnal desires, get pregnant and be ostracized by family and society.
	Because you are not ready to let a man see your imperfect, naked body up close.
BECAUSE YOU WILL HAVE A WILD NIGHT OF PASSION AND NOT DIE A VIRGIN	Because he will not respect you in the morning and think you are a Fast and Loose girl who sleeps with men on the first date.
	Because a concoction of unknown, alcoholic liquids are about to induce nausea and cause embarrassment.
BECAUSE YOU WILL HAVE A WILD NIGHT OF PASSION AND NOT DIE A VIRGIN	Because you have to preserve your virginity like a precious gem for your future husband.

While my two minds were locked in battle and my body was leaning into Rahul and nuzzling him purely out of its own accord, something started chiming in my head like background music—I could hear Amma's words, 'Don't do anything silly! Don't do anything silly! Be good. Be good,' ringing away crazily inside my head like a chastity bell.

I drew apart and looked at him.

'I had a great time,' I said.

'We can continue to have a great time. The night is still young,' said Rahul, holding my hand, his fingers stroking my wrist.

LV: 'So am I. And so are you. So what are we waiting for?'

I ran a mental finger down the length of his face, stopping at the lips.

Me: 'Well, I have a flight to catch tomorrow and I am a bit tired.'

'Are you sure?' He seemed surprised.

LV: 'No, I am not sure at all. I am all muddled up, confused, and a part of me would like nothing more than to spend the night with you.'

'Yeah… Good night,' I said as surely as I could.

'Okay.' He leant forward and kissed my forehead. 'Good night, sweet Damayanthi.'

It sounded incredibly romantic and I wanted to fall into his arms with a little sigh. Instead, I went into my room and fell onto the bed with a huge sob and lay there thinking of all the lost opportunities of my life and felt utterly sorry for myself. I suppose I did the right thing. Maybe I would have felt awful afterwards. Maybe we wouldn't have done anything at all except watch TV and do the crossword. Maybe I misjudged his intentions. Maybe it would have been the start of 'How Damayanthi Balachandran Got Kissed and Got a Life' instead of fizzling out like a rejected manuscript.

Regret is a more miserable bedfellow than guilt.

We will reach Mumbai soon and I will be back to my usual routine. Maybe he has a steady girlfriend and I would have only been a one-night stand. Maybe he was the love of my life and I let him get away. Maybe the plane will crash and I will die a virgin.

Damayanthi, stop thinking these stupid thoughts. Fasten your seat belt and prepare for landing.

Bye,
D.

12

Dear Vic,

It is raining in Mumbai. The rain is nothing like the sporadic drizzles we have in Chennai. It seems as if all the water pipes in heaven have burst, releasing torrents of dull water on us. In spite of the incessant rain, life goes on—with umbrellas, plastic shoes, raincoats and drip-dry clothing. I am sitting in my room, gazing at sodden trees and damp buildings and thinking melancholy thoughts.

'It rains in the city, like it rains in my heart.'

Vic, it is probably not a big deal for you. You probably did it when you were sixteen and that is the average age in your neck of the woods for most people to neck in the woods. I guess it is probably something you want to get over with, like a rite of passage, but it didn't feel right to me. In fact, I seem to be heading for acute depression.

I spoke to Amma this morning and she was very keen to know what had happened in Goa.

'It was a good learning experience,' I muttered. The understatement of the year!

'Did anything happen?' she asked nervously. 'Is there anything you want to tell me?' I think mothers have an in-built radar which senses that something is amiss with their children.

'Nothing happened, Amma,' I replied. I do know that you don't get pregnant after kissing, so that is no cause for concern.

She was relieved, but I continued to mope.

It has been almost a week (five days, including the Sunday when I returned) since I returned from Goa and I have not heard from Rahul. In the beginning (Tuesday evening), I made excuses for him. Something must have happened.

1. He had a terrible bike accident and is lying bandaged and bound in a Goan hospital, calling out 'Damayanthi, Damayanthi!' in a weak voice.

2. He lost his legs in the terrible accident and is too proud to let me see him in his handicapped state.

3.   He lost his memory in the terrible accident and has no recollection of having met me.

4.   He met his long-lost girlfriend/wife, whom he had given up for dead, and now he had to do the honourable thing by her.

5.   He was whisked away by his parents to his ancestral village to be betrothed to the girl they had chosen for him when they both were little children running barefoot at the village fair.

Then (on Wednesday), I became angry and cursed him for being a philandering rake who played with the hearts of innocent young girls and then left them. He was a jerk just like all other men who just wanted to have a good time with a good-time girl. Who did he think he was? I would never think of him again.

Then (by Friday), I became unhappy and cursed myself for being attracted to a man who had his pick of women (Indian and international) and foolishly expected him to call after knowing him for just three days. I was filled with self-loathing for behaving like a wanton tramp and kissing a man I had barely known for two days. I was really silly to read so much into a kiss. Maybe sophisticated people kissed each other all the time and thought nothing of it. Maybe the kiss was the new handshake. I should be called Dummy and Dumballs for expecting anything to happen. I should stick to my numbers. At least they are safe and predictable, unlike human beings.

I am stuck in the unhappy, self-pitying phase right now. I think I ate too much chocolate in the past week and can just about button my jeans now. Logically, I should be refusing food and wasting away in sorrow. Instead, I feel really hungry all the time and eat whatever is at hand. I have a sudden craving for a large chocolate chip cookie dipped in chocolate sauce and topped with a swirl of Jamoca Almond Fudge. I am on my way to becoming a useless lump of lard.

Get a hold of yourself, Damayanthi.

Yours helplessly,
Damayanthi.

⚘

Dear Vic,

It did sound too good to be true. Too bad Algernon turned out to be gay. After all, what can you say about a man whose needlepoint is better than yours? But look at this way, you may have lost a boyfriend, but you have gained a boy friend. I have neither.

I have got hold of myself since Rahul seems to have no desire to get hold of me. I will now devote myself to my career. There is much more work to be done on our special project, with just a month to go for our confirmation. Even Jimmy seems to have become serious. CG has shared some quality tools and techniques with us, which we will now apply to various problem areas that we have uncovered in all the processes. By doing this, we will miraculously uncover ways to save money and make money for First Global.

Somehow, ever since I got back from Goa, I have been unable to concentrate on work. I have had several out-of-body experiences, where my mind has wandered back to the Goan beaches, leaving the shell of my body behind. This morning, when CG asked me a question, I responded with a blank stare. CG seems to have loosened up a bit, but he still fixed me with a scrutinizing frown. He had already had a session with Jimmy when I had been away in Goa and now I was the sole student in the class, revising the application of some statistical tools to our project.

'Do you understand the Pareto Principle?' he asked. Was this a pop quiz?

LV: 'It explains why I spend 80% of my time thinking about someone for whom I probably have less than 20% importance in the scheme of things.

Why 80% of all women want only the 20% of the total male population that they cannot have. Why 80% of all men want only the 20% of all women who look like asparagus and have baingan bharta for brains.'

Me: 'Yes, I do.' Thankfully, I had studied it in economics in college.

CG: 'So are you comfortable with the statistical tools?'

LV: 'No. I am still trying to understand my non-standard deviation from the desired behaviour and do a variance analysis of the factors that can lead to an above-average specimen of the male species to call a girl at the other end of the bell curve.'

Me: 'Yes.'

I was getting a little bored with all this talk of statistical tools. I wished he would say something interesting. I had quite enjoyed our little chat at the COps lunchroom. I liked seeing the lighter side of him that came to the surface occasionally, rather like an interesting sea creature which rose from the depths of a flat, quiet ocean.

'So if you are comfortable, we'll wrap up for today,' CG said.

Thank god! My listening skills were being severely challenged and my mind desperately needed to de-clutter.

'I am going to pick up some coffee. Do you want some?' I needed my caffeine shot and I was being a good hostess.

We headed to the coffee vending machine in the small pantry on our floor. The coffee we get from this outdated contraption is actually dish-washing sludge disguised as mud disguised as coffee. Often, we drank a concoction of uncertain parentage since the various beverages seemed to get mixed up with each other inside the machine, resulting in something even more vile. They must be adding some narcotic substance to it, since I was becoming quite addicted to the brown fluid.

We both sipped our beverages sitting at a little round table.

'So how was your training in Goa?' asked CG.

LV: 'Great. I met someone very interesting.'

Me: 'Great. Very interesting.'

CG: 'Did they demystify the First Global way of banking? How they calculate the PLR and ROI and all?'

LV: 'I spent more time wondering how to convert the short-term floating interest expressed by one party into a long-term fixed interest bond. I was too busy controlling the wild rate of imagination to worry about the rate of return on investments.'

Me: 'Yes, we went through all of that.' I tried a knowledgeable nod.

CG: 'Did you get to see any of Goa?'

LV: 'I didn't get to see much of it, but I think Goa saw a new side of me!'

'Not much. Have you been there?' My mind was already recreating my beach encounter and I thought it best to deflect the question.

'Couple of times. My two friends and I hitchhiked to Goa from Delhi a few years ago.' He smiled.

'Wow! That must have been amazing. Is that the wildest thing you have done?' It was my turn to play quizmaster.

'Hmmm… sort of.' CG's face creased into a little frown, as though he was calculating a complex maths equation. 'The wildest thing was when we three got drunk at a really shady liquor shack with a bunch of truck drivers. Those guys were crazy. The next morning we were sick in the back of some truck going to Amritsar. We had to get off and change direction before the driver realized what a mess we had made in his vehicle.' He was smiling again.

I can't imagine CG doing something like that—so reckless, spontaneous and crazy. Was that the same consultant guy who never used less than forty-seven words in a typical sentence?

'What about you? What has been your wild thing?' CG looked interested, as though I was going to come up with some exciting titbit.

Yes, Vic. I had to confess again. The wildest thing I have ever done was probably my little outing on a Goa beach which I could not confess to anyone.

Think, D, think. Surely you have been a little crazy, reckless and spontaneous in your life?

In sheer desperation, I came up with a mild rather than wild event from my late adolescence.

'I think it must have been the time when I became a wild animal. Does that qualify?'

'Whoa! Yes! I would like to know about that.' CG looked surprised. Did he think I had morphed into a man-eating tigress?

Vision of me in a tight cat suit, crawling on all fours across a carpet in a room done up in a Jungle Deco style. Rahul appears from behind a vine-covered pillar with a whip and growls, 'I am going to tame you, you wild cat.'

'Judging from your expression, it must have been quite a wild experience,' said CG.

I felt myself flush and quickly rattled off some inane version of my youthful venture into animal transmogrification.

'Well, you be the judge. My class in college had put up this dramatized version of *The Jungle Book*. I was Bagheera the panther for a while. I wore a black velvet suit and was so uncomfortable that I kept scratching all over, as though Bagheera was suffering from bad flea attack.'

'And?'

'And that was it! The itching became so bad that I ran out in the middle of the play, saying something stupid like, "I must go now. Mother Wolf is calling Mowgli." I went and took off the horrible suit and another girl went back on stage in my place. That was the end of my theatrical career.'

'Hey, that is unfair! That wasn't really wild.' CG made a mock protesting gesture, but he looked more amused than annoyed.

'Were you ever a wild animal?' I asked in a mock aggressive tone.

'Never. I guess you win.' He grinned at me.

'It's okay. I am not keeping score.' I smiled back.

We talked briefly for a few minutes and finished our second cup of sludge.

I went back to work. The work is not so bad here, Vic. Though, on some days, I feel that I should be doing more worthwhile work—like saving the environment or educating little children or eradicating poverty. If I had some skill or talent, I would devote myself to Art—singing, dancing, writing poetry or painting. But I am only fit for some number-crunching

job in a financial institution. If I had to be in a bank,
I should at least be making more money so that I can
retire by thiry-five and live off my savings. Maybe
I should be in treasury, where the guys make fatter
bonuses. Like Rahul.

SHIT. I almost made it through the day without
thinking about him. Another ten years, and he will
be a distant memory.

Good night, Vic,
D.

Hello Vic,

I am happy to inform you that communication
channels have been opened between r.kumar@
firstglobal.com and d.balachandran@firstglobal.
com.

I saw this email in my inbox today:

To: d.balachandran@firstglobal.com
From: r.kumar@firstglobal.com
Re: Hi

Hi Damayanthi,

How are you doing? I remember the
wonderful time we had in Goa—not just
at the training! ☺ Guess you are back
in Mumbai. Would you like to meet up
sometime? I don't seem to have your number.
Send it to me at 9820255667.

Rahul

I couldn't stop smiling for almost two hours after
that. Jimmy was curious to know why I was so cheerful
after being down in the dumps the whole of last week.
Of course, I didn't tell him. Vic, I have replied with
my contact details and have expressed willingness to
meet up sometime. I waited till the end of day to reply,
drafting my response, sneaking a look at the mail filed
under 'Personal' just to make sure it was real.

The writing in brackets shows the logic and
analysis behind each sentence:

> To: r.kumar@firstglobal.com
> From: d.balachandran@firstglobal.com
> Re: Re: Hi

Hi Rahul,

What a pleasant surprise to hear from you.
(Am not desperately waiting to hear from him

like a frustrated spinster, but at the same time am glad to—tone is friendly, not eager.) I am back in Mumbai and have got busy with work. *(I do have a life and did not spend the past five days thinking about whether I will hear from him.)* I would like to meet up sometime. *(Call to action—firm yet positive tone, finally replaced 'love to' with 'like to' after deleting about ten times.)* Do call/message me on 9820266778 when you are free. *(Giving options to call or message indicates there is no pressure—tone is cool, casual.)*

Damayanthi.

Now I just have to wait for him to call.

Bye,
D.

꘎

Dear Vic,

You have much more experience in matters like this, right? So please be my agony aunt and help me out here. Why would a man ask you for your number if he had no intention of calling? Did he expect me to call? If so, why didn't he say so in the mail? Should I call without an explicit invitation? What would he think if I did? Would a missed call be an indication of intent or an accident? What if he didn't return the missed call? What about an SMS? Maybe just a mysterious '?' in the text? What did people do when they did not have mobile phones? How did I live for twenty-six years without a phone when I now gaze at it as though it is the true object of my affections?

Why am I troubling my mind with all these pointless questions? Instead of Rahul, I got a call from Amma. The parents have discovered a boy in Mumbai.

Amma said, 'Damayanthi, at last god has listened to my prayers. We have received some wonderful news. Yesterday, we got a response to the advertisement. There is a boy in Mumbai.'

Me: 'Oh!'

Amma: 'He is very smart, doing PhD in America. His parents live in Matunga, so he is visiting them. His father is not well, quite old. So they want to finalize everything quickly. The proper thing will be for us to be there with you also and arrange for him to visit you in your house.'

LV: 'Ooh, exciting! I can just see a girl-seeing ceremony in 124 Pine Crest. You cooking onion pakoras in my kitchen and me wearing the good maroon sari with jasmine flowers in my hair and Sonya collapsing in a fit of laughter. Over my dead body!'

Me: 'Amma, I don't think that is possible. We are not allowed visitors in the bank flat.' A wise lady once said, 'You can tell a thousand lies to avoid a marriage.'

Amma: 'Oh. Anyway, it will be too expensive for Appa and me to travel all this distance. So we have spoken to the boy's family. The boy wants to meet you first, alone. It is not at all proper, but what to do, we are the girl's side after all. There is no other proposal also now. We cannot say no, Daamu.'

Me: 'Okay, Amma. I will meet him.'

Once again, the good Damayanthi agrees to meet a strange male with the parental hope of taking an immediate decision on matrimony.

What the hell! It is not as though I have plenty of men grovelling at my feet for my favours. It will be better than waiting for Rahul to call. Maybe this boy will be a charming, intelligent man and it will be love at first sight and we will fly off to live the NRI dream.

Vision of myself and charming, intelligent man having coffee and conversation at swish coffee shop of five-star hotel. I murmur a witty comment and we both laugh like old friends. Rahul walks in alone, wearing a tatty shawl, looking anguished, with Devdas-type stubble and bottle of cheap liquor in his hand. I ignore him. He looks pleadingly at me and says…

'I am so happy that you agreed, Damayanthi,' Amma's relieved voice floated down the line. 'I thought you might be shy to meet a man alone. We have brought you up with all good, traditional values, so I know it can be awkward. But what to do, there is no other option at the moment.'

'Don't worry, Amma, I will manage.' Damayanthi the brave volunteers to meet boy alone.

'I will give the boy your mobile number then and he will call you. His name is Ramanathan, but they call him Ram. I have not seen the photo, but his height is six feet. He is a bit old, thirty-four, but…'

'It is all right, Amma. I am no apsara either.'

Stunned silence from Amma, who is wondering about this new, improved Damayanthi, but is too grateful to question the sudden change of heart.

'Please take care, Daamu. If this alliance happens, I will break ten coconuts at Amman Kovil.'

I miss Amma.

Good night,
D.

Hi Vic,

I don't think you still get the idea of an arranged marriage. Answering personals on a singles website is kind of like scanning matrimonials in the newspapers. Except that you have disintermediated the middlemen and have taken matters into your own hands.

My arranged-for date Ram called. He had a pleasant voice and I was hopeful that this encounter would turn out better than the others. We have arranged to meet at the coffee shop at Taj Lands End. After all, he earns in dollars and can afford to spare a few for the Indian economy.

I got off early from work, went home and changed into appropriate clothes. This was not a date. Technically, it was a girl-seeing ceremony, minus parents. After doing a complete analysis of my wardrobe, I wore a blue kurti with a silver paisley print teamed up with a white salwar and small silver earrings—traditional yet contemporary, just like the Indian woman of today.

Ram was tall and gaunt and wore a slightly anxious look. He wore dark trousers and a pale blue, formal shirt and his black shoes were polished to a shine. He looked as though he had dressed a little too carefully, not with Rahul's casual elegance. STOP. I will not mention the R-word again.

We made some small talk and went into the coffee shop.

He scanned the menu quickly and said, 'I am not really hungry. What about you?' He asked somewhat fearfully. I later realized that he was calculating how many dollars this would set him back.

'Oh, the food here is quite hygienic,' I said, mistaking the cause for his apprehension. 'I will have a grilled sandwich and a milkshake.' I was hungry.

'That's Rs 240,' he said after checking the menu. 'That is about $5—$5 for a sandwich and milk in India is too much, isn't it?'

'Well, it's actually $4.45 at the current exchange rate,' Damayanthi the banker informed him.

'Things have become very expensive in India,' he said sadly. Warning bells should have gone off here, but good-hearted Damayanthi went on blithely.

'Yes. Are you coming back to India after a long time?'

'Yes. First time in nine years. Things have changed a lot.'

'Yes. They have.' I thought we were going to engage in an interesting conversation on the reforms, the telecom boom, the variety of cars on the street, the burgeoning urban migrant population and the new moralities in Indian cinema.

'I remember, we could get a good coffee at Madras Tiffin House in Matunga for just Rs 3, but now a tumbler of coffee is Rs 10. And look, it is Rs 80 here,' he said pointing at the menu.

Cheapskate alert, cheapskate alert! The alarm was now beeping in my brain.

'This is a coffee shop at a five-star hotel,' I said politely. 'Maybe I can treat you. After all, you are my guest.'

At this point, any self-respecting man would have refused and chivalrously offered to order anything at all for me.

But Ram's face lit up and he ordered a masala dosa, two plates of chaat, a cup of coffee and a plate of gulab jamuns. It was only 7:00 p.m. and he was having his dinner at my expense. I wondered if he earned anything at all in America.

'You have no idea how much I miss Indian food,' he exclaimed with a satisfied burp.

'I can imagine.' I sipped my milkshake thoughtfully.

'You must get a work permit immediately when you come to the US. We do need the extra dollars. What you bring as dowry will not be enough. My job as a teaching assistant hardly covers my living expenses. You have done computers, haven't you? Then it will be easier to get a job.'

'I am an accountant,' I quickly corrected him. A little bubble of anger was boiling within me. Did he want a wife or a cash cow?

Just then the bill was placed in front of Ram, who looked meaningfully at me. I pulled out my First Global credit card and pushed it along.

'Oh. Then… what skills do you have? Apart from cooking good Indian food, I hope!' Ram continued shamelessly.

LV: 'Maybe you can rent me out as an exotic oriental virgin who is highly skilled in all the three hundred and twenty-three fine arts of the Kamasutra.'

Me: 'Maybe you can rent me out as an exotic oriental virgin who is highly skilled in all the three hundred and twenty-three fine arts of the Kamasutra.'

The bill was almost Rs 1,000, but the look on Mr Ramanathan's face was worth every paise.

I have saved Amma ten coconuts.

Good night,
D.

13

Dear Vic,

Amma was not thankful that I had saved her ten coconuts, or that her daughter had been saved from marrying a nutcase. She was sure that I had done something wrong which had caused the prospective in-laws to indicate that a newly found family astrologer had discovered that our horoscopes were incompatible. No more unchaperoned girl-seeing ceremonies for me. Thank god that there is at least one happy outcome of the saga of stingy Ram!

After what seemed like an eternity, Rahul finally called. I was torn between sounding cool, like an ice queen who had a host of admirers, and gratified, like Damayanthi who didn't. At the end of three minutes of polite conversation, I was the grateful recipient of an invitation to watch a film on Saturday night. We will catch the 7:00 p.m. show of *The Pursuit of Happyness* at Fame Adlabs, to be followed by dinner somewhere there. There is only a small cloud in the silver lining.

I was moping around in office yesterday with Jimmy, cursing the rains, the trains, the drains and the pains of preparing project reports. Since I had nothing much to do, I agreed to Jimmy's invitation to hang out with him and some other guys. I didn't even ask who the other guys were—sheer loneliness and desperation made me say yes.

Usually, Sonya is out partying Saturday nights while I warm our living room cushions, pretending that reading *The Collected Works of M.K. Gandhi* is more important and worthwhile than wasting energy on frivolous pastimes. She usually leaves by the time I emerge from my room in the morning and returns late at night after her Platinum dinner dates. I am sure she has a boyfriend. I have heard her use a special, intimate voice on the phone sometimes—a throaty laugh just to let me know that she is the kind who has boyfriends while I am the kind who is stuck in the house on Saturday nights.

Jimmy and I had agreed to touch base on Saturday. Now I will have to make some excuse without hurting his feelings. The path to true love does not run smooth. I mean, not that I am in love or anything. It is too premature to feel anything but a strong attraction and a desire to further the relationship. Okay, to start a relationship. What relationship?

Good night, Vic,
D.

Hi Vic,

It is another lazy Sunday morning and I am gazing out at the rain-drenched city, feeling romantic, listening to 'Rim jhim girey saawan' on FM and sipping a cup of coffee. I should be feeling really wonderful after my first (or is it second?) date, but there is a nagging sense of disquiet inside me. I may have gained a boyfriend, but have I lost a friend?

I spoke to Jimmy yesterday morning. Obviously, I couldn't tell him that I was going out for a movie with Rahul after agreeing to hang out with him and the guys. I weighed the pros and cons of confessing. If I told Jimmy, he wouldn't stop me. In fact, he might be happy for me. Unless he was harbouring a secret crush for me, which he most certainly was not. My feminine intuition is not that bad and I get purely brotherly vibes from Jimmy, unlike the purely non-brotherly vibes from Rahul. But then he might joke about it. He might think I have a boyfriend when the fact is that I don't really know what I have. It was all very confusing. In the end, I decided to do the most sensible thing. I lied.

'I don't think I can make it, Jimmy. I am not feeling too well.'

He didn't push me. I guess he was secretly relieved that they could do the male-bonding thing over cars or whatever he had planned with the guys. I got ready for my big date with Rahul. I washed my hair, conditioned it, used an apricot face mask (which didn't seem to make too much of a difference) and then put another orange peel face mask (which, again, didn't make my face glow like that of the bleached model on the pack). I wore a new, dark blue, empire-cut top which, in the latest fashion, was cinched under my chest and flowed freely till mid-thigh, covering my sins and accentuating my assets. As I put on the war-paint and looked at my reflection, I couldn't believe this was the same girl who quoted from *The Beauty Myth* and swore off lip gloss for three whole years. Who was I turning into? A bimbo, primping and powdering for a man? A teenager who experienced a hormonal imbalance every time she thought about a certain encounter involving lips on the beach? This is not me. Or was not me.

Vic, I had to go with the flow. There was no time to play shrink to myself. I took an auto to Fame Adlabs. Since Rahul lives in Andheri, it didn't make sense for him to come to pick me up from here. He was already there when I reached the theatre. It was quite crowded, with throngs of fashionably dressed people out for a Saturday night. For a change, I was among them instead of biting my nails at home. Rahul looked smart in brown linen trousers and a cream shirt. He had already picked up the tickets, which was very thoughtful. He complimented me on my choice of clothes—here was a man who noticed what a woman wore! We went into the plush theatre as the film began and enjoyed the story of a man and his pursuit of happiness. Well, I enjoyed the parts I paid attention to, but a part of me was also wondering if Rahul was going to hold my hand.

If he did, should I let him? How long should my hand stay held? What if I felt itchy and had to move my hand away? Would he feel offended? What if I then held his hand back? Would he feel I was being possessive? Would he put his hand around my shoulders, along the back of the seat? What should I do if he did? I might as well have enjoyed the film because he did none of those things. I was a bit puzzled, somewhat relieved and partly worried that he didn't want to have further physical contact with me. But when the picture got over, he did put a hand on my back as we were leaving.

Rahul suggested dinner at a new Chinese restaurant a few blocks away and we rode there on his bike. I liked riding pillion again, and putting my hand around his waist seemed only natural. Did he own a bike and not upgrade to a car so that girls could sit at the back and put an arm around him? Was I not the only girl he had taken for a ride? Was he taking me for a ride?

STOP, Damayanthi. You don't have a jealous or possessive bone in your body, I had to remind myself.

We entered the restaurant—Great Wall of China. It had red Chinese lanterns hanging all over and oriental pictures of dragons and daggers on the walls. Luckily, we managed to find a table for two in a corner and settled down for a cosy dinner. I left the ordering to him, not being too familiar with Chinese food. Rahul recommended the Manchow soup and we ordered crispy honey potato for starters. It was a good start.

'So how was your week?' I asked.

'Busy, hectic. The markets are volatile and a lot of our clients have open positions, so it was a bit crazy.'

'Oh...' I tried not to think of open positions. Or any other positions.

Just as I was about to carry on with our scintillating conversation, I heard a familiar voice behind me.

'We can sit there,' said someone who sounded like Jimmy. I had my back to the rest of the restaurant and was facing Rahul, so I couldn't see the source of the voice. In the next minute, I watched in horror as the table for four next to us was occupied by Jimmy, CG and a couple of men I didn't know. I had never felt the space constraint in Mumbai before, but at that instant I was wishing that I was in some place where the distance between the chairs at restaurants was more than two feet. I still remember Jimmy's shocked face, CG's mildly surprised look and Rahul's bemused look.

'Hi, Damayanthi,' said CG politely after a few seconds of silence.

'Hi,' I muttered.

'How are you feeling now?' asked Jimmy in a mock solicitous voice, an evil glint in his eye.

'Much better.'

'I can see that.'

'Were you unwell?' asked Rahul, looking puzzled.

'No, not really. Just a headache.'

'Oh,' chorused Jimmy and Rahul, though the tones of the 'ohs' were very different.

'It has gone,' I said with a bright smile, sounding like the old Amrutanjan ad.

Then the introductions were performed, the tables almost joined together, and we were one big happy family. The gentlemen discussed the races and the latest cricket match. Then they all discussed the stock market, the movements of which were carefully analysed and interpreted. While Jindal Steel and Infosys have been going up, Damayanthi's share of mindspace at this table has been rapidly declining.

The romantic mood had completely vanished. We said goodbyes and Rahul dropped me off in front of 124 Pine Crest. This would have been a great opportunity to ask Rahul to come up for a cup of coffee. I didn't know if Sonya was around, but the temptation to take a handsome man into my room and see her envious look was very strong. But I was feeling bad that I had lied to Jimmy, feeling irritated because CG had ignored me, as though he didn't know me at all, and upset because Rahul had been treating me like one of the boys. Was he ashamed to be seen with me? Maybe he was used to a sophisticated woman who cooed happily at the boys and focused all the attention on herself. I was struck by analysis paralysis.

'I had a great time,' I said to Rahul as I got off the bike. 'Thank you.'

'You don't have to thank me,' replied Rahul. 'I had a good time too, though an additional foursome was not what I had expected.'

'I know. I am sorry.' Maybe I should make it up to him and invite him in for dessert. I did have half a tub of chocolate ice cream. I could slip into something comfortable, like my yellow negligee, and we could switch on the TV and settle ourselves on the carpet and lick the ice cream off each other's...

'Hey, it isn't your fault or anything,' Rahul was saying. 'Next time, we'll go to a deserted island.' He smiled at me.

There was going to be a next time. Hurrah! I almost called him in, but then I saw the night watchman get up from his bench and come towards us. I knew he was a watchman, but did he have to watch us so carefully? I am sure he had seen plenty of people being dropped off at night. What was he expecting us to do? What would he think of me if I took a man home with me in the dead of the night? Didn't Sonya entertain male visitors late at night? Why was the watchman staring at Rahul suspiciously? Why did I care at all?

'Yes. Good night,' I said hurriedly. Did he look disappointed or was that just the shadow of the moon on his face? Maybe he looked relieved. Maybe I will never know. I stupidly put out my hand and he shook it with an amused smile. I ran up to my lonely home and slowly finished off the half tub of ice cream by myself, blindly surfing channels on TV.

Now I will spend the rest of the weekend feeling confused, frustrated and angry with myself.

Bye,
D.

Hi Vic,

Today, I thought about bringing up the matter with Jimmy. I thought I should apologize to him for lying about my health. Then I reasoned that I had become better by the evening. Now that I recall, I was feeling a bit queasy in the morning when I spoke to him. It isn't that I owe him an explanation or anything. Except that he is the closest thing I have to a friend in this city. You don't lie to friends. When I was dithering about what to do, Jimmy brought up the topic himself.

'So, how is your love life, Dummy?' he asked. Normally, I would have responded in kind, but today I was in more a defensive rather than attacking mode.

'Non-existent,' I said and tried to concentrate on checking my mail.

'Look, Damayanthi, if you wanted to be with someone, you could have told me,' he said, sounding very serious.

If Jimmy sounded serious, it meant trouble. That was the cue to apologize.

'I am sorry,' I said humbly. 'It is just that I wasn't sure and…'

'I would have given you up, Damayanthi. It would have hurt me for a while, perhaps, but I would never stand in the path of true love,' Jimmy continued in a sad voice.

I stared aghast. Was he really nurturing a secret passion for me? Maybe there is no such thing as a platonic relationship between a man and woman. My feminine intuition was all wrong.

Then he burst out laughing. 'I wish I had a camera to capture that look on your face. Relax, Dumballs. You are really not my type at all.'

'Thank god for that!' I composed myself.

'So how long has it been going on? Come on, spill the beans, D.' He put a mock serious look on his face like a police interrogator and waved an imaginary truncheon in front of me.

'There is nothing going on,' I said and pretended to find the mail from system security fascinating.

Luckily, I was spared the grilling by the arrival of CG in our meeting room. Then we both became serious and immediately opened up the Excel spreadsheets we were working on. Sometimes, I feel that CG is our teacher and Jimmy and I are the students in the remedial class. One of these days, we will greet him with a 'Good moooorning, sir!'

Harish called us for a meeting in the afternoon. He looked quite serious. Usually, we don't see him much.

'Guys, we need to hurry up on the project,' he said the moment he got in. 'There is a lot of pressure from AB to get this done by September.'

Jimmy and I glanced at each other. The moment he heard the word pressure, he looked a little deflated. Sometimes I think Jimmy is totally detached from our work and is doing timepass. I like this new word—timepass, like eating peanuts on the train, chumma. Amma will be shocked to know that chumma does not mean timeplass in Mumbai but kissing, as I discovered a few days ago, much to my embarrassment and Jimmy's amusement.

'We are waiting for some data from the Delhi branch,' I said finally. That was true. I had sent an email to the branch manager asking for some information, but he had not responded. None of the branch managers had responded.

'Have you sent reminders? Have you escalated this?' he asked anxiously.

I hadn't done either. Harish gave me a pitying look. 'Damayanthi, no one will respond to a request for information unless it is important for them. You have to be more assertive in getting information. You can't sit around waiting for things to happen.'

'It has only been four days,' I said by way of explanation.

'Four days is too long. Send them a reminder now and copy me and Atul Vaidya on the mail.'

Atul is the northern regional head and a bigshot. I didn't want to copy him on the mail, but I figured Harish knew what he was talking about. Such is the way of the world.

'So how much is the estimated cost savings across the process improvement initiatives?' Harish continued.

'About half a million,' said Jimmy, who had come alive. He wasn't sure and neither was I.

'Look, guys,' said Harish sternly. 'We need to show a saving of at least $1 million in this project for it to get noticed. I don't care how you do it—just do it. If you get me $1 million, I will arrange for you to make a presentation to AB himself. And if Nadeem is here, he will also be there for the presentation. It could be a huge opportunity for you guys.'

Nadeem Hamid is the regional head for the SAME countries (South Asia and Middle East), based out of Dubai. He visits once or twice a year to keep a check on his subjects. According to Jimmy, the entire bank will run around like a headless chicken for two months before the visit, preparing reviews, presentations and cleaning up workstations. It sounds exciting.

Vision of myself pointing to a presentation and saying, 'That is how we can save $1 million for First Global and positively impact CSat scores as well. Any questions?' AB whispers to Nadeem, 'Damayanthi is one of our rising stars. She has an amazing grasp of all the functions and a brilliant analytical mind.' Nadeem nods approvingly. 'Why don't you send her for the Global Leadership Programme we have at Harvard?' Harish beams proudly and says...

'I need to see some positive results within a month. You guys make sure that ASTC is also delivering. Just get it done. We will do weekly reviews from now on.'

Yes, Vic. I will be a focused career woman now. My personal life, or what little of it there is, will be put on hold. I immediately sent off reminder emails for all the earlier ones I had sent, copying the respective regional heads and Harish.

Within a few minutes, I saw that Harish had added his bit and replied to each mail with, 'Please treat this as urgent. AB needs the information by the 10th.'

That was news to me, but the line worked. Each of the branch managers who had ignored me for a week soon replied with 'Will revert ASAP' mails. I feel powerful, Vic. I have discovered the secret to getting things done. I am a woman of action now.

Except when it comes to my non-existent love life.

Bye,
Damayanthi.

14

∽

Hi Vic,

I guess you are making some progress with the personal ads. HotSexyman157 does sound promising, but are you sure you want to meet someone who says 'I vantu meke friendsheep with u'? He does not sound like someone you want to be seen with in public. Then again, maybe you will not be seen with him in public, preferring to discuss matters privately. You will never know till you check him out.

Today we had a meeting with CG and conveyed the news about the $1 million savings that we were supposed to provide. After doing some juggling around with numbers, the maximum we could come up with was $4,50,000.

'Let us brainstorm some ideas,' suggested CG. This meant jotting down whatever came into our heads without evaluating the ideas. In the beginning, we were serious. Jimmy jotted down the ideas on a flip chart.

'Reduce courier cost by not returning returned cheque to people. Send them an SMS instead.'

'Use one-sided paper for deposit slips.'

'Avoid deposit slips by installing scanning machines at ATMs that will capture cheque details.'

'What about cost of scanning machines?' I asked.

'No judging now. We'll eliminate ideas later,' said CG.

The ideas flowed thick and fast.

'Eliminate travel budget of AVPs and above.'

'Eliminate AVPs and above.'

I thought CG might disapprove, but he was smiling. After a while, he joined us in giving even crazier ideas.

'Replace all COps people with robots,' I said.

'You mean they are not robots? You could have fooled me,' CG remarked.

'Install an automatic mechanism that will switch off ACs at 6.00 p.m., to save electricity.'

'Install a mechanism that will switch off the lights at 6.00 p.m., to save employees.'

'Anyway, most of us are totally in the dark about what we are doing through the day!'

'Use single-ply toilet paper in the loos,' quipped Jimmy.

'Eliminate toilet paper,' I added.

'Use traditional Indian way of hygiene.'

'Yeah! Anyway, there are enough people who do nothing but lick ass all day long.' CG grinned.

Of late, I was getting to see a side of him I hadn't before. Was that a sense of humour beneath that pseudo-intellectual exterior? He seems so decent during our brief encounters, and then it is as though a grim mask comes on when he is working. Still, I hadn't had so much fun at work in a long time. However, nothing concrete came out of all the storms our brains churned up. Jimmy and I have to sift through all that chaff to come up with even a grain of a million-dollar idea.

Now I feel rather gloomy about our loser project. It doesn't seem like we will be able to meet our deadline. Harish will fire us or we will languish in a corner of the clearing department, sorting and flinging cheques along with Balki.

Good night,
D.

Hi Vic,

Rahul has not called. Sonya is back. It is raining again. I have an incipient cold. It is a weekend and I am alone again. This is the story of my life. I am tempted to pick up the phone and call Rahul. Just a casual 'Hi, what are you doing?' Or 'Just wanted to get your opinion on the global recession.' Or 'I was passing by Andheri and wondered if you were free for coffee?' I rehearsed the lines about a hundred times and once almost picked up the phone, but couldn't bring myself to do it. I don't think it is because of any old-fashioned reticence, but because I might find out that he was having a great time doing interesting things without me, and that would just make me more miserable.

Sumi called me this morning. I wanted to complain to her about the general insensitivity of men and get some advice from her. Instead, she was depressed because things are not well between her and Deb.

'He is being such a damn jerk, D,' she moaned.

'He is a man, Sumi. They all lapse into jerkiness. It is an occupational hazard.' For a change, I seemed to be the one giving her advice.

'I can't believe it. He thinks that if I learn to speak Bengali and cook fish, his parents will come around. What a fuckall idea!'

'You mean he wants you to give up your ways and change into the perfect Bong bride to please his parents?'

'Yes. I can't believe this is the same Deb who urged me to get a tattoo and express my individuality.' Sumi sounded baffled.

I was indignant on her behalf. 'That is so unfair. Why don't you ask him to learn to speak Tamil and to cook aviyal?'

'D, you won't believe it—I did. And you know what the jerk said? "Come on, babe, be realistic,"' she mimicked Deb's deep voice.

'Did you say "Don't call me babe"?' I put on a mock American accent.

She laughed then. I guess I had cheered her up a bit.

'D, this is all so screwed up now that I don't know if I want to get married at all. I mean, I thought I loved him and all that, but if he really loves me, he wouldn't ask me to change the way I am. Maybe we should do a trial separation.'

'This whole love thing is so screwed up.' I sighed, thinking about my sad non-love life.

'Ah-ha! Fee-fi-fo-fum, do I smell the presence of a real man?' Sumi immediately perked up and forgot about her own miseries for a while.

'No, not really,' I confessed. Not really is the way I felt about Rahul. Sometimes, he didn't seem to exist in my life at all.

'Which means there is someone. Come on, D. Tell Sumi akka yeverything. Is he hot? Have you done it?'

'Shut up, Sumi. We haven't done anything.' I gave her a brief, watered-down version of my close encounters with Rahul.

'He sounds yummy,' sighed Sumi. 'Go for him, D. Don't feel shy. That doesn't get you anywhere. Just pick up the phone and call him. Don't get despo, but let him know that you are interested. There is nothing that attracts a man more than a woman who is attracted to him,' she said, sounding like a love guru on TV.

We signed off feeling a little better. I hope things work out and her bong Babu comes to his senses and realizes how lucky he is to have Sumi just the way she is.

Now I am feeling at a loose end. I am writing to you on a Saturday afternoon after coming back from office, with no prospect of anything exciting to do. I have this strange, restless feeling that cannot be subdued by TV, reading, cupboard-cleaning or sleeping. I am still not ready to call Rahul. I am going to go out by myself and buy some books.

Bye,
D.

⁂

Hey Vic,

I am sorry that HotSexyman157 looked about a hundred and fifty-seven years old and did not live up to his moniker. You can't trust the pictures posted on these sites. But if he had called himself DirtyOldman157, he would not have got a single hit.

I am glad I went out to buy books. I ended up having an interesting evening. I took an auto to Crossword and enjoyed a happy half hour of browsing. I ended up at the kids section, standing nostalgically in front of the Enid Blytons. I used to love those books as a kid, even though it seemed as if wonderful adventures only happened to blue-eyed children in faraway islands. You, my dear Victoria, must have had a lot of these adventures. I remember the folks from the Faraway Tree and the different lands that used to appear at the top of the tree. At one point of time, there was nothing I wanted more than to be a heroine in an Enid Blyton adventure, eating buttered scones, capturing crooks in Cornish castles and saying 'Come on, old boy' to a Scottish terrier. Later, I wanted to be a Regency heroine coming out in an elegant ball amidst the cream of London society and flirting from behind my delicate, lavender-coloured fan with dashing, witty rakes. Now I just want Rahul to call me. What a comedown!

As I was flipping through *Five Go Off in a Caravan*, I heard a familiar throat-clearing sound behind me. And there was CG, holding a hard-bound edition of *The Argumentative Indian*. Trust him to see me with a children's book in my hands.

'So you like Enid Blyton books?' he asked with an amused look.

'I used to read a lot of them,' I muttered. 'Not any more!'

'I read a few as a kid.' He shrugged dismissively.

'I guess most people did then,' I said. 'I don't remember any other children's books.'

'You know, Enid Blyton was quite racist,' CG said. 'I don't think kids today should read these books any more.'

'What do you mean? They are just harmless books.'

A why-do-I-have-to-give-an-explanation-to-this-woman look appeared on his face. 'They are not inclusive. You don't find any coloured or non-Caucasian characters in the books. If at all they are there, they are objects of ridicule or fun. Only the blond, blue-eyed ones get to be brave and noble.'

I had never thought of them like that at all. 'Well, I guess that was a function of the times she lived in. Besides, you needn't do a deep dive into the subtext and instead just enjoy a good adventure,' I retorted.

'That is at a very superficial level.'

'It is supposed to be at a superficial level. These are children's books, not political treatises.' I was annoyed at the righteous indignation he displayed—at the same time, I was enjoying the argument.

'So you are saying that it is all right for children's books to have racist and sexist messages in them because children won't understand them?' Maybe CG was also enjoying the argument.

'No. I am saying that the messages are not overt and do not impact the story in any way. These secret messages are too subtle to be misinterpreted by the target audience.'

CG wasn't giving up. 'Well, on one hand, you can say that children won't consciously find a deeper meaning in the seemingly innocuous stories, but on the other hand, there will be subliminal messages that get ingrained into their consciousness and impact their behaviour even as adults.'

I tried to suppress the small smile that I could feel creeping across my face. He sounded like he was making a corporate presentation on 'The Political Correctness of Enid Blyton in the 21st Century'.

'What is so funny?' he asked, looking a bit perplexed.

'Nothing. Forget it.'

'What?' he persisted.

'You were talking like you were making a serious presentation on "The Political Correctness of Enid Blyton in the 21st Century" to a bunch of schoolchildren,' I confessed. I half expected him to take offence and sneer coldly at me, but he gave me a completely disarming grin instead.

'Yeah! Sometimes I get carried away. My kid sister tells me I can be a pompous ass at times.' A hint of a smile showed on his face.

'Only at times. Everyone has the right to be irritating at times.' I smiled back. I hope he didn't think of me as a kid sister. Suddenly, the thought was not at all appealing.

'Hmmm. So what is the most irritating thing that you do?' he asked.

'Irritating? Me?' Hand on heart, I feigned an astonished look.

'Does that mean that you are the perfect girl who never gives anyone any cause for even mild annoyance?' His tone was teasing, but not in an offensive way.

'I try to be good and almost perfect in everything. But I guess sometimes I end up sounding a little sanctimonious, and that can be irritating.'

'But only sometimes,' he retorted quickly.

'Rarely. Hardly ever. I mean, almost never. Usually, I am just good and perfect.'

'You win. These goody-goody, sanctimonious types are more irritating than the pompous asses.'

We laughed together.

Somehow, we had moved towards the café in the store and ended up having coffee. We must have talked for more than an hour. He seemed vastly knowledgeable about all sorts of things. We discovered that we both enjoyed *The Lord of the Rings* and Philip Pullman's *His Dark Materials* trilogy, but I had never heard of movies called *Snatch* or *Dog Day Afternoon*. Nor could he appreciate the fact that I could watch *Chocolat* ten times without getting bored. We argued a bit, but CG managed to avoid sounding like a pompous ass. He listened well and we moved from one topic to another fluidly. When he came down from his pedestal, he could actually mingle quite nicely with the hoi polloi.

I suddenly realized that it was almost 7: 00 p.m. Still no call or message from Rahul. It was going to be another quiet Saturday night.

'Well, I guess you need to go,' said CG after we slowly finished the second coffee. 'I am sure you have plans for the night.' Maybe after seeing me at dinner with Rahul he thought I had a swinging social life. Little did he know that I hadn't spoken to Rahul in a week and spent most of my time wondering if I had a life at all.

'Err... I suppose you do too,' I mumbled quickly.

He gave a noncommittal response. I had a strong feeling that he knew I was free and I had a strong feeling that he had no plans for the Saturday night either, but we still behaved like two mature, single adults and decided to part ways. As I waved goodbye to CG and hopped into an auto, I realized that I hadn't bought a single book after three hours in a bookstore. Now I am wide awake with all that caffeine in my system, still feeling restless and trying to find some TV channel that can divert my mind from thinking about Rahul. I might as well try to sleep.

Bye,
D.

Dear Vic,

I am surprised to hear that you want to join a convent and become a nun. I guess it is just a temporary desire for a simple life after a series of unfortunate events with men. Sort of like the urge to purge after a heavy meal. You know, not all nuns become Mother Teresa, but it is still a lofty ambition.

I too have a good mind to run away to an ashram and take on a vow of celibacy and austerity. Wait a minute—I am already living a life of celibacy and austerity. I need to run away to a luxurious spa and get foot massages from gorgeous gigolos instead.

At times, I wish I had telepathic powers to figure out what goes on in the minds of men—at least, one man. Rahul called today. I saw his name flash on my mobile. Jimmy gave me a curious look and I had to pretend to nonchalantly walk out from Kroner to take the call.

'Hey, I hope I didn't disturb you in the middle of work,' he started.

I would have been disturbed if he hadn't disturbed me, but I managed a casual, 'No, not at all.'

'I've been really busy. The markets have been crazy and clients even crazier.'

'Of course,' I murmured sympathetically.

'So I got a few minutes to myself today and thought I'd catch up with you.'

'Oh? I had been wondering...'

'I do want to spend some more time with you, but it has been quite stressful.'

He *did* want to spend time with me. It is the thought that counts after all. It is not his fault that the markets are behaving crazily. It must be quite stressful.

Vision of me giving Rahul a stress-relieving massage. My fingers knead his flesh. I move from the neck to the shoulders. He takes off his shirt. I feel the smooth skin on his back, cool under my warm hands. He moans in appreciation and says...

'Are you okay? You haven't said anything.' I hoped I wasn't moaning on the phone!

'I am fine, fine. Er... I want to spend more time too...' There! I said it. From being a passive recipient of his attentions, I have become an active attention seeker. I know it was bold on my part to say that, but being quiet isn't getting me anywhere.

'Great. Maybe I can take you out to one of the clubs? There is a new place that has opened—the CopaCabana. It is somewhere on a private beach, sort of like a fancy shack in Goa.' Was that a smile in his voice?

'I would like that,' I said slowly. I would happily *kill* for that. 'I remember the Goan shack.'

'So do I,' he said softly. 'I think we have a lot of catching up to do. This time, I will make sure we have more to remember.' Was he flirting with me? What did that mean? How would he make sure? What does he really want?

'Umm,' I whispered. This time, I was going to silence that little bell in my head and make sure I did something to remember—something I would definitely not write home about.

'Take care. See you soon.' He signed off.

I could feel a silly look on my face for the rest of the day. I would remember what he said, right in the middle of working on my spreadsheets, and smile. Jimmy was curious.

'You are looking strangely happy for a person on a loser project who has no hope of meeting the deadline, Damayanthi,' he remarked.

'I believe in positive thinking. I am deeply motivated to find a way to do... whatever,' I replied, still smiling.

'Ah-ha! Clearly your positive thinking has nothing to do with finding cost-saving process improvement measures for the bank.'

'Oh, no! Jimmy, I am totally dedicated and completely committed to... to... whatever.' Smile still on!

'D, be careful,' said Jimmy, suddenly serious. He has started calling me D these days and I don't mind this nickname. I think of it as Dee, which sounds rather like a possible name for a Southern belle in *Gone with the Wind*.

'What do you mean?' I asked, the smile slipping a bit.

'I mean, don't do anything just because you think you should.'

'Meaning?' I was still clueless.

'Never mind.' He shrugged, but I hung on.

'You are a good person, D. Just don't do anything stupid that you'll regret, okay?'

God! He sounded like my mother and looked just as uncomfortable as Amma does when offering me advice on resisting temptations. But that was perhaps the nicest thing he has ever said to me and I appreciated it. He was more perceptive than I thought.

'Jimmy, all my life, I have never done anything really stupid that I regretted,' I reassured him, though I was feeling far from reassured myself.

'I know. Don't start now.'

'I won't. Actually, I can't. Old habits, you know.'

'Yeah, at the age of fifty-five, it must be difficult to change.' He laughed. I was glad he was back to his usual self. So was I. The smile had faded from my face, but was lingering behind the façade.

Vic, I just realized that Rahul and I had not discussed dates—a simple detail as to when we will recreate the Goan shack experience. Now I will have to wait again for him to call.

Bye,
D.

15

Dear Vic,

Good thing you reconsidered the convent option. The Order of the Penitent Servants of St Louisa, members of which lead a life of mortification and self-denial, does not sound right for you. I don't believe in self-denial and restraint any more either.

I don't know where the week went, but it is Saturday again. I went out with Jimmy for dinner. He seems to have become a little protective of late, as though he has to keep me from doing something stupid. I have reassured him that I am in full control of my life.

This time, Rahul messaged me saying that he was tied up with a conference somewhere in Lonavla. It was for a bunch of private banking customers, where he was giving a talk on some new treasury products that First Global has devised. Sonya is out as well, so I have the weekend to myself.

I have decided to be proactive instead of inactive. Instead of waiting for Rahul to call, I will transform myself into the Girl Who Must Be Phoned Right Now. Maybe he is ashamed of taking me out to a posh club. I would look so out of place there, among those slinky models with short skirts and long legs. So I have to become the woman he would like me to be. This desire for a makeover has also been spurred by the sight of Sonya in her designer togs. I saw her as she left for dinner, clad in some small white napkin that clung to her curves like shrink wrap on a sausage. She had on high-heeled silver sandals and a matching silver bag. Her hair has now been coloured to a rich golden brown and hangs down her back in a silken swathe. I had a horrible vision of her bumping into Rahul when he came to pick me up the next time—he would immediately be smitten by her outer beauty and forget about my sterling qualities.

I need to take preventive measures. I am finally going to get my hair cut. Not the tepid trim that I have gone in for all these years, but a proper new hairstyle.

Vision of myself looking fabulous with spiffy new hairstyle and in sexy clothes. 'You look drop-dead gorgeous,' says Rahul, his eyes alight with adoration. He holds me in his arms and whispers, 'I didn't think you could look more beautiful than you always do, Damayanthi, but tonight you are stunning. I am a lucky man.' I sigh deeply and say, 'Deep down, I am the same girl you kissed on the beach that night.' Eric Clapton's 'You look wonderful tonight' plays in the background as we dance together on a moonlit beach.

I will do it, Vic. I will be a woman who runs with the wolves and takes the bull by its horns.

Yours truly,
Damayanthi.

❦

Dear Victoria,

Let me introduce you to the new model-in-waiting, Ms Damayanthi Balachandran. I couldn't recognize myself after my makeover and that, I suppose, is a very good thing. This morning I had made an appointment at this chic but not intimidating salon called 'Hair's the Place'. We do not say beauty parlour here.

I was greeted by a lady with purple hair and a nose ring, who was happy to hear that I wanted a completely new style.

'Ooh, I love makeovers,' trilled Jessy. She called another girl and they both opened out my hair and examined it from all angles.

'Traditional bone structure,' said the other girl in a husky voice. She had very short, spiky hair, kohl-rimmed eyes and an Om tattoo that peeked from beneath a sleeveless T-shirt. 'Typical oval face.' I didn't like her very much. She held my chin and turned my face around. There were silver rings on all five of her fingers, each embedded with a different stone.

'I don't want anything too different. Not very short,' I insisted. I was ready to take a leap of faith, but not a quantum jump.

'No, dearie,' assured Jessy. 'It will have to be at least shoulder-length with your face. We'll give you a soft, layered look. Walter will cut your hair. He is very good.'

I looked around for Walter, but Miss Spiky Hair seized a pair of scissors and got to work. Oops, it was Mr Spiky Hair, aka Walter. I closed my eyes and put myself in his hands. After what seemed like ages, I saw a small black pool at my feet. My hair, which had been halfway down my back, was now swirling around my shoulders in soft black waves.

'You are looking very nice,' declared Walter, who now stood over me like a proud parent. Jessy came over to hold the mirrors and show me my newly shorn tresses. A small part of me said, 'Amma and Appa will be shocked to know that you have cut your long, lovely hair, carefully nourished over the years with many litres of coconut oil.' The main part of me said, 'Go for it, girl.'

Jessy urged me to try their premium pedicure and manicure. I might as well go all the way, I thought. I sat like a princess as two minions scrubbed my heels and buffed my nails. After that, I was led to a facial and someone else rubbed cream on my face, slathered mashed bananas on my forehead and plopped pieces of papaya on my cheeks. Anything that felt yucky had to be good for my complexion. Then the facial lady massaged my neck and shoulders in a most stress-relieving way.

By the time I stepped back out into the afternoon, I had spent the equivalent of a whole month of SSV salary in four hours. Now all I need to do is stop eating for a month and I will be able to pass myself off as a small-time model. Okay, maybe not a model yet, but a modern, attractive woman of the world.

Next was the wardrobe upgrade. I went to Shoppers Stop and tried on the office-wear. None of the trousers seemed to fit well and I decided to buy a long, black skirt instead. The skirt, made of some wrinkle-proof, crinkly material, had a slit at the back, but it showed only a glimpse of my calves as I walked.

Sexy, but decent. I teamed it with a pale pink top and was quite pleased with the effect. High-heeled black pumps completed the ensemble.

I can't wait to go to office and see the look on everyone's faces. A part of me is a little scared that Jimmy will laugh and CG will look down on my attempt to become a proper corporate lady. But what is done is done. I can only hope for the best.

Good night,
D.

Hello Victoria,

I don't think wearing a hot pink mini skirt with a tank top to work will work as part of the makeover. I suppose I can hope to just fire up Rahul and other men with it, but FG will probably fire me for violating dress code.

Vision of myself in said costume sashaying into the lunchroom. Men drop their thalis and their tongues and gaze at me in adoration. Rahul appears amidst the slobbering crowd and says, 'Damayanthi, you look incredible.' He holds out his hand and we neatly step over heartbroken men and half-broken plates and waltz off slowly into the sunset.

The day was a success, sort of. Unfortunately, I did not see Rahul. I am at the main office these days. I keep hoping that I will bump into him at the elevator, but it doesn't seem like we inhabit the same office space.

I said a jaunty 'Good Morning' to Jimmy, who was already in Rouble, our office for the day. He looked at me and whistled.

'Somebody has been busy this Sunday,' he remarked. 'I see you have decided to do self-improvement in place of process improvements for the bank.'

'At least it is an improvement.'

'Anything would have been an improvement, D.'

'Thank you, kind sir, for your encouraging words.' I made him a mock bow.

'Hmm…' He gave me an appraising look. 'Not bad, not bad at all. But what happened to the girl who valued inner beauty and all that stuff?'

'I think the inner beauty has been suppressed for too long. No one can see it. It needs some help from the outside to escape.'

'So who is the beneficiary of all this escaped beauty?' he asked with a mischievous grin.

'Why, the whole world, of course. Think Global, First Global.' That was our latest slogan. We had posters all over the office urging FG employees to build a boundary-less culture and have a 'global mindset'.

'Okay, maybe you would like to start on the fourth floor with treasury and then work your way down, globally.'

I felt my ears turning red and quickly switched on my laptop. I wonder how much Jimmy knows or thinks he knows. Does my face give away what I am thinking? I hope not.

'Let's get to work, Jimmy,' I muttered.

CG walked in after a while. He didn't even look at me. I was quite upset for the first few minutes. Just when I thought we had broken the ice, just when I had started thinking that he was a nice person, he completely ignored me.

'Where is Damayanthi?' he asked Jimmy after a while. How could the man not notice a woman sitting literally in front of his face?

Jimmy grinned and pointed at me. I looked up from my laptop and said, 'Hi CG,' a little tersely.

He just looked at me. I couldn't tell from his expression what was going on in his mind, but somehow he didn't look even mildly appreciative.

'You look different,' he said finally.

I said, 'Just had a haircut.' A casual shrug of the shoulders, as though I had makeovers done every day.

'Oh!'

That's all he could come up with? I was disappointed.

He didn't say anything else, but started off with a process update. He had another project to handle as well and we chalked out a schedule of roles and responsibilities for the next month. This meant that Jimmy and I had to do most of the work. We had barely managed to get up to $5,50,000 worth of cost savings and had no feasible idea for the next half a million dollars.

My mind did not work most of the day. Maybe this is what happens when you start focusing on the exterior. The interior turns to mush. I was a little disappointed at CG's reaction to my new made-over self. But some of the attention I got at LR compensated for it a bit. Ajay Mahtani, who usually ignores me, came over to ask about our project. A couple of people Jimmy knew came up to say hello to us. Maybe it was just a coincidence. Maybe they didn't recognize me and wanted to know who the new girl was.

'So do you think the launch of the new, improved, ultra-hip Damayanthi with advanced image boosters has been a success?' said Jimmy as we were finishing lunch. He sounded like one of those reporters on NDTV. He even waved a spoon under my nose like a microphone.

'I don't know.' I sighed. I hadn't set out to launch myself into the social stratosphere. I didn't want to attract hordes of men into my inner circle—not that it was going to happen. The one-man target audience I had in mind was not around and I had never seen Rahul at LR. I didn't know if and when he was going to call.

'Initial reactions seem positive,' urged Jimmy. 'Miss Damayanthi, what impact will it have on your target market?'

'I don't have a target market,' I mumbled.

Just then, I saw Balki heading towards us. Before I could scoot, he came up to our table.

'Damayanthi, is that you?' he asked, putting down his tiffin dabba on the table. 'I did not recognize you in those clothes.'

At least someone was going to say something nice about the new, improved me.

'Very modern dress,' he continued. 'Don't mistake me, okay. Traditional clothes like sari are also good for Indian women. These days, we are not preserving our tradition and culture. So many girls are wearing western clothes when we have such beautiful Indian attire.'

LV: 'Saari, saar. Sari will be worn next time. I will wear it in very traditional style, without a blouse, like they did in the good old days.'

Me: Polite smile.

Jimmy managed to keep a straight face and jumped into the debate. 'Yes, yes, that is what I was telling Damayanthi. She is getting corrupted by watching too much TV. So much exposure is not good.'

I excused myself from the table and left. At least now I was off Balki's list of eligible women. I had proven myself to be a non-traditional woman with corrupt, modern values.

So much for my makeover making an impact. Maybe I am better off in my sari or salwar kameez and ponytail. At least I would have no expectations of admiration from the members of the opposite sex. Now I felt like the hostess who had slogged in the kitchen the whole day for a grand dinner party only to have all the invitees decline at the last minute. All that lovely food gone waste...

The rest of the day passed without incident. Maybe the whole thing was a stupid idea. I confessed as much to Jimmy.

'I feel silly,' I said. 'I spent a bomb on this haircut, new clothes and shoes, and now I feel I don't look good. I should oil my hair and change back to my usual self.'

'No, D. You look good. Keep the change.' He

smiled kindly. 'It suits you and you are still you, inner beauty and all.'

Maybe I will.

Good night,
D.

16

～

Dear Vic,

We have spent the last week racking our brains for the process improvement measure that would save us half a million dollars. I just couldn't think of anything. Nor could Jimmy. The only good news was that we were to finally get a workstation. Not that I was complaining about hopping from one conference room to another—at least it made for some variety in my life. My hope is that one day we will be forced to move to Lira, which is on the fourth floor, right next to the dealing room. At least then I would be able to see Rahul. More importantly, he would be able to see me.

Yesterday I got a message from Rahul. I still have it saved and peep at it from time to time. It reads:

'Thinking of you… talk to you soon.' Not much, but it is the only message I have from him, the only romantic message I have ever received. The 'talk to you soon' bit had me a bit confused. Did he mean that I should call him soon or he will call me soon? How soon is soon?

The novelty of my makeover has worn off. I alternate between salwar kurtas and long skirts. There is still hope that Rahul will see me. I just cannot understand his behaviour. Aren't men supposed to chase their women with single-minded dedication? Is he taking it slow and easy for my sake? Maybe he feels he shouldn't rush me. Maybe he is just too busy. Maybe he is playing hard to get. Maybe he is playing 'Don't want to be got'.

I am becoming a horrible, obsessive person. Maybe I am just a step away from becoming one of those manic stalkers who haunts her object of affection until he gets a restraining order.

Shame on you, Damayanthi. Try to find a way to save half a million dollars and do your job instead of mooning over a man.

Bye,
D.

Dear Vic,

Today we found the answer to our process improvement problem. I should be happy, but instead I have a nagging feeling of disquiet bubbling inside me. Jimmy was clearing out the workstation to make place for us—the workstation is in an awkward place, a dingy corner close to the washroom. Obviously, it was the last resort for desperate, floating nomads like Jimmy and me. There were a bunch of drawers under the table that needed to be cleared out for us. So Jimmy got the keys from the admin guys and started going through it. I was plugging away on the laptop (which was actually on top of my lap), trying to see if some calculations could increase our cost savings numbers, when suddenly Jimmy shouted, 'Eureka! I have found it!'

'What?'

'The mother lode! The holy grail! The answer to our problems!' he declared grandiosely.

I almost forgot all about my laptop and jumped up.

'What is it, Jimmy? Have you found a secret stash of a million dollars?'

'Something like that.' Jimmy grinned, brandishing a spiral-bound folder.

He had found a report by a summer trainee on process improvement measures in operations. He showed me the last page—'Projected cost savings: $7,00,000.' The magic numbers gleamed at us.

I felt as though we had really found buried treasure. We quickly flipped through the book. There was no duplication of ideas. The summer trainee, a girl called Malavika Mehta from the Indian School of Business, had worked hard. Her suggestions were sensible, the cost-savings calculations were prudent and the areas were ones we had not covered previously.

She had created an Excel macro which updated outstation check details directly onto the system. This is being done manually still. This saved not only two employee headcounts but also reduced cycle time. There were other meticulously detailed process analyses and improvement measures.

'This is amazing, Jimmy,' I said happily. 'We must tell Harish that we found this. He will be really happy to know that we can get these savings.'

'Whoa! Wait a minute,' said Jimmy. 'We should verify it ourselves. This report is a year old.'

'Of course, Jimmy. After verification.' I wasn't that stupid.

'We will tell Harish, D, but there is no need to mention the report,' Jimmy explained in a slow, patient tone, as though he was talking to a child.

'What do you mean?' I asked, a little puzzled.

'We do not have to reveal the source of the data. There is no... no... fun in saying that we got these ideas off a summer trainee's report.'

'Why? What will happen?'

'D, are you a fool? How do you think the system works? Do you think you will get any credit for a project where the main ideas are from a year-old summer trainee report?'

'So what are you saying? We steal the ideas?' I was a little indignant. How could he call me a fool? I knew the system well. Stealing was not the done thing. First Global had a clearly defined integrity policy.

'This is not stealing, D. This is best practice sharing.' He was sounding like Harish giving one of his management spiels.

'Oh?'

'Look, the summer trainee is long gone. I don't think she is with the bank now. She has put in so many long hours in preparing this report and nothing has been done about it. We owe it to her to ensure that the ideas are implemented.' Jimmy was making idea stealing sound like donating money to provide for starving little orphans.

'I am not so sure. We can use the ideas, but shouldn't we mention the trainee's name or cite this report as a source? And what if some people know that she is the one who had made these suggestions earlier?' I was still not convinced.

'But why? This Malavika babe doesn't care any more. She has probably moved on to another job. Her summer project guide, Ranjit Dhar, has quit the bank. I know because there was an announcement three months ago.'

'But…'

'We are supposed to use all possible resources in our project, and this report is a resource. Just like the table, the laptop, the process manuals, the post-it notes, you know. We don't mention them in the report.' He seemed very confident.

'Are you sure?' I was still doubtful.

Jimmy nodded. 'Of course. Relax, D. It is not a crime for which you'll get capital punishment. You needn't look so guilty. We are just doing our job, that's all.'

'So we just include these suggestions in our report and pretend as though we thought them up?'

'D, we will verify them first. We will check out the calculations, we will factor in some changes for this year's manpower cost projections. It is not as if we are not going to do any work.'

'But is it enough?'

'Of course. First Global is all about working smart, not working hard.'

'We will be able to finish the project before the deadline,' I said as I thought things over.

'And we will not have to slog our butts off on useless process manuals and pointless focus group discussions. We will be recognized as resourceful team members,' Jimmy pointed out.

'Do you think we should tell Harish and get his okay?' I was still a little doubtful, though I was finally beginning to understand the advantages of best practice sharing.

'Of course not. We won't tell anyone.'

Not even CG? Were we going to take an oath of secrecy? I thought we should tell CG. He might be able to give us some suggestions.

'Why?'

'The need-to-know policy, D. CG doesn't need to know. Think how impressed CG will be when he sees that we have come up with these brilliant ideas.'

Vision of CG looking impressed when I tell him about the brilliant idea. 'I had no idea you were so brilliant,' remarks CG, shaking his head in wonder. 'Why didn't I think of it before? Damayanthi, on one hand, you have an incisive, analytical mind, and on the other, you have the creativity to come up with amazing solutions.'

I was almost convinced. There was a little niggling doubt at the back of mind, but I couldn't see anything risky or really wrong with the solution. It would be only a minor sin of omission. If I ever meet this Malavika Mehta, I will definitely thank her and acknowledge her efforts.

So Vic, it looks like we will meet our deadline and our target. Verifying the data will not take too long. At last, I will be able to goof off a little at work.

Bye,
D.

Hi Vic,

Today, we shared our cost-saving ideas with CG. Jimmy had put the data into a presentation and I took him through it. He asked some probing questions, for which I had all the answers. Jimmy and I had split the work between the two of us. He copied the data and important points into the presentation. I understood the process improvements and verified the data. It has taken us more than a week to do this. We were taking it slow because we didn't want people to get suspicious that we had too many brainwaves all of a sudden. I am now a master at corporate dissembling—how to look busy and do little work.

'You guys have done some good work,' said CG after we finished. I sent a silent prayer of thanks to our saviour Malavika.

'Damayanthi did most of it, really,' added Jimmy. It was nice of him to say that. I flashed him a look of gratitude.

CG did look impressed. At least it was a different look from the one he usually had. There was a hint of approval even. I felt like the time I received the Best Conduct Award from Sister Theresa at school. I half expected him to pat my head and say, 'Good girl.'

'Good job, Damayanthi,' he said. High Praise from the High Priest of Presentations!

He gave us a couple of useful suggestions and told us how to make the presentation better. After a few hours, Jimmy and I felt like we had actually completed the project successfully.

'This calls for a celebration,' declared Jimmy.

The three of us decided to go out for lunch. We headed towards Fountain Café, a favourite hangout of First Globalites. I was glad that I was in my corporate attire. My dark blue skirt was a little shorter than the previous ones, the white shirt a little tighter. I knew that I looked better than I had in many days. Suddenly, at that minute, walking with CG and Jimmy on the Mumbai streets, I felt comfortable, carefree. This was my place, my time. I was a swinging banker who was successfully completing a project and could happily walk between two men on the road without worrying or wondering about other people, about tomorrow.

Vic, the best part is yet to come. As we walked into the café, I saw Rahul. It had been ages since my makeover and I had almost given up all hope of meeting him again. I had been itching to call him and my fantasies had become even more bizarre in terms of imagined meeting places.

Finally, when he was there in front of me, I ignored him. That was a stupid thing to do, because there was nothing I wanted more than Rahul to notice me. Jimmy noticed him right away. Rahul was with a couple of other First Global treasury types. One of his companions was wearing red suspenders!

'Oh, there is your friend, D,' remarked Jimmy. 'The one we met the other day at that Chinese place. Rahul Kumar, right?'

CG looked up in the direction, but didn't seem too pleased to see Rahul, unlike Jimmy, who was grinning like an idiotic Cheshire cat.

'Oh, really?' I feigned ignorance and pretended to notice him for the first time.

'Should I ask him to join us?' continued Jimmy.

'No,' said CG and I together. I was a little surprised at CG's instant reaction.

'I mean, we shouldn't intrude. He is with his friends,' said CG, looking a little uncomfortable. I guess he didn't want to entertain 'my friend' and I didn't blame him.

I didn't want to call out to Rahul either. Really, that would be so obvious. Just then, Rahul saw us. I guess he and his friends were leaving after their lunch. He came up to say hello to us. Maybe he didn't recognize me.

'Hi,' I said in a flat voice—polite, but not pleasant. After obsessing about meeting him for days on end, I felt rather angry. How could he just walk up to me and say hi, as though I was a casual acquaintance and no more? I didn't care. I would show him that. I would be the ice queen. Distant and disinterested.

'Damayanthi,' said Rahul, looking at me as though nobody else existed in the whole world, 'this hairstyle suits you. You look really stunning.'

Just then, something weird happened. I remembered a scene from this film I watched sometime ago on TV—a French movie called *Amelie*, where this girl suddenly melts and turns into a puddle of water. Swoosh! One minute she is a sane, solid woman, the next moment she is all liquid mush. That is exactly what happened to me. All my thoughts of ignoring him dissolved in that puddle and I was gazing up at him and murmuring my thanks. I felt myself simpering, my cheeks turning red. Some banking small talk was exchanged between the men, but I wasn't paying any attention.

'Bye, I'll call you,' said Rahul softly when the treasury guys were leaving, his hand on my shoulder, his head bent close to mine. The gesture seemed intimate, as though he knew me well, really well. As I lifted my head to smile and nod in assent, he seemed close enough to kiss or be kissed again. For a moment, I wished that I could cast a spell and make everyone disappear—or transport me and Rahul to a remote but picturesque island, where there would be no one but him and me cavorting on the bleached sands beside an aquamarine sea.

Rahul waved to me as he walked away and I dragged myself back to the present, my eyes devouring the sight of his retreating backside as he disappeared out of the door.

'Shall we order or have you had your fill, D?' I heard Jimmy ask, a naughty little grin on his face.

I glared at him. I was back to being solid, sane woman.

'Let's order quickly,' said CG briskly. 'I need to get back to a meeting soon with the structured products team.' He seemed to be in a hurry. I guess he was irritated that our brief interlude with Rahul had delayed the lunch.

The meal proceeded quickly. I smiled through most of it, Jimmy talked a lot and CG looked bored. The conversation, which had flowed so naturally between us just a few weeks ago, seemed stilted. I laughed at Jimmy's jokes and made occasional inane contributions. My mind was still processing the way Rahul had looked at me. I could still hear him say, 'You look stunning.'

Vic, at the end of the day, I am happy. Professionally, I will complete my project successfully. And the look on Rahul's face said that he would call soon, so my personal life is also looking up.

Sweet dreams,

D.

Dear Vic,

I got into office ready to work hard and re-present the summer project report. CG, Jimmy and I were supposed to have a review meeting with Harish. But CG was nowhere to be seen. We hardly see Harish these days. His phone is constantly busy and he rarely seems to be around his cubicle. He believes in the MBA theory, according to Jimmy—Management by Absence. We see his emails now and then, indicating that he is still a presence in our life. According to the LR grapevine, Harish is busy lobbying for his promotion and schmoozing with Veronica to get time with AB. I guess it is better than having a boss who breathes down your neck.

I was wandering around the fifth floor looking for Harish when I saw a strange sight. CG was talking animatedly to… to Veronica? I didn't believe it. Why was he here? What was he doing with Veronica? Veronica wore a tight red silk blouse which, as usual, presented a clear view of her anatomy. He said something and she smiled up in a desperately arch and coy way and batted her mascara-coated lashes at him. Disgusting! Didn't she have enough bankers dangling after her that she had to flirt with external consultants? I marched up to them to disrupt their cosy conversation. We had a serious meeting to attend and here he was here leering at Veronica's lungs. Double disgusting!

'I am sure you won't have any problems with that,' CG was saying and smiling warmly. He never ever smiled like that at me or Jimmy. 'Aww, that's sweet of you,' giggled Veronica.

I made loud throat-clearing noises behind them. Veronica gave me a baleful stare, as though I was a termite that had crawled out of the woodwork. I was too far down the ladder for her to know me.

'We have a review meeting with Harish,' I informed CG as coldly as I could. He excused himself and Veronica looked a little disappointed. 'Catch you soon.' She giggled again and waggled her fingers at him.

'I didn't know you knew Veronica,' I muttered.

'I don't. I just met her now,' he said, looking bemused. 'I was looking for Harish.'

'You seem to have made a conquest,' I said more accusingly than appreciatively.

'Really, you think so? Good, she is quite attractive.'

LV: 'If you like exhibitionists with IQs that match their bra size!'

'If you like that type,' I retorted sharply, annoyed with myself. How did it matter if he liked Veronica? I mean, it is not like I care about his personal life or anything. He was looking pleased with himself and ran a hand through his hair. His hair looked a little unruly today and he seemed more relaxed than before. Was this the Veronica effect? Why should I bother about CG? I should be worrying about why Rahul hasn't been in touch.

I had forgotten that I had come looking for Harish and suddenly I didn't care about the meeting either. CG and I trooped silently to the lift to make our way down. The lift was crowded and we had to almost squish up against each other. It wasn't very comfortable and I glowered in the crowded silence. I almost stepped on CG's shoes as someone else climbed into the lift and I was pushed back. He winced, but put out a hand to steady me. 'I swear I will never be late for a meeting again. Please don't stomp all over me,' he whispered into my ear. I didn't smile. I wish I had stomped on him. Hard.

Just then, my mobile phone beeped. It was Rahul. I felt my mood change, almost as if the clouds had parted and given way to warm sunshine.

'Hi, r u free for dinner tom nite? Wld like to catch up,' the message said.

'Yes,' I wrote back.

'Gr8. Will leave from office at abt 7.30. OK?'

'Sure.'

Tomorrow is Friday, and I have a date. What a great start to the weekend! Maybe we would even spend the entire weekend together.

Vision of me and Rahul in a luxurious five-star hotel room, the kind where they serve champagne in long-stemmed glasses for breakfast. I am asleep in bed, with clean white sheets drawn up to my neck. Rahul is beside me. He kisses my exposed shoulder softly, strokes my back and nuzzles me awake. 'Wake up, beautiful,' he says. I turn around and gaze up at him. 'Last night was so good,' he whispers into my neck. I smile widely like a contented cat.

'Have you won some contest?' asked CG, looking curious. Was I smiling foolishly at him or the phone?

'No, no, nothing like that,' I muttered and hurried towards our meeting room.

Harish had materialized there. Our review went off well. He seemed satisfied with our process improvement measures. He kept asking, 'Do we have data for this?' and 'What is the data source for that?' Jimmy and I had our answers ready. For a moment, I wanted to tell him about Malavika's summer project, about the real source of most of the work. Luckily, the moment passed. The summer project report was safely in Jimmy's house. Jimmy had asked around about Malavika and found out from a junior from ISB that she was working with Merrill Lynch in New York. We were safe.

'Great show, guys,' declared Harish. 'I will tell AB about the work you have done. In fact, let me see if I can get a slot with Nadeem when he is here next week to show him the improvement measures we have recommended.'

'That would be great, Harish.' I was excited. This could mean a huge career boost for Jimmy and me. We could move on to real jobs at First Global!

'Why don't you guys do something? Prepare a presentation on the entire project along with exact cost savings. But for not more than ten minutes. So put only the really important slides. Make it really slick. If we get a slot with Nadeem, you both can make the presentation to him.' Harish was also looking excited.

Normally, bottom-of-the barrel juniors like us would never get face-to-face time with someone like Nadeem. I had heard that he usually addressed the whole group in a town hall and had meetings with a select bunch of seniors. Only vice presidents and above.

'That would be great.' Even Jimmy, who was a little cynical about such things, had perked up.

'Guys, you send me this presentation by day after tomorrow. I will take a look at it as well. Nadeem is here next week. I didn't think we would have this thing ready by then, so I didn't ask Veronica to put it in his agenda. But now I'll see if he can spare about fifteen minutes for us. You leave that to me. You both work on getting together a really impressive presentation.' Harish appeared to have ingested a large can of Gatorade—he was more energized than I had ever seen.

Jimmy and I started to put together a short and snappy presentation. I have realized that making presentations is a critical skill they did not focus on during my CA exams, nor during my stint at SSV.

Here, at First Global, making them is a way of life. I have managed to figure out how to make simple slides and tables, but Jimmy is a pro at doing all the jazzy stuff. It's 11 p.m. and I have just finished working on my part. Tomorrow, Jimmy and I need to burn the midnight oil to finish the thing.

Oops, I just remembered that I have a big date tomorrow night. Why does everything happen together? Somehow, I have to escape unobtrusively at 7.30, without seeming to shirk work. Normally, Jimmy and I are through by 6.30 every day, but I know it will take a long time tomorrow. Harish needs to see our presentation day after morning.

Pray for me, Vic.

Love,
D.

Dear Vic,

What a day! What a night!

I decided to be super efficient today and finish off as much as possible. Jimmy's efforts to goof off were met with stern reprimands. I knew we had a long way to go. Somehow, Jimmy and I ended up arguing more today than ever before. Normally, he is content to go along with what I say. But today, he gave his own inputs. We even had a disagreement about who would talk through which slide. This time, in the interests of meeting my 7:30 p.m. deadline, I went along with some of his ideas.

It was almost 7:00 p.m. and we still had two slides to wrap up. It is difficult to condense six months of work into ten minutes of presentation and I am still not sure if we got it right. I messaged Rahul that I would take till 8.00 and he was okay with that. Finally, at 7:45 p.m., I had to tell Jimmy.

'I have to go,' I said.

'D, even I am tired. We'll be through in an hour,' he said.

'Jimmy, can you please finish off just one slide? I hate leaving you like this, but I have er… er… another… appointment,' I muttered sheepishly.

'Appointment—like with a dentist or doctor?' Jimmy looked suspiciously at me.

'No, a dinner appointment.'

'Like a dinner date?' he asked.

What's the big deal? I did have a dinner date. Why was I being so coy about it?

'Yes, I am going out to dinner with Rahul,' I said, with a serious, straight face.

'Cool, D. Why didn't you just say that you had a date with your boyfriend?'

'He is not my boyfriend,' I answered a little too quickly, maybe a little regretfully.

'A maybe boyfriend?' he enquired.

A maybe boyfriend probably described our relationship well. I am still not sure when a boyfriend becomes an official boyfriend. Vic, do you think three dates and a kiss qualify? Do you need to make a public statement to that effect and wear matching His-and-Her love bracelets? Do you need to have a declaration of interest from one party and reciprocation from the other? Do you have to sleep together at least once?

The truth is, even now, I don't know what Rahul and I have. I know I am strongly attracted to him—I dream about him often, I imagine us walking happily off into the sunset, sometimes I think I would do anything for him. I glow when I feel his eyes are on me, melt when I feel his skin against mine and burn thinking about him when he is not there. Yet, I don't know how he feels about me at all. Maybe after tonight…

Jimmy was looking at me expectantly.

'Maybe,' I said.

'Hmmm, in that case, I think you should take the chance to convert the maybe to a definite yes.'

'Really?'

'You carry on, D. I will finish up. CG is around somewhere. He said he will also take a look at it. You have done a lot of work today. So go ahead, have fun.'

'Thank you, Jimmy. You are so sweet.' I gave him a spontaneous hug and he looked pleased.

I dashed off to the washroom to change. I was carrying a change of clothes and cosmetics with me. After ten minutes, I emerged from the washroom with my new, dark blue silk blouse with small pearl buttons down the front. It went well with my grey skirt and made the outfit go from discreet to dressy very easily. A fresh coat of lipstick, eyeliner and a generous spray of perfume made me feel ready for a night out with my maybe boyfriend.

I came back to my workstation to find CG already there.

'Going somewhere?' he asked quizzically, raising an eyebrow. I couldn't figure him out at all. Sometimes, he could be so funny and a delight to talk to and yet, of late, he seemed distant and more like the superior boor I had originally thought him to be. Anyway, there was no point in trying to figure CG out. I was determined to go out on this date.

'I have a prior commitment,' I mumbled. Why did he make me feel like a truant sneaking away from school?

He raised a sceptical eyebrow.

'An appointment with the dentist,' I found myself saying.

'She has a date,' said Jimmy simultaneously.

'A... a date with the dentist,' I blabbered, glaring at Jimmy. Oh god! Why was I saying such stupid things? What was the big deal?

Just then Rahul walked onto the floor and approached me with a wave.

'The dentist?' enquired CG. His eyes were cold—angry.

' Er... er... uh...'

Jimmy came to my rescue. 'I said I would finish up. Won't take me too long.'

'Are you sure?' CG still looked sceptical. I am sure if he had a date with the woman of his dreams, he would have left too. 'I think we all need to go through this together to make sure we are properly aligned.'

I gave Jimmy a pleading look. I grovel at your feet, my eyes said to him, I will do anything you want, but please take care of this tonight.

'No problem, CG,' said Jimmy. 'We both can go through it now and I will brief Damayanthi tomorrow. We just have one more slide.'

CG nodded grudgingly. He was worse than Parvathi Miss, my tenth-class maths teacher, who refused to give the girls permission to go answer nature's call during her class. We all had to stifle any biological urges while desperately trying to master trigonometry and calculus.

I looked gratefully at Jimmy. 'Thanks,' I mouthed behind CG's back.

'It isn't often that she has a date, poor thing,' added Jimmy. 'We, as friends, must be supportive,' he explained to CG, who did not seem supportive at all.

'I have to go. I will finish everything early morning tomorrow in case anything is pending. We can send it off to Harish by 11.' I collected my things and walked off—actually, ran off. I could feel them gazing at my rapidly retreating back—Jimmy, like an indulgent parent, and CG, like a disapproving one. I'm sure he would have given me a curfew time and ordered me back to work if he could have. For a minute, I actually wondered if I should call off my date and stay back. I somehow didn't like the idea of incurring CG's displeasure. When I sneaked a peek back at him, I couldn't quite read the expression on his face. He certainly didn't look happy.

Too bad! I am an adult woman, living my dream life with a dreamy guy, and no one was going to spoil that. Rahul and I left for dinner. He had thoughtfully got his car along. He did have a car, after all. I guess he used it only for special occasions. Hey, that meant our date was a special occasion.

'There is a great restaurant near where I live. Would you like to go there?' he asked as we sat in the car.

'Sure, anything is okay with me.' I wasn't there with him for the food. I would have gone to a roadside dhaba with him and just gazed adoringly at him.

We had a lovely ride all the way to Andheri, listening to music, making small talk while I tried to ignore a restless, hungry feeling which had nothing to do with food. Was I imagining it or was the air humming with sexual tension? Sting singing 'Desert Rose' in the background seemed to enhance the ambience and I could feel my skin prickle every time Rahul moved. Once, when we stopped at a traffic signal, he put his hand on mine as it lay on my lap.

'I am glad we could make it today,' he said softly.

'So am I,' I said. The warmth of his hand seeped into mine and then spread through my whole body. I was disappointed when he lifted it to change gears.

Dinner was over rather quickly. We were early, by Mumbai standards, on a Friday night and the restaurant was not very crowded. Rahul spoke about his job, his travels, his opinion on the bank, stock market, politics, films and technology. I made all the appropriate listening noises and looked interested, but my mind was wondering how the evening would end.

'Would you like some coffee?' asked Rahul as we finished. I usually don't have coffee at night. I guess sophisticated people like Rahul do. They probably sip it black and make love through the night after the enhancing dose of caffeine.

'Er…' I wasn't so sure.

'Or we could go to my place and have some wine. I have some really good wine, a Chilena Pinot Noir. You would like that.'

'Okay, sure.' That made up my mind for me, Vic. I had a strong feeling that tonight was going to be *the* night. I just needed the wine for some Dutch courage.

Rahul's place was a cosy two-bedroom apartment, furnished tastefully in black and white, with a large flat TV dominating the living room wall. The wide, black leather couch was soft and springy and I sank into it. Rahul put on some music, and as the soft notes rippled across the room, I leant back and closed my eyes.

When I opened my eyes, Rahul was standing in front of me with two glasses of wine, looking down at me with a smile.

'Did you fall asleep?' he asked.

'No.' I sat up straight. Sleep was the last thing on my mind. But I think my mind had gone to sleep. All my thinking cells were being taken over by the feeling cells. As I sipped the wine, I could feel my thinking cells doze off completely.

Rahul sat down next to me, close enough so that I could lean back against his shoulder. The lighting was muted, the music seemed softer.

'Comfortable?' he asked.

'Yes,' I whispered.

We didn't talk any more. He turned my face towards his and kissed me. It was just as good as the first kiss and I felt like I was back in Goa again, a warm flush spreading slowly through my body. We kissed for a long time. I could feel my face flush and a delicious numbness in my brain. I felt his body hard against mine, our skin touching. Then his hand was on my shirt, expertly opening my little pearl buttons. This was it.

My thinking cells were suddenly jolted into wakefulness. This is the point of no return, Damayanthi. Is this what you really want? To give yourself to this man here whom you don't really know and probably are far away from marrying—a man to whom you might be nothing more than a passing fancy?

Rahul's hands were through with the buttons and my bare flesh felt the sting of cool air and the unfamiliar touch of a man's mouth.

Damayanthi, my thinking cells intruded, do you have any idea what you are doing?

'I don't… I haven't…' I muttered feebly, trying to move his hand away.

'Relax. It's all right, baby,' he murmured soothingly. 'I won't do anything you don't want.'

The thinking cells tried once more. Do you know what you want?

I didn't. I did. I wanted this. All thoughts of unwanted pregnancies, fear of being seen naked and becoming a social outcast vanished from my mind.

I was flowing along a strong current and was going to go wherever it carried me. My hands reached into Rahul's hair and did what they had been longing to do—I clenched a handful of hair and pulled him towards me in a very definite gesture.

That was when the bells went off. But instead of Amma's voice chiming like a chorus singing 'Don't do anything silly', which would have been expected, I heard the sound of real bells—the strident, urgent sound of a mobile phone ringing. It was mine.

'Leave it,' said Rahul fiercely, his hands still on me. But I saw the number flash on the screen. Home.

I gasped in shock. I had heard about mothers having eyes at the back of their heads, but this was too much. Surely she hadn't had a premonition that her dutiful, demure daughter was going to do the exact thing she had been warned about? What was even more worrying was the fact that it was late at night, way past Amma's bedtime.

I got up, fumbling, and grabbed the phone. I rushed to the next room, which happened to be the kitchen, and finally breathed out a hushed hello.

Vic, the news was not good. My grandmother was admitted to the hospital with chest pain this evening. Amma was calling from the hospital. She was anxious and upset. Patti is seventy-eight, not the age to go to a hospital without wondering if you will come back home. Amma wanted to know if I could come home for a couple of days, just in case. I am Patti's favourite grandchild. Amma takes after her. Both are genetically predisposed to giving large doses of unsolicited advice and frequent bouts of unnecessary worrying.

Now I was worried. I slowly buttoned up my shirt. The romantic mood had vanished, any stirring within me was completely extinguished. I felt bad that I was behaving like a wild, wanton woman when my grandmother was in the hospital. The logical part of me said that there was no connection between the events, but I felt guilty and stupid nonetheless.

I saw Rahul sitting with his head in his hands. He looked irritated. But when I stepped into the room, the irritation was replaced by concern.

'All well?' he asked hopefully.

'My grandmother is not well. She is in the hospital,' I blurted out.

'I am sorry to hear that,' said Rahul. He came towards me and put an arm around my shoulders. I stayed still, but inwardly I shrank away. Rahul seemed to sense my mood and stepped back.

'I'm sorry,' I said. 'I want to go home.'

Rahul looked at me for a moment and asked, 'Are you sure? Do you maybe want to take your mind off things?'

'No.' I was very sure. My mind was back in place and I didn't want to take it off just yet.

We drove back to Pine Crest in silence. I guess, after this, Rahul will never call me again. I will never be able to recapture that moment.

I said goodbye to Rahul at the gate.

'I am sorry,' I apologized again. 'I didn't want to run off like that. I guess our… our meetings are jinxed.' I attempted a small smile.

'It is all right, Damayanthi,' he said. 'I understand. We have lots of time.'

'I hope so.' I really do.

Now I feel terrible that my grandmother is in the hospital and I can't do anything about it, terrible that I lost yet another opportunity with Rahul and will not be able to do anything about it.

Hope I get some sleep and don't have bad dreams. Have a lot of work tomorrow.

Good night,
D.

Hi Vic,

Well, there is da good news and da bad news. The good news is that my grandmother is well. Tests have been done and nothing is wrong with her heart. The chest pain was probably due to a bad case of gas. Which is great, and I am really happy for her, but I feel stupid that I ruined what could have been a momentous night because of a case of geriatric flatulence.

The bad news is that Rahul did not call or message. I think he has given up on me. He isn't going to waste his time any more with a girl like me. I don't know what I can do. Maybe I should call him and explain. Maybe this is a break-up and he doesn't really want to talk to me again. I think it is mean and insensitive of him to not call or check on me. He is nothing but a selfish SOB out to have a good time. I was just another conquest, a scalp—a special virginal one—in his collection of scalps. I will never think about him again.

I have to focus on work today. Though it is a Saturday, we are working. I reached office at 8.30 and saw what Jimmy had done with the presentation. We both went through the whole thing and sent it off to Harish. Harish was surprisingly prompt in his reply. He wanted us to make some changes. Add some graphs and tables, change the font size, make it more colourful and some other cosmetic modifications. I think we will be working on Sunday as well. Nadeem is here on Monday and we have to be ready then. I am not sure when our slot will be, but Harish has said that we have to be on standby all day. CG was not around. I hoped he was not too angry with me for running off last evening. Serves me right, I guess.

Hey, my phone just beeped. These days, every time my phone beeps or I get a new mail in my inbox, I rush to it thinking it might be Rahul. Usually, about nine times out of ten, I am disappointed. Sometimes I try to resist peeping at it, but end up giving in to temptation and feel even more disappointed.

Okay. I can't resist any more.

It *was* a message from Rahul. 'Hope all is well at home.'

He is not a selfish SOB after all. I think it was very thoughtful of him to wait till the end of day to send the message. He was giving me time to handle my emotions. Actually, he is a kind, sensitive person and I misjudged him too early.

Vic, there is still hope.

'All well. Thank you. Sorry I had to leave like that,' I messaged back.

'Cool. Catch you later,' Rahul replied.

Cool. I was cool. I would make sure he caught me later. Maybe he saw me as a challenge now—the one that got away. It probably brought out the adventurous spirit in him. Vic, I have another chance. He is busy this weekend with some relatives who are visiting Mumbai. I believe his aunt and uncle are staying at his apartment en route to the US. That is what he said. I have magnanimously let him be with his family. There is always next weekend.

Good night,
D.

17

Dear Vic,

Has it ever happened that things that happen to you don't seem to have happened to *you* after a while? Almost as if you are watching a flashback sequence in a movie and seeing someone else playing you? I know I seem confused, but I have had an utterly surreal experience—a scene from a tragic movie or a horror flick.

It is past midnight at 124 Pine Crest on a Sunday. Damayanthi has been a good girl, working the whole day, and she should have been fast asleep. But she has had a dream about her maybe boyfriend, Rahul, a dream that made her blush in her sleep and wake up feeling hungry and thirsty. She goes out of her bedroom and heads for the refrigerator. To her surprise, the fridge is open, and in the dim light she sees a man—a semi-naked man. The man rummaging through the fridge looks familiar. The well-muscled smooth back, the crisp dark hair and the clean profile makes the man look exactly like Rahul. Damayanthi wonders if she is still dreaming and pinches herself so hard that she screams a little scream.

The man looks up. It *is* Rahul. He looks horrified and astonished and his mouth opens in a loud gasp. As Damayanthi switches the lights on, she has a horrible feeling that it is not a dream but a nightmare. The horrifying facts stack up.

One, she is wearing a hideous, purple, frilly nightie.

Two, she had oiled her hair for the Sunday hair wash and is wearing it in a most unbecoming single plait which, along with the white anti-puffiness cream smeared in great concentric circles around her eyes, makes her look like a bleary raccoon emerging from an oil spill.

Three, Rahul is wearing only a pair of boxers.

Four, the fact that he has not emerged from her room means that he has been in the only other possible room—Sonya's.

Five, the fact that he has been semi-naked in Sonya's room means that they have certainly not been doing the crossword in there.

Rahul makes as though he will slink off quietly to wherever he emerged from.

'What are you doing here?' asks Damayanthi. Her voice seems to come from far away. She desperately hopes that he will say something like, 'I came to meet my long-lost sister Sonya.' Or 'I climbed in through the window and was coming to your room and thought I would pick up a bottle of chilled wine from the fridge.'

'Damayanthi! Is that you? What are you doing here? I thought you were out of town,' whispers Rahul, looking at her as though she is an unwelcome worm in an apple that he has just bitten into. Surely she doesn't look that bad? Does he think all that outer beauty came at no cost? Oh god! Why did Damayanthi choose to wear that horrible nightie on this fateful night?

'I live here and am still here. What are you doing?' Damayanthi is still hoping that there is some rational explanation for this. Maybe he will say, 'I couldn't sleep thinking about you. So I got up and ran all the way from Andheri and just stopped to grab some water from the fridge before I woke you up and took you in my arms.'

'Nothing,' Rahul continues to whisper. He looks a little uncomfortable.

'What do you mean nothing? Why are you wandering around half-naked in my house at two in the morning?' Damayanthi's voice becomes louder, as though someone has just turned the volume up. She detects a note of hysteria in her voice, but can do nothing about it.

Rahul pauses, as though he is sorting through lies and trying to figure out which one will get him into the least trouble.

'Okay, fine. What the hell! I was with Sonya,' he finally replies. He doesn't seem apologetic or horrified.

'And what were you both doing? Researching private equities? Getting a handover? Doing an inventory of your joint assets?'

Damayanthi can't believe that he has been sleeping with Sonya and dating her at the same time, without knowing that they are flatmates. Or did he know that and think of it as a great adventure? Surely he has been here before? She has been in her room the whole day. She has not heard Sonya go out or come in. She hasn't seen Rahul either, but she did hear some noises from Sonya's room, which made her stay out of Sonya's way.

'Look, be reasonable. What's the big deal? You should be grateful that you had a good time with me,' Rahul shrugs nonchalantly.

'Grateful!' Damayanthi cannot believe she is hearing him right. 'So what was I? Your corporate social responsibility goal of the year? Show poor little Damayanthi a good time and earn cheer points from HR?'

'Come on. It isn't like that. Life is too short, Damayanthi. You have to have as many different experiences as possible.' Rahul sounds as though he is propounding a new creed—the cult of sleeping-around.

Damayanthi is reeling from the revelation. 'So I was an experience for you? One more in your large collection of women? Do you have a whole harem or what?' She is now furious with him, but more with herself.

'Why are you getting so upset? It is not as though I promised you marriage or anything. These days, everyone wants to have a good time. But you are so uptight. You could learn a lot from me. But you are so old-fashioned. You just don't let yourself go,' Rahul rambles on glibly.

'So I am old-fashioned and uptight! And Sonya? Sonya is…' Damayanthi cannot find the words to complete the sentence. Anger chokes her larynx.

'Sonya is hot. We both have a good time.' He appears very casual about the whole incident, almost as if the norms of society doesn't apply to him.

Damayanthi cannot believe what she is hearing. Here she has caught her maybe boyfriend red-handed and he is telling her that *she* is uptight and old-fashioned and he is only having sex with her flatmate because she is hot. She can't figure out if she is going to cry or scream.

'How can you do this?' she manages to say. 'I trusted you. I thought you liked me.'

Rahul says smoothly, 'I do like you, Damayanthi. I did enjoy the times we spent together, even though you were a bit… shy. Sonya is a passing thing. It's just sex, not a big deal.'

Before he can say anything more, a shoe comes whizzing out of the dark corridor and hits him squarely on the head.

Damayanthi hears a furious voice floating towards her and sees Sonya emerge from her room. She is wearing a thin white T-shirt which barely covers the top of her thighs. Her normally straight hair is tousled and her eyes are blazing.

'You fucking bastard,' shouts Sonya. 'How do you like this for a big deal?'

She throws another shoe at him. A big, brown, male shoe which hits him on his butt. He puts his hands protectively over his groin to ward off the next missile. She darts into the room and comes back with a bunch of clothes which she hurls at Rahul. They scatter around him.

'Get the fuck out, you lying, cheating son of a bitch!' Sonya does not mince her words. 'I don't want to ever see you again, you fucking bastard.'

Rahul quickly assesses the situation and thinks that exit is the best option. Sonya does not give him time to get dressed. She is throwing other things at him—a pillow, a book, his mobile phone, his car keys, his wallet, a large pink teddy bear, a pink towel, an ash tray that shatters against the wall. Rahul runs out of the house with his clothes still hanging from his hands, his black belt trailing behind him like the devil's tail. Anyone else watching this movie would have laughed.

This is where the movie ends. I remember the rest very clearly.

After Sonya slammed the door behind Rahul, she turned to me. I was too stunned from all this drama and destruction to even register what was going on.

'You bitch! How dare you steal my boyfriend?' Sonya screeched as I was trying to ignore her and walk back to my room. I would have maintained a dignified silence, but all the anger and resentment I felt against Rahul, against her, bubbled up to the surface.

'*Your* boyfriend!' I screeched right back. 'Since when did he become your boyfriend? You deluded fool, you heard him—you're not a big deal!'

'He has always been my boyfriend,' she retorted.

'If he is your boyfriend, why did he kiss me and take me out to dinner instead of being with you?' I twisted the knife. At least he was only my *maybe* boyfriend.

'I am sure you threw yourself at him. You shameless bitch! You've probably never had a man in your life and are frustrated like hell. I am sure you were all over him with your gross curd rice hands, begging him to take you to bed.'

'And your so-called boyfriend is of course a little baby who had no choice in the matter. Maybe I tied up his hands and forced him to have dinner with me.'

'Yeeew! Just look at you in that gross purple sack and all that third-rate, cheap cream smeared on your face. And your stupid hair looking like a fat rat's tail!'

Well, I could get personal too.

'Just look at you in that skimpy little T-shirt, advertising your stick-insect body so blatantly, trying to show off your non-existent boobs.'

'How dare you speak to me like that? You are such a loser! What I can't figure out is how a guy like Rahul could even be seen with such a tasteless, fat, fashion disaster like you.'

'Whereas anyone can figure out that he was with you only for unlimited free sex!' I can't believe I said that. Even Sonya looked shocked and was speechless for a second.

'You are nothing but a screwed-up, desperate weirdo,' she spat out.

'You are nothing but a screwing-around, immoral slut!' I spat right back.

There was another brief moment of silence. While Sonya was frothing at the mouth and trying to figure out what to say, I turned my back on her and flounced back to my room. I shut the door hard and a second later heard the loud slap of Sonya's door slamming shut.

I should have felt a sense of elation at having, in some strange way, got the better of Sonya. Instead, I found myself crying. I must have sobbed for a long time. I cried for my pitiful, wasted life, my maybe boyfriend who never was, my silly romantic dreams that never were. Is this what they call heartbreak?

I think I fell asleep sometime in a damp patch of tears. I have gone through the weekend feeling uncomfortably numb. There has been no sign of Sonya. Her room is shut, soundless. Now I can feel only a cold hatred. Bitterness pokes at my lungs like shards of glass. I finally find one man, the only man who ever seemed attracted to me, the one man who made me feel like I was a normal, attractive girl, and he was gone. My prince turned out to be a frog—a lying, cheating, horny toad who was oblivious to his own lying, cheating, horny toadiness.

A part of me was happy that I had not slept with him, that I had not thrown myself away on a worthless man, but another part reminded me that I might never get another chance to be with a man like him. Vic, I just can't figure it out. It seemed so good and right when it lasted. I loved being with him. I was almost convinced that I was in love with him. How could it all have been a farce? I just don't know anything any more.

Things can't get worse.

Bye,
D.

Hello Vic,

I was wrong. Things have got worse.

Just when you think you have hit rock bottom, you realize that it was a false bottom and there is yet a long, dark fall to the real one.

I was miserable this morning. It was more than the usual Monday-morning blues. Having your heart broken and your dreams shattered does not help when you have to prepare for the most important presentation of your career. I put on more make-up than usual, wore my best corporate attire and tried to paste a plastic smile on my face, but my mind and heart were atrophied.

Jimmy, on the other hand, was keyed up like an energizer bunny. He paced the floor, the corridor, and looked at our presentation several times. He Googled images and tried to beautify each slide. He changed the font size a dozen times. He wanted to insert a flowchart after the first slide, sneak in an Excel spreadsheet and do some hyperlink stuff with the others.

'D, Harish called and said that he will try to get us fifteen minutes in the afternoon. Just be prepared.' Jimmy was all ready to go.

'Okay,' I muttered as I tried to go through the presentation and focus my thoughts.

CG came in later. He was finished with our project. There were other, more important things for him to do, but I was glad he took the time out to come and see us. He was in his trademark suit and red tie, but there was less gel in his hair and it threatened to spring up any minute and take on a life of its own. I had not spoken with him in a while. He seemed to have forgiven me for lying and running away the other evening.

I was mechanically going through the slides—
seeing them, but not registering anything—when CG
asked, 'Are you okay?' His voice was kind—there was
a sympathetic note in it that I had not heard before.
Maybe I looked really miserable.

LV: 'No, I am falling apart. My head hurts, my
eyes sting and my life is one awful mess.'

I nodded dully, feeling far from okay.

'It is all right to feel nervous,' he continued. 'Even
I get nervous before important presentations.'

That was surprising. I couldn't imagine CG
nervous. He always seems so self-assured! In fact,
even during normal conversation, he seemed to be
making presentations—holding forth with supreme
confidence.

'Do you?'

'Yes.' He smiled. 'Even though some people think
my usual conversation is like a presentation.' I knew
he was referring to our exchange at the bookshop. So
he remembered what I had said.

I think I gave him a weak smile in return. Actually,
I was not feeling nervous. I wasn't even thinking about
the presentation. Despite my best efforts, scenes
from the previous night would pop into my head. I
would hear Sonya's voice calling me a screwed-up,
desperate weirdo. I would hear Rahul saying I was

so uptight. With great difficulty I dragged myself back to reality.

Jimmy and I spent the next few hours doing a kind of rehearsal, with CG as director, indicating what we should say for each slide. I tried to put a bright, confident smile on my face and waved the red dot of the pointer over the slide and pretended to address the actual audience. Jimmy piped up in the middle, 'Hey, D, you should use an example here. Talk about the customer who complained about the lost cheques. Point to the data when you say "This saves us $2,50,000 and gives us priceless goodwill with the customer".'

'Why don't you say it, then?' I was getting a little irritated. 'I will do the last slide. The one that says "Thank you".'

'Don't get so uptight, D. I am only trying to help,' Jimmy retaliated in annoyance.

'I am *not* uptight,' I shouted almost hysterically. What had happened to me? I had ruined my love life and I looked set to ruin my career as well. Maybe I was embarking on a terrible, self-destructive journey without the help of alcohol and drugs. But I didn't care—this was the second time someone had called me uptight. And this time, it was my friend.

'What has happened to you today, D?' Jimmy now looked concerned. 'Just relax. You are hyperventilating.'

A part of me said, 'Get on with it, D. That jerk Rahul is not worth it.' Another part was still crying. Yet another part was seething with cold fury.

'It is okay. Don't worry, Damayanthi. I think you'll do a great job,' CG said. 'You have prepared well, put in a lot of hard work and I am sure it will go off well.' His voice was soothing and, strangely enough, therapeutic. His vote of confidence meant a lot and suddenly I was thankful to have him around.

'Thank you,' I said to him. 'I hope so.'

By 3.00 p.m., we were tired of rehearsals and just wanted to get the show over with. The dog and pony show, as CG called it. The hours ticked by and we had no news from Harish. His mobile phone was not reachable and no one seemed to know where he was. By 6.00 p.m., we were disturbed. Jimmy and I didn't know what to do. We knew Nadeem had arrived. There was some talk of his cancelling the town hall meeting due to some crisis back at headquarters. Jimmy had heard that he was due to fly back tomorrow. Maybe no time slot could be had for our presentation. Maybe Harish was still trying to get us in. The management committee was having meetings through the day.

'Let us go home, Jimmy. Nothing is going to happen,' I finally said at 7:00 p.m. All that preparation and hard work had amounted to nothing. Suddenly, nothing at all was working out. I was more dejected than I had ever been before.

'No. Let us go to the fifth floor. Maybe we will find out something.' Jimmy wouldn't give up.

We went up to the fifth floor, AB's domain, which was out of bounds for us. Only the management committee members had rooms there. The inner sanctum of the fifth floor was very sleek, very exclusive. Instead of the glass and Formica of our cubicles, there was wood panelling, carpeting and oil paintings on the wall. It looked more like a five-star hotel than an office. The meeting was going on in the board room.

As we headed into the passageway leading to the board room, we noticed two senior VPs talking outside the room. They looked at us enquiringly.

'We are looking for Harish Chopra, our manager,' explained Jimmy. 'He was supposed to tell us about the presentation to Nadeem.'

'Oh, Harish finished the presentation about an hour ago,' said one of them.

'I think he has left,' said the other.

'What? Harish made the presentation himself?' Jimmy almost yelled.

'Yes, about the process improvement project,' said one of the VPs in a matter-of-fact manner, and then ignoring us, they continued to talk to each other.

'This time Harish will get the promotion. His ideas were good, for a change,' said one.

'I think AB was quite impressed with the $1.5 million projected savings. His research seemed quite thorough. Must have got someone else to do it,' responded the other.

The first VP laughed. 'As usual. I think Harish might get the Singapore job.'

'He has been angling for it since we came to know that Arvind was moving.'

Jimmy was looking furious. It still hadn't registered with me.

'We will ask Harish tomorrow,' I said. 'Maybe there wasn't enough time.'

'Damayanthi, you fool. That SOB has screwed us both royally. Do you think he mentioned us even once during the presentation?'

'Then why did he ask us to prepare the presentation and promise us that we would make it to Nadeem?' I was quite puzzled.

'So that we would do a good job and finish it on time. That sicko dangled the bait in front of us and we took it.' Jimmy was shaking his head in disbelief. 'He had no intention of giving either of us the spotlight. Now he has taken all the credit for the project. I am sure he said that all the ideas were his and we were just flunkies who put it together.'

I couldn't help thinking that there was some kind of grim justice to this. We had first stolen the ideas from Malavika's summer project. It was bad karma. Just as Amma always said. If you do something wrong, it will come back to you. We were being punished for our greed and laziness by someone else stealing our work.

'Let us go home, Jimmy. There is no point hanging around here now.' I was resigned to my fate, which could now involve an actual resignation.

'How can you just take it like that, D? It is unfair. I am going to take this up with Harish.'

'Okay, we will do that tomorrow.'

I feel like the dumbest woman in the world. The only woman who has been cheated by her maybe boyfriend and boss in the same day. It is hard to believe that just two days ago I was gloating about my professional and personal life.

Bye,
D.

Hi Vic,

I dragged myself back to office today. I couldn't bear to sit at home and mope around any longer. Jimmy was there, feeling just as angry as yesterday. We got an email from Harish. The gist of his mail was that he was forced to do the presentation by Nadeem, who apparently insisted on the team leader making the presentation. He thanked us for our contribution. He was going to Singapore on some urgent work and would be back after a week.

Jimmy and I are now nobody's children. I feel like an abandoned orphan. Harish will probably get the Singapore job and we will be jobless. In these times of global recession, I won't be surprised if I find a pink slip on the workstation one of these days.

Jimmy was complaining about Harish to all and sundry. No one seemed very surprised. Some of them smirked as though Jimmy and I had fallen for the oldest trick in the book. I think Jimmy is going to quit. I don't know what is going to happen to me.

Vic, I want to go home. Back to Chennai. It's strange how 32 Amman Kovil Street seems like a sanctuary of peace and love now. I want to hear Amma's voice. I want to look at Appa's kind, quiet face. I want to walk aimlessly with the cows on the Adyar roads. I want to light a lamp and pray at the neighbourhood temple. I want to eat a whole bowl of payasam. I want to crawl into my little room and lie there till eternity.

Bye,
Damayanthi.

18

~

Hi Vic,

I am back home. I am sitting in my room watching the November rains. It starts raining in Chennai when the rainy season ends in Mumbai. In my life, there seems to be a continuous depression.

I have slunk away from Mumbai without telling anyone except Jimmy. I sent him an SMS and he replied saying that he is also taking a few days off. It is not like anyone is going to miss us. It is an ignominious return rather than one in a blaze of glory. I have crawled back home with my tail between my legs. I can't even tell anyone here what happened. So I have to pretend that everything is okay.

I had called Amma from the Mumbai airport. She doesn't like surprises and immediately assumes the worst. In this case, she wouldn't have been wrong. I have told her that I have been given leave after completing a project, and because I am also worried about my grandmother, I have taken a few days off to be with the family.

It was so good to see Amma and Appa at the airport. Amma hugged me and almost burst into tears.

'How thin you have become,' she said accusingly, scrutinizing me from head to toe. 'I know you have not been eating well at all. And your hair! Aiyo! You have cut it so short. What will everybody say?' I would have been irritated with her a few months back. Now, I am actually glad to be back with the people I know and care about. Amma and Appa wouldn't cheat me and stab me in the back. I felt my eyes prickle with tears and I hugged Amma back.

I drank in the Chennai scenery as we drove home from the airport. The large hoarding of our chief minister next to a larger hoarding of the latest Rajni film, the desperate darting cyclists, the rumbling green Chennai buses, women with white-and-orange flowers in their hair walking briskly in cotton saris that rode above their ankles. I hadn't been away from home very long, but it all seemed strange and familiar at the same time. We passed the Raj Bhavan, the Guindy IIT campus, the old flyover and I smiled to see the same old Hotel Traffic Jam next to the Adyar signal. Amma insisted that we stop at Grand Sweets to pick up my favourite Mysorepak and rava laddoos. Somehow, this time, I didn't quite feel like eating sweets. The house doesn't seem to have changed at all in the last few months. I felt a little different stepping into it. Maybe I had changed. Maybe it was a greater change than just the makeover.

Amma is on a culinary binge. She seems determined to make up for all the months I have apparently starved myself. I don't really care about dieting any more. I eat everything she puts before me. I am totally at a loose end now. Nothing to look back on, nothing to look forward to. I wonder if I should resign from First Global before they fire me. I wonder if Rahul is thinking about me, if he and Sonya have kissed and made up after dismissing me as a moment of insanity on Rahul's part. I wonder what Jimmy is doing, what presentation CG is making.

I can't help feeling there is more to life and I am missing out on it. I sometimes can't believe I was spending most of my time thinking about a worthless man while I should have being doing something more worthwhile. I can't believe the purpose of my life is to improve the process of depositing cheques in a bank. Maybe I was better off with SSV Iyer & Sons. At least I could dream about the good life then, believing that it was there somewhere. Now I just don't know anything any more.

Good night,
Damayanthi.

※

Hello Victoria,

I have spent four days at home doing absolutely nothing. I wake up late even though I can't sleep too much at night. I wish I could waste away and become a pale, ethereal figure which flits around in a white gown—instead, I am packing in the pounds. I watch mindless television and go for long, lonely walks along the Adyar streets, dodging cows and cyclists.

I think I am getting over Rahul. It is amazing how every little thing that seemed so wonderful and adorable in your object of affection seems just the opposite when you fall out of love. I can now clinically see Rahul for the feckless philanderer that he is. I thought he would be my soul mate, but he clearly didn't believe in having a sole mate. His inability to hold on to one job for too long was a sure sign of commitment phobia. His desperate craving for variety and different experiences was an indication of a fickle soul incapable of steadiness. His conversation, which I used to find so fascinating, was only the boastful ramblings of a self-centred, selfish man. On one hand, I can still admire his outer beauty, and on the other, I am repelled by his inner ugliness. He appears to be a modern-day Dorian Gray, descending into the depths of depravity with every passing minute.

Gawd! I sound like CG. I wonder if he thinks of me. I guess CG must be busy with work. I feel a little bad that I misled him into thinking the process improvement measures were my idea. I guess I deserved it.

I think Sonya deserved it too. It must have been worse for her. At least Rahul was only my maybe boyfriend, but Sonya believed that they were an official couple. I can't help a little feeling of schadenfreude when I think that I, 'the fashion disaster', had stolen away her boyfriend. She must be hurting even more. Good! That is the only ray of light in this dark cavern of my life.

Bye,
D.

Hey Vic,

What do you think about me getting married and going off to Sunnyvale, California? There is still a late entrant in Damayanthi's marriage race.

Amma seemed a little hesitant to bring the topic up this time.

'Daamu, the boy's family is very good. Parents are very well off and he is the only son. Six feet tall, thirty years old, working in California in a place called Sunnyvale. He has an MBA from Stanford. Very good senior job with CISCO.'

He sounded too good to be true. I was waiting for the catch.

'But there is only one thing,' Amma's voice dropped to a whisper. She looked as though she was about to spill a guilty secret.

LV: 'It is okay if he has a venereal disease, Amma. I have sworn off sex for the rest of my life.'

'He is divorced.'

Divorce is still a four-letter word in our community. It happens only to wicked, sinful people who bring it upon themselves. I couldn't believe Amma wanted me to marry a divorcee. Only social outcasts, hopeless cases and complete rejects were married off to divorced men. She must be really desperate.

'We have checked everything. It is not the boy's fault at all. Both Vimala Maami and Appa's colleague, Vishwanathan Sir, know the family very well. The girl he married was a mental case. Vimala says she ran away with someone else only two months after the wedding. Such a pity. It was a good arranged marriage. The horoscopes were a perfect match.' Amma shook her head wonderingly.

LV: 'How could the horoscope lie? That is like the sun rising in the west!'

The silver lining to this sad story was that the family does not believe in horoscopes at all any more.

'They just want a girl of good character.'

LV: 'Sorry, Amma. Then I am out of the race. I almost slept with a Casanova, cheated in my job and am currently lying to my parents about my career prospects.'

Appa, who had been silent so far, gave me a steady look. 'We won't force you to do anything, Daamu. If you don't want to even meet, it is okay. I know California is very far away from here. So you may not want to relocate.'

Actually, that was the best part. I wanted to put as many miles as possible between my past and my future. Go somewhere where I wouldn't bump into Rahul or Sonya or that horrible Harish. It didn't matter if it was

California or Cambodia. I could make a fresh start—a clean beginning in sunny Sunnyvale.

'It is all right,' I said. 'I don't mind meeting him. You can't blame him for the divorce if those were the facts. He is what they call an innocent divorcee.' I suddenly felt sorry for the man, for the mental case girl who ran away, for all of us humans who do silly things and repent later.

Vic, I have made up my mind. As long as this prospective groom is not repulsive or odious and wants to marry me, I will marry him. There is no use dreaming about true love and finding the right man. Eternal fidelity and everlasting love are stuff only for novels. Reality is marrying a stranger and cooking sambhar in Sunnyvale.

Bye,
D.

Dear Vic,

Today, I got a call from Jimmy. My mobile phone has been switched off for the past few days. I have no desire to be in touch with anyone. Then I realized that I had some old messages that I should delete. I had stupidly saved all of Rahul's messages. Now I needed to trash that man out of my phone. Just as I switched on my mobile phone, I saw that there was a message from Jimmy from a day ago: 'D, call me.'

I was wondering whether to call him when the phone jumped in my hands. It was Jimmy. I wouldn't have wanted to speak to anyone else.

'D, where the hell have you been?' he sounded annoyed.

'Home,' I replied shortly. 'How have you been?'

'Good! At least I feel fine now that I have decided.'

'Decided what?'

'I am quitting, D. I am putting in my papers tomorrow. I am joining my father in the family business.'

'Jimmy, are you sure? You said you would never do that. What about all that making it on your own and stuff?' I was surprised.

'Yeah, that was fine for a while. But I am the only son and Dad is growing old. He needs someone he can trust. And it is not like he is making me MD from day one.'

He sounded positive and I was glad for him.

'At least you get to be the boss—or the boss's son, which is even better.'

'Yeah! The first thing I am going to do is get an executive assistant like Veronica and announce a dress code that doesn't allow women to wear anything but miniskirts.' I could sense his smile.

'Well, those are the perks of being the boss. What are you going to be doing?'

'Dad set up this new business a few years ago. It makes software for the entertainment industry. You know, digital animation and cool stuff like that. I am going to be looking after that for a while.'

'Wow! That is great. It sounds very interesting. More interesting than shipping and textiles, which is what I thought your family was doing.'

'Dad is selling off the shipping component and we are getting into new-age businesses. One part of my job is to tie up with film producers and production houses. So maybe I'll get to schmooze with the stars and all. Maybe I can even get to meet Katrina…'

'Sounds more fun than anything you would be doing at First Global.'

'Of course. Now I can't imagine going back to that dump with that sleazeball Harish.' Jimmy was still angry. He didn't think it was some form of divine punishment for stealing Malavika's ideas—that was a smart thing to do. Getting ripped off by Harish wasn't.

'What are you going to do, D?' he asked.

'I don't know. I am still figuring it out.' Somehow, I didn't want to tell him that I was contemplating marriage with a complete stranger.

'Are you thinking of quitting? We have only a fifteen-day notice period since that slime Harish didn't confirm us either.'

I hadn't realized that. I think I can resign by mail once my marriage has been fixed. I will wait and see how it goes.

'So, D, come back soon and we'll catch up. CG was also asking about you. He was wondering where you had disappeared.'

'Oh! I didn't tell him anything.' I felt a bit guilty about sneaking off after all the help and encouragement he had given me on that fateful day. Jimmy's life seemed to be falling in place. It was good to have a family business to go back to. I wish I had something or someone to go back to.

D.

Hey Vic,

CG called me today. I was a little surprised when I saw his name flash on my phone.

'Hello, Damayanthi, how are you doing?' I was happy to hear his voice. It sounded comforting, familiar, even though we had had hardly any conversations over the phone.

'Hi, I am okay. How are you?'

'Oh, fine. Er... I heard from Jimmy about what happened with Harish. I believe he didn't even mention your work during the presentation and has not given your confirmation letters. I am sorry that it happened this way, after all the hard work that you did.'

CG was polite and pleasant. He sounded genuinely sorry that we didn't get the recognition he thought we deserved. I don't know why, but suddenly I found myself telling him the truth.

'I deserved it, CG.'

'What do you mean?'

'Jimmy and I took most of the ideas for the process improvements from a summer trainee's project. We didn't even mention it when we presented it to Harish. That is why we didn't get any credit for this project. It was all wrong. And I am sorry I let you think it was all my idea.' The words burst out of me like a flash flood.

There was a longish pause. On one hand, I felt better now that I had confessed, but on the other, I was unhappy that I had destroyed any good impression I might have made on him. I had lied again.

'Why did you do that, Damayanthi?' CG sounded more puzzled than disapproving.

'I don't know. Jimmy said it was okay to do it. It was like best practice sharing. And it saved us extra work. It seemed like a smart thing to do.'

'I don't know whether it was smart or not, but it is understandable. I may have done the same thing in your place. But why didn't you tell me? I might have helped in some way.' He was being very understanding and kind. I felt a little lump in my throat and hoped I wasn't going to burst into tears.

If you are confessing, you might as well go the whole way. Now that I believe that honesty is the best policy after all.

'I thought… I thought that if you thought that I thought up those ideas, you would think that I was smart and intelligent.'

That sounded completely incomprehensible. I was babbling. I had just about destroyed any chance of recovery.

'I do think you are smart and intelligent,' CG said slowly. 'You needn't have tried to impress me.'

'Oh?' That was news to me.

'And I think you are brave to tell me this. You could have just kept quiet about it. It requires guts to own up to your mistakes. Though I don't think mentioning the source of your ideas would have made any difference to what happened, Damayanthi. There is no direct cause-and-effect relationship between many events that happen in the world. Things just happen and we try to rationalize them afterwards to make some sense of this random existence.'

Normally, I would have argued with him. Now I found myself agreeing with this philosophy. I am also trying to make sense of my random existence.

'You sound very wise,' I remarked.

'Nah. I am just trying to make some sense of my own random existence.' It was eerie to hear him echoing my thoughts like that.

'Well, on one hand, you say you are trying to make sense out of life, but on the other, you sound very sensible.' I could hear the smile creep back into my voice.

He laughed with me then, a nice, companionable chuckle.

'When are you coming back to Mumbai?'

LV: 'Why? Did you miss me? I missed you.'

What was I thinking? I shushed that voice immediately.

'I don't know. I think I can resign by sending an email to HR.'

'Resign? Why?'

LV: 'Because it is better to resign than be fired. I have to save what little face I have.'

'I don't want to go back. I don't think I am cut out for the corporate life.' I had known it all along. I should have quietly languished in SSV & Sons or married that ghastly Gajalakshmi guy.

'So what are you going to do?'

LV: 'Why? Do you care?'

'Get married.' Now why did I say that?

'WHAT?'

LV: 'Why? Did you think I would never find a man?'

'Why not? Any reason I can't get married?'

'No… I mean… no reason… So who is the lucky guy?' Was he being sarcastic? He didn't sound sarcastic. He sounded strange. Definitely not happy to hear the news of my impending matrimony.

'No one I know.' Play it cool, Damayanthi. Act like it's no big deal.

'Oh! I thought there was someone you…' His voice trailed off.

LV: 'If you are thinking about a certain lying, cheating, no-good SOB who I once thought was a potential candidate, then you can think again.'

'No,' I said firmly. 'There isn't anyone. I will probably see my prospective husband for the first time next week. It will be a good old-fashioned arranged marriage.'

'So you are going to marry a complete stranger?'
LV: 'Stranger things have happened.'
'Yes.'

'Is that what you really want?' He sounded serious. No one had asked me what I really wanted before. Now, with that question looming in front of me, I wasn't so sure.

'I don't know. If I marry this person, I will move to California. I have always wanted to see the Golden Gate and walk along Hollywood Boulevard,' I said.

'In that case, take a vacation, go on a world tour. Damayanthi, running away is not going to make things easier. You might always regret the things you didn't finish.'

He was right. I was running away. Running from facing Rahul, Sonya, Harish, my miserable life and ruined career. Running away, which seemed like the safest option, was actually thoughtless and stupid. CG was right. I did have unfinished business.

'You are probably right,' I sighed. Damn the man. Why was he never wrong? It wasn't easy to do the right thing.

'Come back to Mumbai, Damayanthi.' CG's voice was insistent. 'See how things are and then decide. You might have had one bad experience with Harish, but it doesn't mean that you have to throw your career away. You don't want to do anything premature without thinking it through.'

'Yes. I will,' I found myself saying. I owed myself that.

'Come back soon. I… I will see you then.'

'Okay.'

Vic, I have to go back. I will get the meeting with prospective husband postponed. I have to face up to my life. And if I have to leave First Global, I need to do it properly.

I am going to Balaji Cyber Café to book my ticket to Mumbai. I have to tell Amma and Appa that there is some work-related emergency. Resigning gracefully before being fired *is* an emergency.

Ciao,
Damayanthi.

19

⤳

Hi Vic,

Being back in Mumbai feels strange. There is very little of the excitement I felt the first time. Nor is there the comfort of coming back to an old friend. There is only a looming sense of uncertainty. I will go to office tomorrow and formally put in my papers. I haven't checked my mail in ten days. I remember the time I used to be almost addicted to it. Now I don't want to see the bad news in black and white.

Jimmy has informed me that he is no longer coming to the bank. He has served a one-week notice period and is happily in between jobs right now. He has gone to Lonavla with a gang of friends and will be back after three days. I will meet him before I leave. I wonder what CG is doing. I need to tell him that I am back after all. I do not care what Rahul is doing. I don't think I will see or talk to him ever again.

I am in my room now, after dinner. 124 Pine Crest seems empty. I don't know where Sonya is. Maybe she is back in the arms of her old boyfriend or cavorting with her new one. I know I never liked her and have often wished she would vanish in a puff of smoke like those witches in fairy tales, but I now feel a little bad that I shouted at her and called her an immoral slut. Rahul was probably her boyfriend even when we were at Goa together and maybe I did steal him from her. The thought was actually not unpleasant. Damayanthi Balachandran, boyfriend stealer. No one would believe it. I have a sudden urge to talk to Sonya and explain things. I think this urge will pass soon and I will hate her slinky self again.

I just heard a sound outside my room. I hope a burglar hasn't entered Pine Crest. I will have to be an intrepid, investigative girl and see what is out there.

Will be back soon if I don't get knocked on the head by a goonda.

Intrepidly yours,
D.

Vic,

I am back after a very strange interlude. Just as I opened the door of my room, I found myself staring into Sonya's face. I noticed that she was wearing baby pink pyjamas, respectable ones that covered her from top to bottom. Although, a burglar might have looked more friendly.

'Oh, you are back,' she said, glaring at me as though I was a bed bug on her pink duvet. 'I had hoped you were gone for good.'

I stifled all the natural responses that immediately came to my lips. Beneath that sullen surface, I thought I could see a girl who had been hurt, who still hurt.

'Sonya, we need to talk,' I said evenly.

She looked surprised. 'What is there to talk about?' she asked, frowning.

I took a deep breath and launched into my little speech.

'I never stole your boyfriend. I met Rahul at Goa during the FGE training. I never knew he had a girlfriend or was seeing anyone. We just went out a couple of times. There wasn't anything between us.'

She looked disbelievingly at me.

'And I am sorry I called you an immoral slut. I... I didn't mean that. I was angry and upset. I hope you and Rahul can work things out and get back together. I don't want to see him ever again.'

Sonya was still staring at me and shaking her head in a disbelieving way. In fact, I couldn't believe I had actually said that. I felt relieved, though, that I had got it off my chest. I felt even more relieved that I could think of Rahul dispassionately, in a detached sort of way, like I would think about a chair or a plastic mug. A dumb, inanimate thing—just like him. I was finally over Rahul. I didn't care one way or the other. It had only been a superficial infatuation. Sonya was welcome to him.

She gave a small smile then, just a little upward curve of the lips. 'Did you know that Rahul already had a girlfriend in Delhi and one in Calcutta as well?'

'Wow! A girl in every metro. I... I can't believe it. How many girls did he think he could handle at a time?' So he really did have a harem!

'Well, clearly two at a time was too much.' Sonya actually smiled. She looked more human, not like a Page 3 picture.

'You mean, all along, he was taking both of us for a ride?' I shook my head.

'Yeah. It is over now. I am never going to see him again either.'

'Neither will I.' I was happy now. I wasn't the only girl he cheated on. There is some justice in the world.

'Just my luck! I always end up with bastards or babies,' sighed Sonya.

'What do you mean?'

Sonya pulled out two Breezers from the fridge and expertly opened both. I took a swig from the cranberry one as we settled ourselves on the sofa. It tasted like fizzy fruit juice. I got the packet of brownies I had picked up from Barista and we nibbled on them. She seems to love brownies. I don't know where all those carbs go in her body.

'You know, almost every man I have been with falls into one of those two categories,' Sonya continued. 'The babies want to be pampered and spoilt. They make you run around wanting to do things for them and make you feel that they just cannot get along without you. The bastards pamper you and spoil you and you feel that you just cannot get along without them. You have to dump the babies because they get too needy and clingy and the bastards end up dumping you because they have got tired of your neediness.'

'How about Rahul?' I asked.

'He is the most dangerous type. A bastard you want to baby. To think that I actually spent so much time and money in doing up his house! What was I thinking? That one day we would live there together or whatever!' She seemed disgusted with herself, although her remarks explained the smart interior decoration in his bachelor pad. It had a woman's touch to it.

'Someday, someone will get even with him,' I said. 'He will meet a femme fatale who will break his heart and leave him for a fat, balding billionaire.'

'We should get even with him,' declared Sonya. She was already on her second Breezer. 'Make him really sorry that he ever fooled around with us.'

'Maybe we should hire some bhai to beat him up,' I suggested.

'Nah, that is too tame. He will have his current girls giving him tender, loving care at the hospital after that. Maybe seduce a couple of nurses as well.' Sonya dismissed that idea.

'We could sneak into his house and cut up his designer jeans,' she said after a while. 'Actually, we could chuck all his clothes and shoes into the garbage dump. And I will take back those curtains I put up in his house.'

'Hmm… something more original and drastic,' I thought out loud.

'What about inviting him over and getting him drunk? We'll strip him, take naked pictures of him and then blackmail him for the rest of his life.' Sonya sounded excited by that idea. The Breezer was doing interesting things to my senses. I was feeling a little fizzy-dizzy myself.

'What if we just put his pictures on the net or something?' I suggested. 'The rest of the girls in the world deserve to know the kind of guy he is.'

'Great idea,' chimed in Sonya enthusiastically. 'We'll force him to say, "I am a great, big asshole and a complete bastard, who is fit only for scrubbing ladies' loos," and post the video on YouTube.'

'We'll tie him to a chair and make him look ridiculous. Put a red clown's nose on his face and give him a pair of horns and write "I am a jerk" with red lipstick on his naked body.'

'We'll tattoo a sign on his forehead—"Statutory Warning: Being with this man is seriously injurious to your love life." We'll wrap him up in toilet paper and put a clown hat on his head.'

We were letting our imagination run wild. For a few minutes, we happily contemplated the sweet feeling of revenge.

'The strange thing is that he was really good to me while it lasted,' said Sonya after a while, looking rather pensive.

'I know,' I had to agree. 'He made me feel as though I was the only woman in his life, even though I was probably the forty-fifth.'

'He is like a serial killer—the kind who tastes blood once and just has to go on killing to satisfy his blood lust.'

'He is a serial philanderer. I don't think he even thinks it is wrong. It is just something he does.'

'Like a psychopath,' added Sonya. 'A psychopathic gigolo.' She giggled.

I remembered that time long ago when I had just come to Mumbai and the watchman had asked me if I wanted a 'boy'. I guess I had found the hunky gigolo after all. I couldn't help smiling.

When I think back on those times with Rahul, I don't feel any misery, only a dull sense of loss. He did make me feel attractive, like a woman who could be loved. I suppose I owe him that. Now I can think of the Rahul episode as just another episode in the serial of my life. There will be no reruns. No revenge either. That episode was over.

'I am off men now,' declared Sonya. 'I will devote myself to my career and my passion.'

'Isn't your career your passion?' I asked.

'Arey nahin.' She giggled. The four Breezers were beginning to take effect. 'Maine interior decoration ka courshe kiya hai. That ish my real interesht.'

I should have guessed. 'Then how come you are at a bank?'

'My parentsh thought I should do shomething more worthwile. Sho I did my MA in developmental economicsh from Delhi University, aur bash, yeh job mil gayee.'

Sonya was a serious economist. I couldn't believe it. My face must have shown my disbelief.

She looked defiant despite her tipsiness. 'I know. No one sheemsh to believe me. It is sho unfair. Jusht because I look glamoroush and shtylish, people think I have no brainsh. Most of my shilly, idiotic platinum cushtomersh shpend more time gazing at my pershonal asshets rather than focushing on their liabilitiesh.'

'I have never had such problems.' I laughed. Life was full of irony.

'You are lucky. You look brainy.'

In other words, not glamorous or stylish. I didn't feel bad. It was true.

'Anyway, I am doing thish interior decoration project. For one of my private banking clientsh. He ish letting me decorate hish new apartment. If it goesh well, maybe I'll get some more offersh... Kya pata, I'll become a full-time interior decorator only.' She was about to open her fifth Breezer—she guzzled the stuff like it was fruit juice!

We talked on. Sonya drunk was better company than Sonya sober. I suppose I let down my hair a bit as well. We discussed FGE, the meanness and jerkiness of our bosses, working in a man's world, movies and our favourite serial—*Sex and the City*. This was the closest I had got to female-bonding in a long time. It was good to discuss the painfulness of threading and share the best remedy for pimples and wail about the unfairness of carbohydrates.

'I am shorry I called you a fashion dishashter and a deshperate weirdo,' said Sonya as we finally got up.

So she did remember. 'It is okay. I guess I don't have your kind of fashion sense,' I admitted.

'If you need a wardrobe conshultant, let me know,' Sonya offered. It was probably the nicest gesture she had made towards me. I could imagine her taking me on shopping expeditions and giving me a proper makeover.

'Thanks, Sonya. I will. But I guess I am okay with the way I am.' I gathered my orange nightie around me as we said our good nights and headed back to our respective rooms. I think I have lost a maybe boyfriend but found a maybe girl friend. Too bad I have to leave First Global now.

D.

Dear Vic,

I went back to First Global today. It was lonely without Jimmy. No one seemed to notice me or ask me anything. I might have been the invisible woman. I hooked up my laptop and proceeded to trudge through my emails. There were about two hundred of them, a hundred and ninety of which were routine, useless junk mails.

I clicked on the one from Madhurima from HR which cryptically said 'Urgent'. I opened it with some trepidation, expecting a curt firing letter. Instead, there was a request to meet her ASAP. She had sent two reminders as well. I guess First Global believed in firing people in person. She was probably going to shout at me first for being AWOL. Suddenly, I just wanted to get it over with. I would meet her and tell her I wanted to resign. There were a couple of mails from Harish, but I didn't want to look at them. I also saw a standard farewell message from Jimmy to some of us and one from CG.

It just said: 'Damayanthi, have been trying to get in touch. Do call or email. Regards, CG.' It must have been before he spoke to me. I suppose I will say a formal goodbye to him, to Jimmy, to First Global, to Mumbai.

I called Madhurima and went to meet her.

'Where have you been, Damayanthi? You know, I have been trying to get in touch with you for the last three days. You didn't give a leave application either.' Madhurima looked more harassed than annoyed.

LV: 'How does it matter when you are going to fire me?'

'I am sorry,' I mumbled. 'The project was over and my grandmother was admitted in the hospital, so I took a week off to go to Chennai, my hometown. Harish was not around. So...'

'Oh, okay. The next time, remember to fill in the e-leave form on the intranet. That way, I will also get a copy as your HR manager.'

LV: 'What did you say? The next time? There isn't going to be a next time.'

'I needed to discuss something important with you,' I said. Might as well get it over with. That way, I would make it easier for Madhurima as well. She looked more cheerful now. Maybe she got her kicks from firing people. You never know with these HR folks.

'So do I,' she said. 'First of all, congratulations.'

I was confused.

LV: 'Is getting fired from First Global a good thing? Is the bank becoming bankrupt? Is this how you do it as per the new HR policy?'

Maybe these HR managers were trained to make firing seem like the start to a great new career outside the bank. After all the managementitis I suffered under Harish, I won't be surprised.

'You have been confirmed. Didn't you see the mail from Harish?' Madhurima asked, looking surprised.

I shook my head slowly. This was crazy.

LV: 'So what devious form of torture is this? Why confirm me as a permanent employee and then fire me? Is it like the feast before the hanging?'

'Harish couldn't sign the letter because he had to rush to Singapore for his new assignment, but he sent a mail with a strong recommendation for your confirmation. You know, you and Jimmy have been confirmed, but Jimmy wanted to quit before he even saw Harish's email.'

Harish confirmed us! Was that penance for stealing our ideas or a bribe so that we wouldn't raise the issue? I don't think I will be able to figure him out. I am sure there is a catch. Now I will have to serve a one-month notice period during which they will make me do menial jobs and slave for the release letter. I guess they had some dirty work lined up for me for a month. I didn't care. I wasn't going to do it.

'Actually, I wanted to put in my...' I began.

'You know, I wanted to discuss your next assignment. There is a great opening and I thought it would be just right for you. I checked with Harish and he also felt that you would be great for this new role,' Madhurima rattled on.

LV: 'Madhurima, have you not attended any communication skills training? What about listening to your employees and all that? Did you hear what I wanted to say?'

'You know Renu Kamath, the senior VP who was heading credit?' asked Madhurima.

Wait a minute. What had happened to *my* listening skills? Did she say new assignment? New role? I wasn't sure I had heard correctly. I had heard about Renu Kamath, though. She was the only woman who was a senior VP and a business head at First Global.

I nodded slowly. I could hold back my resignation for a few minutes and see where this was going.

'Renu is now going to be heading our new microfinance company. It is a joint venture with MKS Microfinance, which is the leading provider of microfinance in the country. She is hiring people for the new company and I thought it sounded like a great opportunity for you. In fact, Renu wanted to meet you ASAP. She is handpicking people for a few important roles. If she likes you and you want to join as well, it means you can get promoted to senior manager immediately. The opening is for a senior manager role. I will call her right away.'

My head was spinning. It was still spinning after the meeting with Renu. Renu, contrary to my expectations of an Amazon with a booming voice, turned out to be a short, feisty lady with a thick mop of grey hair. She wore an elegant, dark green, printed silk sari and rimless glasses. Though she had a friendly look and greeting for me, I could sense the steel behind the smile. For about half an hour, she spoke to me about microfinance. She was passionate about the subject and showed me a presentation on what it was all about.

'If you want to change people's lives for the better, if you really want to make a difference in your life, this is the job for you,' she declared.

Vic, microfinance is about giving loans to poorer people who normally don't have access to bank credit. These people have a better record of repaying loans than many big companies. I had heard about Muhammad Yunus's Grameen Bank in Bangladesh and the difference the bank had made in the lives of rural women. But I had never thought about doing anything like this.

She asked about me and what I wanted to do. I answered her as honestly as I could. There were no clever lines learnt from websites. Only my own little voice and me telling her that I did want to make a difference, that I dreamt about being a part of something great and noble, but that I had no idea how to go about it.

'There is a project we are going to be working on first, Damayanthi,' Renu said. 'It is for weavers who make saris in a village in Tamil Nadu. These people, mostly women, have to borrow heavily to get raw materials and get paid a fraction of what a rich woman will pay for a sari like this in a city shop. Through our project, we provide them with low-cost loans and help them to market their saris and make a decent living from their trade.' She showed me pictures of smiling women weaving saris on an old-fashioned loom.

'Do you think I can do this job?' I was unsure. I hadn't had any experience with credit.

Renu smiled at me and said, 'I believe you can and you will do a great job.' She really sounded as though she believed it. For a minute, I believed it too. I felt a small frisson of excitement at the thought. I could be a catalyst for change, I could help people, I could use my skills. And I could get paid for it!

Vision of myself in a village in Tamil Nadu. I am distributing wads of money to smiling women in colourful saris. They thank me and look at me as though I am their saviour. 'Akka, you have changed our lives,' says an old lady. 'Thanks to you, I can support my old parents and make a decent life for ourselves,' a young girl says, sheding tears of joy. 'Long live Damayanthi akka!' shout the women with one voice. ' Long live Damayanthi akka…'

'Can you see it?' asked Renu. She was smiling at me. Did she know what I was thinking? 'Can you see the difference this organization can make to people?'

I nodded. I had always wanted my life to mean something. Maybe this was my chance. But something held me back. I needed to talk this through. I had rushed into the First Global job just to escape my dreary life. Now I wanted to think about it a little more. I guess this is what they mean by being older and wiser.

I said I would get back to her the next day. Renu and Madhurima were quite understanding about it. This was not the most glamorous role in First Global. They probably thought I was weighing it against other options in the bank. No one was fighting to get into microfinance.

Vic, I need to talk to someone who can give me sane advice. On one hand, I have the option to marry and go off to California and live the NRI dream with a stranger. On the other, I can be in Mumbai and…

I just don't know.

Bye,
D.

❧

Hello Vic,

I guess you have guessed who I called. CG seemed surprised to hear from me.

'Are you back?' he asked. I thought he sounded pleasantly surprised.

'Yes. I am in Mumbai.'

'Good. Did you go to work? What happened?'

'I got confirmed.'

'Congratulations! I knew you would.'

'You did?'

'Yes, Damayanthi. I did. What now?'

'I have been offered an assignment with the new microfinance company which Renu Kamath will be heading. I am not sure if I should take it or not.'

'Why not?'

'I don't know for sure.'

'What do *you* want?' There was that question again.

'I don't know,' I whispered.

'Do you want to talk some more about it?'

'Yes. I was hoping you could... er... help.'

'Where are you now?'

'At home, in Khar. Why?'

'Well, I am not far from there. Do you want to... meet somewhere... where we could talk... er... Of course, if you would rather not… we could… er…'

'We could meet at the Barista on Carter Road. I have been there before. It won't take me more than ten minutes,' I said decisively.

'Okay. I know the place. I'll be there.'

We reached at the same time. I felt absurdly pleased to see him. He seemed taller, bigger than the last time I had seen him at the First Global office. His hair was tousled by the sea breeze and the smile on his face when his eyes fell on me, though slight, said he was happy to see me.

'Hi,' I said, feeling a little shy, a little nervous now that I was burdening him with the responsibility of career-changing advice. We settled down after ordering our coffees.

'So tell me about this new role,' he invited.

I told him. I told him about the poor village women, the idea of changing the world one micro loan at a time. I told him about my fears about the responsibility, my dreams and dilemmas. He listened.

'You sound as though you will enjoy the new role. I think it will be challenging but fulfilling. You seem to be the kind of person who needs a cause, something great and noble which you can be a part of.'

I just nodded. He seemed to just look into me and read my mind. Strange, I thought. I never felt this way with Rahul. With Rahul, everything was about him. I don't think he ever asked me what I wanted.

'What other options do you have?' CG was asking.

'I could marry the total stranger, go to California and take my chances.'

'You could also stay here in Mumbai and take your chances,' CG said slowly, looking at me, straight at me as though he was seeing me for the first time. I had never noticed before, but his eyes, beneath those gold-rimmed glasses were like pools of hot chocolate. Soft, warm and delicious.

I found myself nodding. 'Yes, I could.'

Vision of myself in 124 Pine Crest. I am just back from a trip to a village after significantly improving the lives of the weaving women who have gratefully bestowed a lovely silk sari on me. Sonya admires the sari and I admire her little home improvement touches to our apartment. Jimmy is lounging on our living room couch with the remote. The doorbell rings and I open the door to let CG in. He pauses for a minute when he sees me and says, 'You look nice.' 'Thank you. So do you.' He does look nice in dark blue jeans and a white linen shirt. We hug. It feels normal, comforting, nice. He saunters in as though he has been here many times. There is an easy sense of camaraderie between all of us. It seems as though we are going out for dinner.

I liked the life I had just imagined. It could be one of those rare visions of mine that could actually come true. I smiled to myself.

'What are you smiling about?' asked CG.

'Nothing.' I continued to smile.

'More secrets?'

'No, I was just thinking—rather, imagining—how it would be if I stayed here…'

'And?'

'I have a great imagination.'

'I think you do. So what is the most incredible thing you have imagined?'

I hesitated only for a second. I felt I could tell him anything, everything.

'Well, I had this beautiful doll when I was small. My uncle got her from England. She sort of grew up with me and has been my friend for a long time…'

For a minute, I thought he was going to laugh derisively. Only a wacko would have a doll as a friend.

'An imaginary friend?' He didn't even smile, just seemed very matter-of-fact about it. And I found myself telling him my biggest secret.

'Her name is Victoria. She has long, blond hair, changes boyfriends and designer handbags every week and lives a wild, bohemian life in London. I imagine her world, her friends, what she does during the weekend. I still write to her almost every day.'

CG looked at me wonderingly. Now he definitely thought I was a weirdo. A crazy girl, out of touch with the real world.

'Your turn. What is the most incredible thing you have imagined?' I was sure he wouldn't be able to come up with something better. Or weirder.

'You know that comic *Calvin and Hobbes*?'

'Of course. I love reading it.'

He paused for a moment, as though he was on the edge of a swimming pool, wondering whether to take the plunge or not.

'Okay. Like Calvin, I have this stuffed lion called Booga, with whom I have been having the most incredible adventures ever since I was a child.'

This was not what I had expected. I simply stared disbelievingly at him.

'Do you still?'

'Not so often now, but he still lives in a corner of my bed that transforms into the African Savannah. I talk to him sometimes.'

We both laughed. An I-don't-believe-I'm-telling-you-this kind of laugh.

'So who wins?' I asked him.

'I guess we are about even this time.'

'Yeah, I think we are.'

There was a long pause. Not an uncomfortable silence but a deep, companionable one. The kind which lets you breathe easily despite a slight hammering in your heart and a sudden rush of adrenalin through your system.

'So what have you decided?' CG finally asked.

'I am staying here.'

'You are?'

'Uh-uh.'

'Just like that?' He didn't seem convinced.

'Yes. Just like that. I will stay here and take up the microfinance role.'

'What about seeing the Golden Gate and visiting Hollywood Boulevard?'

'I could go on a vacation or a world tour.' I shrugged.

'Are you sure?' I saw his expression—hopeful yet doubtful, puzzled yet pleased—and I felt very sure.

'Yes. It doesn't make sense to go abroad when the whole world is coming to India, right?'

'Well, on one hand, it is good to get global exposure, meet new people and new places...'

'On the other, it is much better to have coffee with the same old friends at the same old places,' I finished his sentence. On an impulse, I reached across and put my hand on his. He turned his palm up, so that we ended up holding hands. It felt good, really good.

'Cheers to that,' said CG, raising his coffee mug with the other hand.

'Cheers to that and more!' I clinked my coffee mug against his and we smiled at each other. I was vaguely aware of the world whirling around me, other people's voices, sounds of laughter and a blur of colours, but was more aware that something was swirling and churning within me.

Vic, I feel a strange combination of tranquility and excitement, a sense of having arrived and yet a sense of anticipation about the road ahead. Somehow, I feel I may not be writing to you very often from now on, but I know you will always be there for me.

Take care of yourself and have a wonderful life.

Love,
Damayanthi.

Acknowledgments

My parents, for their unconditional love, unstinting support and the writing genes. Dad, the first author in the family, who believed that you must be the change you want to see—you will always be an inspiration. Mom, thank you for being there, for everything.

My sister Niranjana, the seriously good writer, for all the insightful comments and suggestions after speed-reading the manuscript.

My first readers who encouraged me to finish the book, especially Abhijit Bhaduri and Vivek Govil, for feedback and fundas on getting published, and V.R. Shankar, for the counsel.

My ex-colleagues and friends in Citi (The Bank) for helping me navigate corporate corridors and the good times outside office.

My friends Rohini Ganesh and Rima Sharda, for moral support, child support and the promised sales support. Dear Core—you rock!

My editors at HarperCollins, Karthika and Pradipta, for believing in the story and helping me to make it 'more sexy', Shuka, for the cover design, and the team, for taking it through to publication.

My husband Rajesh, for the title, the photo—you actually made me look nice!—for giving me the space, time and motivation to keep writing. I couldn't have done it without you.

My daughter, my angel, Kaavya—everything is for you.